REDEPLOYED

DANIEL J. NORMAN

Published by Daniel J. Norman

Redeployed
Copyright © 2012 by Daniel J. Norman

1

Her ribs cracked against the tree ending her slide down the mountain. She jerked to her feet and tried to scamper on all fours back up the mountainside. It gained on her. She clawed into the turf. Thankfully, fear numbed the pain in her side although she soon lost the use of her arm. The damp overcast covered the undergrowth in a slick coating. The undergrowth pulled at her. Her damp clothes weighed her down. It took all her effort to make inches of progress. She had to reach the top to escape. She needed to reach the top before it did. A wall of rhododendrons blocked her. She threw herself over them and churned her legs while balancing herself with her good arm. She heard it plowing through the bushes after her. A fern tangled her leg and she slid down the mountain again. Her head slammed into an outcropping and halted her skid. She bolted up and furiously drove her legs into the ground. Lactic acid burned in her legs and lungs. It breathed heavily on her neck. She strained to see the top. If only she could make the top. Pain radiated through her body. She focused her brain on forcing her body to accelerate. She grabbed a fir sapling and launched herself into the desert.

The sand ate up her legs. She needed to move them quicker than the dune consumed them. Faster, faster! Her mind pleaded with her legs as they mushed their way up. It was in the dunes just behind her. She had to make it to the top of the dune before it did. The sun roasted her skin. The air pulled at her tongue. Fire poured out of her lungs. The sand grew deeper as she ascended. She closed her eyes to concentrate on her movements. The ground fell away from her. She landed on the wet sand.

She sprinted for the water. She could hide from it in the water. All she needed to do was make it to the water and she would be safe. She hammered her arms up and down trying to coax her legs along. Her legs failed her and she tumbled into the sand. She dug her hand into the sand and pulled herself forward to the water's edge. It was too late. It had a hold of her arm.

"Excuse me, miss," the flight attendant said. "We're about to land and I need you to power down your computer." The flight attendant continued her check as she passed down the aisle. The twelve-day trip stripped her of energy. All she had to do was get to the JFK employee lot, drive home and go to bed. She looked down a row of seats— tray tables up, electronics off. The seat closest to her was reclined. "Excuse me, miss." The lady was asleep. The flight attendant brushed the back of her fingers across the back of the lady's wrist just the way she was trained.

The lady snapped like she was electrocuted. Her eyes bulged. Her legs shot out. She grabbed the flight attendant's wrist and bent it back and against its elbow. The flight attendant fell and spun smacking her head into the back of the chair in front of the lady.

"Oh my, God! I'm so sorry!" Stephanie cried. "Oh, I'm so sorry. Are you all right? Did I hurt you?" She covered her mouth with trembling fingers.

"It's okay. I'm sorry to have startled you," the flight attendant said as she braced herself on the armrest to get back up.

"No, I mean it. I am so very sorry."

"It's okay, dear. Don't worry about it." The flight attendant saw the redness in the woman's eyes. She was traumatized by something. All the flight attendant wanted to do was fall asleep in her own bed. The flight attendant moved on to the next row and finished up her check before buckling in for landing.

"I apologize again for what happened—for what I did to you," the woman said to the flight attendant once more as she exited the plane.

The flight attendant reached our and touched the woman's arm again. "It's nothing to worry about. I'm sorry to have startled you so badly." The woman's eyes were redder and dried tears laced her cheeks.

"Come in. Come in!" Lucy opened her door and greeted Stephanie. Lucy was half of the on air personalities of the morning talk show *Lucy and Lou*. Lucy played the spunky X-genner and Lou was the crusty old Baby Boomer. Lucy immediately saw something haunted Stephanie. A spark was missing. "So tell me, how was it?" Then Lucy thought maybe it was too early to ask that question. Maybe she should have opened with something benign.

Stephanie's jaw dropped and nothing came out.

"Here sit down. Make yourself comfortable." Lucy led her to her living room and sat Stephanie down. "Let me take that for you." She reached out for Stephanie's computer case.

"You said you were in town to see your agent?" Lucy asked. Stephanie stopped by her agent and then her publisher to finish some final edits, sign some documents and discussed compensation. She relied a lot on Drake's journal and wanted to make sure Drake received a share of her royalties. The preorders were off the chart. Stephanie and Drake would be very well off. Add to that a movie deal that would bring in extra commissions.

"Yes, I had some meetings I had to attend for my book. So, I thought I'd give you a ring."

"Well, I'm so glad you did. I haven't seen you since that time Grace was on the show."

"Yes, it's been awhile."

Lucy paused for a moment to give Stephanie an opportunity to bring it up. When she didn't Lucy asked, "You're not doing to well are you?"

Stephanie shook her head.

"I've been reading what happened and it sounds awful."

Stephanie nodded.

"Is there anything I can do?"

"I don't think so." Stephanie fought to stem the tide of emotion building up.

"This may sound forward, but I do know a wonderful psychiatrist...We had him on the show...He's here in the city...I could give you his number."

Stephanie nodded. "I'm sorry I'm not much fun. But I really just needed a friend right now."

Lucy reached out and held her hand. "Don't mention it."

Stephanie made an appointment for the first opening the doctor had. He set her up with a suite of pharmaceuticals that included anti-depression, anti-anxiety and sleeping pills. On the flight to LA Stephanie didn't even feel like herself. She was out of her mind from the drugs. She felt like a marionette whose strings were being pulled.

The initial set of drugs wore off as she was picking up her luggage. She could feel all her fears creeping up on her, but she felt like she was in control of her body again. She couldn't do the drugs again. She needed help and she needed to be with somebody to take care of her.

2

She knocked on the door before she talked herself out of it. She held her breath. If he wasn't in she didn't know where to turn. With the exception of Grace, who was with her in spirit throughout her Iraq experience, she didn't feel any connection to any of her friends from before the war. Doug English was in a hospital in DC with a butchered leg, and he was a distant second to—the door opened and before she could say anything she threw herself into his arms.

"I was just thinking of you," he said.

Stephanie leapt into his arms and buried herself in his tall frame. She opened her mouth to say something, but her body shuddered too much.

He pulled her away, held her shoulders at arm's length and examined her. With a genuine smile he asked, "Are you okay? You don't look too good." His eyes passed up and down the former lingerie model. It'd been a decade since she modeled and when he last saw her she had a fuller figure. He could feel her bones through her shoulders. Her body continued to shudder. He pulled her in again and held her tighter trying to stop her quaking body. "Are you cold?"

"No."

"You need to eat something."

"I don't have an appetite."

"Doesn't mean you shouldn't eat."

"Just hold me right now. I'm sorry, but you're right, I'm not doing well."

"Okay, but then we're going to get something for you to eat. Do you like Chinese?"

"Doesn't matter."

"Well, Chinese is my favorite, so we're going to get some Chinese whether you like it or not."

"That's fine."

Drake pulled her away and examined her again. The shuddering subsided. On the way to the restaurant they caught up with each other and their individual treks back to the states. They didn't discuss the kiss she gave him when they last saw each other. The *kiss* was from Grace, but they both knew there was more to it and she ran away from him as soon as it was over.

At the restaurant he asked, "So you're having a hard time sleeping?" Drake pulled out her chair for her.

"Yes." Stephanie's phone buzzed an incoming text. *In ny getting refueled.*

"Well, I have the perfect solution to that," Drake said.

"What is that, a fifth of Jack?

"No, PT! Do you have any gear with you? Or is it back home?"

"I don't have a home?" *Dinner with Drake.* Stephanie wrote back.

"What?" He raised an eyebrow.

"I let my lease run out and I put everything into storage."

"So where are you staying?"

"For tonight, or…"

"Okay, tonight."

"Well, I was hoping that you might let me sleep on your couch." She could tell he wasn't tracking. "I'm not doing too well by myself." *What's his #?* The texter asked. "What's your phone number?" Stephanie asked Drake.

Drake told her and then asked, "Who wants to know?"

"I just want to program it in my phone. I was going to call you earlier, but I really needed to see you, see someone, so I just came by."

"So do you still want to run into a firefight?" Drake asked. Stephanie's tour in Iraq drove her to madness. She admitted to Drake that she wanted to kill herself. She contemplated several methods including running out into a firefight.

Stephanie hesitated too long for Drake's comfort. It was a rhetorical question, but she was in fact searching her feelings. Would she run out into a firefight? No, because the Marines she cared for, the Marines she loved, would feel compelled to run out under fire to drag her to safety. No, she would kill herself some other way. In Iraq though she found herself struggling to hold herself back from running out into a firefight.

"Fine, you can stay at my place, but you can't kill yourself tonight." It was almost exactly what he told her back in Iraq. "Are you going to look for a place?"

"No." She smiled coyly. "Grace is going to let me house sit her place."

Drake leaned back in his chair. His eyes widened. "That's so awesome! How lucky are you to let your lease run out only to be able to move into a movie star's mansion."

"Yes, but that is a big house to be in all by yourself." Stephanie brought him back to her situation.

Drake's phone rang.

"Who is it?" Stephanie stifled a smile.

"Dunno," he said with a cocked eyebrow. "Hello."

"Drake?" He thought he recognized the transcendent accent that was somewhere between the Mid-Atlantic and Britain—some called it Britainic.

"Yes."

"It's Grace."

Drake's face lit up. Stephanie beamed with pride. Cupid had nothing on her. "Where are you!"

"New York. We're getting refueled."

"Oh."

The dejection in his voice warmed Grace. "I'm sorry," she said. "I tried to stay as long as I could, but they're waiting for me to start filming."

"Oh, don't worry about it."

"Is there anyway you can take some time off and come out for a week or so? I know it sounds rather strange, but I miss you." Grace's schedule included three back-to-back movie productions in England, Monaco and Africa.

"I know. I feel the same way. Sometimes I can't believe we've never met." Grace and Drake lived a twenty first century romance—almost entirely cyber. They shared emails and video clips. Occasionally a phone call or package slipped into the mix when he was in Iraq.

He didn't want to answer the first question. He needed to spin up for his next deployment. He might get some leave before his next deployment, but right now the Iraq War was in flux. The drive to Baghdad was relatively easy. Was it too good to be true? Military leadership waited with anticipation for the other shoe to drop. Until then, leave was not liberally approved.

Grace continued, "Between your emails, phone calls and Stephanie, I feel like I know you so well. And now we are in the same country, but three time zones away."

"Yeah, I guess this is the closest we've ever been," he said "I..."

A long pause passed before Drake tested the connection, "Grace?"

"I'm sorry but I better go before I start crying."

"Okay."

"Drake."

"Yes."

"I'm so glad you..." She looked for the appropriate term to say she was glad he didn't get killed. "I'm so glad you came back...I just wish I was there to welcome you home. I have to leave now." She choked on her words bad enough that she hung up and didn't give him the chance to say goodbye.

Drake looked across the table. "What are you smiling about?" he barked. His face turned angry.

Stephanie bit her lip to stifle a giggle. "You are just so caught up in her. It's cute."

"Shut up," Drake said and stuck his fork into broccoli and chicken and wolfed it down. "You and I are going to PT," he said with a full mouth.

Drake's phone buzzed. *Miss you so bad it HURTS!!!*

Same here-tear. He wrote back.

"Who's that?"

"None of your God damn business!"

Stephanie leaned her head back satisfied with her efforts.

"I swear, I'm going to run you to death, Chandler. You won't even be able to say suicide by the time I'm done with you." Whenever he was pissed at her Drake called her by her last name.

"There's this place I just found that I can't wait to tryout," Drake said as he drove his Chevy Tahoe towards Camp Pendleton. Stephanie wore running cloths. Drake had boots, Battle Dress Uniform, BDUs, trousers and a sand weighted ruck.

"You're not going to take me on a ten mile run like you did in Iraq are you?" When Stephanie first showed up as an embed with the platoon Drake offered her the opportunity to go on a platoon run. He ran the platoon until Stephanie dropped out. He wasn't going to let any of his guys fall out before she did. At the ten mile point Stephanie asked when it would end. That is when he told her it would end whenever she gave up—which she promptly did.

"No, this one is only three miles. But it is all uphill. It's awesome!"

"Why do you get so excited about this?"

"I dunno. I just do."

"But you think it will help me?"

"Yeah, I think it will."

"Do you ever think you workout, or PT, for the same reason you think it would help me?"

"Huh?"

"Why do you like PT? Does it help you forget about all the people you killed?"

"Nope."

"Iraq doesn't bother you at all?"

"I wouldn't say it bother's me, but I have to admit I'm a little paranoid. Every car is a potential VBIED," Vehicle Bourne IED. "A jihadi could be hiding behind every corner. What really freaks me out is seeing someone walk over an overpass. I keep looking up waiting for them to drop a grenade on me.

"So you don't have dreams or fears?"

"Nope, I sleep like a baby."

Stephanie turned in her seat. "Do you know how angry that makes me?"

"What?"

"That I have to be loaded up with pharmaceuticals to calm down enough to sleep and you have no problem sleeping."

Drake turned serious. The light banter was over. "Hey, I didn't have to go through what you did, so you can't compare it."

"But you killed…what…dozens of people? Doesn't that haunt you?"

"Nope, they all deserved it. And there were some that deserved it that I let get away." He raised a finger to make a point. "If there is anything that haunts me, that is it. That I let someone get away that might have killed a friendly later on down the line."

"I just don't understand how you can be so callous?"

"I'm not the one who cut some guy's balls off, remember."

"Yes, but he had it coming to him."

"Well there you go," Drake concluded. "That is how I feel about the jihadis I killed."

"There was this one man though…" Stephanie's voice trailed off.

Drake sensed a story coming that he needed to listen to carefully. "And…"

"I shot him—at the bridge—when we were in the warehouse. After the firefight was over I went out and he wasn't armed."

Drake ran through the information in his mind. "The ROE allowed us to kill anyone in the area. Remember, I called in mortars, artillery and airstrikes all around us. There were probably some collaterals in there."

Stephanie tilted her head to the side. He provided an answer, but it didn't help her. "You know what the shrink said?" She spun her fork in the air as she finished chewing and swallowed. "I told him about the guy in the farmhouse."

"I give."

"He said that the only good to come of that, was that I knew that killing him didn't solve my problem."

Drake laughed, "Like he can imagine what you went through." Drake reached across his center console to hold her hand. "There are very few people that can empathize with what you've been through. I could never imagine how you must feel. And I think it is arrogant for someone like that quack to say he knows anything about what you're going through. What was he, some New York shrink?"

Stephanie nodded.

"So his greatest dilemma is probably dealing with insecure twits that didn't get enough attention from their mommy."

"I see you are a firm believer of mental health sciences," Stephanie said dryly.

Drake pulled into a gravel parking lot. "You're about to get the best counseling session you ever had."

Stephanie squeezed his hand before letting him get out. She locked eyes with him. "Drake, thank you. I know you don't go for sentimentality but this means a lot to me. It means a lot to me that you care."

"Yeah, well, just wait until we're finished. Then see if you want to thank me, because after running three miles up, we'll do some hills at the end to top it off. And then, if you're lucky, I'll throw in some pushups and situps."

"So why do you PT so much?"

"I get a high from it, and I have a goal in mind," he said as he tossed on his ruck.

"What is the goal?"

"I'd like to go recon."

"Recon?"

"Yeah, SOCOM type stuff."

"Drake, that's dangerous."

"Yep, last time I checked it was."

Stephanie grabbed his arm and stopped him as they started off. "Now hold on."

"What?"

"Are you trying to get yourself killed?"

"No."

"Do you love the danger? Are you an adrenaline junkie?"

"No."

"What is it?"

Drake lowered his voice. "I like it. I like being a leader, and it is the ultimate leadership challenge. I feel like those guys need me. I don't want some loser leading my guys. They volunteered to defend this country. They deserve the best."

"And you're the best?"

"Well, I wasn't going to brag," Drake said with false bravado. "But if you think so." He took a few more steps towards the hill.

Stephanie jerked his arm back. "Hey, listen to me, I'm serious. There are people in your life who are counting on you to be alive." She allowed him time to self assess. "I would have *never* introduced you to Grace if I knew you were going to do this to her."

Hurt flushed over Drake's face.

Stephanie looked him squarely in the eye. "And I need you too. At least right now."

Drake opened his mouth and nothing came out.

"Promise me you'll think of Grace too, not just your guys."

"I promise." He sounded like a scolded child.

3

"So you don't mind me staying here for at least tonight? I just don't want to be alone," Stephanie said as Drake pulled out his apartment keys. She rubbed her sore legs. "Although I'd like to kill you right now for what you did to me."

"Oh c'mon, admit it, you loved it. As for staying over, don't give it a second thought. But I do need to go into work tomorrow for a little bit. Are you going to be okay by yourself?"

"Yes, I have some things to do." She needed to do some writing. "This weekend, do you think you could help me move some of my things out of storage and over to Grace's?"

Drake opened the door and let Stephanie in. He looked at her and let the idea swill around in his head. He talked to, emailed and texted a Hollywood starlet, but it still seemed like a dream. Seeing her house would cement home that the fantasy was more reality than dream.

"Drake?"

"Huh?"

"Would you be willing to help me move in?"

"Oh, yeah, sure. And I could probably get all the help you need from the guys at base that would love to roam around Grace Freemont's crib."

"No, I only need you. I think that between the two of us we can do it all. It's not like I'm going to move any furniture, just some wardrobe items mostly."

"Can I take pictures?"

"Of what? My lingerie?"

"No, Grace's place."

"Absolutely, but it isn't like it will be the only time you ever visit the place."

"Oh, you mean when Grace gets back."

Disappointment crept across Stephanie's face. She reached for Drake's hand and held it. "Well, I was hoping while I was staying there, you'd visit me occasionally." She looked into his eyes. "We are friends, right?"

"Oh, sure, I wasn't thinking about that." He walked over to the fridge and looked in it. "Dammit."

"What is it?"

"I have absolutely nothing to offer you."

"That's fine. Water will be just fine."

"Oh, I do have some wine."

"No, I would just like the water."

"Okay." Drake poured her some water and set her up with a shower. He made up the couch for himself and then put in a Grace Freemont movie. He laughed at himself. He was semi-dating the girl in the movie. He opened his phone, dialed a number and got voicemail. "Hey, it's me. I, uh, I just need to talk to you." He flipped the phone closed and pressed PLAY on the remote.

When the water stopped he got up and raced to the bathroom door. "I forgot to check if there were any towels in there. Are you okay?"

"Yes, there are a couple towels in here. I'll be out in a minute."

They traded spots. She put on one of Drake's T-shirts for a nightshirt. Drake got in the shower. As soon as he was in the shower he heard a knock, "Yeah."

Stephanie cracked the door. "Do you mind if I sit in here and talk to you?"

Drake pulled back the curtain. He was going to ask why, but when he saw her face he understood. "You're still not doing too well are you?"

"No, no I'm not."

"Have a seat." Drake pointed to the toilet. "I'm sorry."

"For what?"

"That you're not doing well." Then he asked, "And you don't want to take a sleeping pill or anything?"

"No."

"Well, I obviously didn't PT you enough."

A knock at the apartment door broke the conversation. "Do you want me to get that?"

"Sure," Drake said without thinking. He ran through who it could be. By the time he figured out who it was Stephanie was opening the door.

Gabrielle's jaw dropped the moment she saw the trollop. She stormed passed the tart wearing Drake's T-shirt. "Where's Drake?" she demanded. She evaluated the woman. She was slightly older that herself. She looked very worn, but she also looked familiar. Her weary eyes sunk into her face. Gabrielle wondered if she was on drugs.

Gabrielle started to fume. Why would Drake call her if he already had a woman over? Evidently whatever he had, or didn't have, with Grace Freemont was over. That was the only woman who could stop Gabrielle from having him. She could steal Drake away from this piece of trash before the night was over. She'd wrestled men away from girlfriends, fiancées and wives. This deal was as good as done.

"He's in the shower," the woman said meekly.

"Oh, did you two enjoy yourselves?"

"No, not really. He tried to run me to death."

Gabrielle cocked her head to the side. That wasn't what she expected to hear. She propped her hands on her hips and inspected the place like she owned it. She didn't understand the sheets on the couch. "So how long have you two been and item?"

"We're not an item."

Gabrielle started to recognize the accent on the woman. A Swaziland native, the woman spoke with a South African accent. "You're not?" Gabrielle reeled. She tried to catch her bearings. "Then why are you here?"

"I, I'm…" The woman couldn't speak.

Gabrielle realized the woman wasn't strung out on drugs. She was traumatized. Gabrielle's face softened. "Who are you?" Kindness replaced the contempt in her voice.

"My name is Stephanie Chandler. I write for *Hollywood Vine*. I—"

Gabrielle gasped. Her eyes grew. She raised her hand to her cover her mouth. "Oh, you poor thing." She reached out for the woman's hand, which Stephanie met her halfway. Gabrielle held it in both of hers. "I'm so very sorry."

"There's no need for you to apologize."

"I know, but I can be—"

"Forget about it."

"Sometimes I can be such a bitch."

"Don't I know it," Drake added. He stood in the bedroom doorway, wearing skivvies while drying his hair.

Gabrielle cocked her hip and shot a disapproving look across the room. She resisted the urge to run across the room and throw herself at him. She didn't fully understand the dynamics of the room. Why was Stephanie Chandler in Drake's room? What about Grace Freemont? "Thank you very much," she said dryly.

"You're very welcome." Drake played as if she meant it.

"Did I interrupt anything?" Gabrielle asked trying to establish some situational awareness.

"No," Drake said running the towel through his hair.

Stephanie sat on the couch and watched the two play mental pugilistics. She knew all the erotic intimate details of their relationship and Gabrielle's reputation. She didn't know why Gabrielle was here though.

"All I have is a cab. Do you want a drink?" Drake asked.

Gabrielle looked at him and then Stephanie. Her eyes darted around nervously. She felt like she was in for a shock. "No, I'm fine."

Drake poured himself a drink. "Steph, do you want one?"

"Sure," Stephanie replied tentatively. Drake's behavior didn't line up with the personality both women knew. The eeriness unnerved them both. He handed Stephanie a glass and then poured one for Gabrielle even though she opted out of his offer.

"I said I didn't want one," Gabrielle said more timidly than Drake had ever heard her. She felt very alone. She and Drake use to be so close. They were one. But she severed those ties, not directly, but implicitly. She wished she could go back to the beginning of the year before he left and change it all. She missed the him and not just in the physical sense.

Drake nodded at it and demanded, "Take it."

"All right," she said demurely.

Stephanie watched intently. She felt sorry for Gabrielle. Stephanie watched her squirm with discomfort. Stephanie tried to think about what she could do for the troubled woman.

Drake leaned up against his kitchen counter. He looked at his wine trying to find a start. Gabrielle grew impatient. Her looks and aggressive demeanor usually put her in control of personal relationships. Sitting on the receiving end and waiting grated her nerves. "So why did you call me?" When she got his message, she thought she knew why, but that theory disappeared when she saw Stephanie. Although she considered herself open-minded, she wasn't into sharing.

Drake swirled his wine. He looked up at her. She saw a glaze in his eyes. "What is it Drake?" She had never seen him this emotional. She never wanted him more either. She reached out for him.

Drake saw her hand but didn't reciprocate. His relationship with her was over. He had the girl of his impossible fantasy. Nothing would ever get between him and Grace.

"What's the matter Drake?" Stephanie asked. Gabrielle's anguish tore at Stephanie.

"I called you because we need to talk." He fell into another crushing silence.

Gabrielle's eyes filled to match Drake's. She didn't know what was coming, but Drake punished her. "Dammit, Drake, tell me already," she choked out over her emotions.

"I called to talk to you about Rodney."

Gabrielle turned away from him and put her wine down. She put her hands out on the counter to steady herself. Private Rodney Saunders was an endearing friend of Gabrielle and Drake. When he had nowhere to go for Christmas before their deployment, Drake invited Rodney to spend it with them and their friends. A foster child with no real home, Rodney incited a matronly spark in Gabrielle. She loved him.

Stephanie stood up. She saw the pain in Gabrielle's face and wished Drake would hold her and comfort her. Stephanie also knew Drake would never jeopardize his budding relationship with Grace.

"Did you hear?" he asked.

Gabrielle nodded. Her face twisted. She was breaking down. Stephanie rushed to her and held her. "How did it happen?" Gabrielle asked.

Drake stood silently. Stephanie squeezed her.

"How did it happen?" Gabrielle asked again.

"He's with God, sweetie. It doesn't matter how it happened. He's at peace now. Trust me, he's at peace."

"I want…" Gabrielle sobbed. "I want to know."

"He was cut up by an A-10."

"An A-10?" It was fratricide. A US Air Force pilot cut down her Rodney. Questions swirled in her head. Did he suffer? How did it happen? What happened to the pilot? But Gabrielle couldn't speak. She sobbed onto Stephanie's shoulder.

"I'm so sorry, love." Stephanie rocked her back and forth.

Gabrielle squeezed her and then pulled back to wipe away tears.

"Are you all right, love?" Stephanie asked.

Gabrielle sniffed, "Yes…I'll be fine."

Drake poured out his wine and filled his glass with water. He sucked it down during the awkward pause.

"I'll let you two talk," Stephanie said backing up to the couch where she sat and watched the former lovers try to establish a relationship under new circumstances.

"I'm glad you're okay," Gabrielle said hoping he would react.

"Yeah, I'm fine. How are you doing?"

"Well, I left active duty. I joined the reserves. I got hired to be a prosecutor." She shrugged. "I need a fresh start."

"Why do you need a fresh start?"

Stephanie cringed. Drake couldn't see the obvious. She pulled up a blanket and rested her head on a pillow.

"I need to move on…like you did."

Drake filtered scenarios trying to imagine what she meant.

"How is Grace?" she asked giving him a clue.

Drake couldn't stop the smile blooming on his face. "Good." He held back the giddy feeling tickling his gut whenever he thought of her. Then he considered his next move in the conversation. He didn't know how to ask about her delicately, knowing her reputation. "I'm sure you've been seeing someone."

Gabrielle took a sip of wine and finished off her glass without answering. She held it out. Drake reached around to the counter behind him. He grabbed the bottle of wine and poured her another glass. She swirled it and threw down a throat full. She bit her lip hard. Her heart ached. Missed opportunities and opportunities stolen from her snapped at her mind. Then she thought of Stephanie and her past and realized some people labored under heavier crosses. "I'm glad she makes you happy."

Drake wasn't observant enough to catch the underlying feelings in her tone. Stephanie rolled over. She couldn't watch the slow torture Gabrielle endured. She also felt somewhat responsible. "She does." Drake beamed.

Gabrielle nodded. She needed to move on. She had her chance. She almost said it. Now it was too late. "I hear she's out of the country."

"Yeah, I just hope she gets back before I deploy again."

"That must be hard."

"It is."

"So you've never met in person."

"No, we haven't. But there is a lot of good to that."

"And what is that?"

"We get to know each other. We didn't just hop in bed and ride another physical fallacy." His spirits soared the more they talked about Grace, all at the expense of Gabrielle.

Another dagger pierced her heart. Her finger crossed underneath her eye to wipe away a tear before he saw. *Oh, is that all I was…a physical fallacy?* She knew she was though. She built and earned her reputation. "When do you think you'll deploy again?"

"I dunno, but it could be soon. I'm meeting with Jon Kim—he's going to be the Company CO—tomorrow and we're going to make some personnel moves."

"Are you going to be his XO?"

"I think that is one of the positions we'll discuss."

"What's there to discuss?"

"I don't want it."

"Why not?"

"I want to have a regular platoon."

"You'll at least have weapons platoon." Gabrielle spat out her reply. She thought quickly and spoke quickly. This conversation took a bad turn. One thing she knew for sure though—how much she cared for him.

Drake cocked his head and lifted a finger off his glass and pointed it at her. "Not necessarily. To fight the insurrection, some company COs are pulling their weapons platoon."

Gabrielle's stomach turned on her. "Drake, don't do this. Don't go back as a line platoon leader." A hint of anger threaded her words.

"Why not?"

"Because it isn't fair to Grace. You can't do that to a girl."

"Do what to her?"

"Make her fall in love with you and then put yourself on the line like that when you don't have to." Only she knew everything she was hidding in the statement.

"What do you mean 'I don't have to?'"

"I mean you don't have to."

"It's what I do." Anger slipped out of Drake's voice. It was like old times. Theirs was a fiery and passionate relationship. "I lead men into battle. And although I might not be the best leader, I enjoy it."

"You selfish bastard, always thinking of yourself. What about her?"

Drake shrugged his shoulders.

"That's all she gets?" Gabrielle mocked him and shrugged her shoulders. She emptied her glass into her mouth and slammed it down. "Look, I've been on the receiving end of this and it ain't pretty. If you're looking to destroy her, you keep this up. Otherwise, if you love her, if you *really* love her, you'll let her go now." The terror gripping Gabrielle wasn't for Grace.

The logic smacked Drake in the face. His jaw dropped.

"You can't have your cake and eat it too," Gabrielle continued.

"You think you know me so well," Drake spat.

"Yeah, I do." she sniffed and wiped away another tear. "I do." She resisted the urge to reach out to him. "And I know how lucky she is to have you."

"Huh," Drake huffed.

Gabrielle hoped for something more reciprocating. When her disappointment wore off she asked, "So how did you get to know Grace Freemont?"

A smile that broke Gabrielle's heart creased his lips. "Oh, she's a good friend of…" Drake nodded towards Stephanie. She was out, but she quaked and fidgeted.

Gabrielle followed his eyes to the woman on the couch and back. She saw the concern, the love of a fellow human being wash away his smile. It was another dagger. He could be a cruel son of a bitch one moment then tender and loving the next. She needed to get out.

"…Stephanie's," he concluded.

"And you took her in?" Gabrielle asked nodding to Stephanie.

"Yeah, I'm worried about her—"

"Goo." Gabrielle poked his belly and smiled. It was a sentiment they shared when they were lovers. She claimed he had a hard shell and a soft gooey middle.

Drake smiled feebly. "She's not doing well."

"I can't imagine what she is going through."

"It's day to day."

"Day to day?"

"Yeah, she keeps wanting to kill herself." Drake paused and looked off. "We were in this firefight once after she was…" Drake looked at Gabrielle.

She nodded indicating she knew the premise of the story.

"It was bad. It didn't look good for the home team." Drake sucked in a deep breath. "Anyway, she starts tugging at my M9."

Gabrielle cocked her head in curiosity.

"So I gave it to her and I said, 'Make sure you point it at the bad guys,' or something like that. She said, 'It's for me, not them.'"

"You didn't give it to her did you?"

"I did."

"Drake!"

He put his palms up to quiet her. "Think about it, if you were her and you were about to be captured a second time. Wouldn't you want to eat a bullet?"

"Oh, I see, yes, that makes sense. But is she suicidal?"

Drake nodded dejectedly. "Yeah, I think that is all she thinks about." Drake looked back at the troubled woman.

"The poor thing. Is there anything I can do?"

"Well, uh, yeah. I'm going in tomorrow. Are you going to be around?"

"Yeah, I'm on terminal leave for a couple months."

"Would you mind checking on her?"

"Sure."

"Thanks."

Gabrielle looked at him wishing there was more. "I better leave. You need to get up in the morning."

Drake walked her to the door and opened it for her. She turned to kiss him like she'd done dozens of times in the past. But that was the past. She reached out to him and ran her hand up and down his arm. "I'm glad your home safe." She turned and walked away before the first tear breached her eyelids.

Drake closed his door and shook his head. "That was strange," he muttered to himself. Gabrielle wasn't the type to get emotionally attached. She certainly acted strangely. It wasn't like she hadn't slept around since he left for Iraq he thought to himself.

4

This time it caught her leg.

Gabrielle heard the faint cry. But it wasn't a cry. It was a guttural shriek of a dying animal. She rolled over and threw a leg over a body pillow. The animal continued shrieking in death throws. It had to be a cat. No, it wasn't a cat. She got up and walked to the window. She pulled back the drape. It wasn't coming from outside. She turned and looked at the door and strolled over half asleep. When the door cracked open she noticed the wails grew louder. She looked down each end of the hall. Her ears zeroed in on the source as she strolled through the hall. Other tenants stood in their doorways. As she drew closer to Drake's apartment she realized the screeches came from his apartment. She pounded on the door. "Drake!"

"Yeah!"

"Are you okay?"

"No!"

"Let me in!"

"I can't get to the door!" he screamed over the cries.

Gabrielle sprinted to her apartment and rifled through a drawer throwing its contents onto the counter until she came across a key. She sprinted back down the hall. She slid in her key and twisted the knob.

"Stephanie!" Drake stood over Stephanie trying to hold her while she thrashed about shrieking. "I can't get her to wake up," he said over his shoulder to Gabrielle. "Stephanie!" Stephanie's hands flailed and clawed at him.

Gabrielle raced to his kitchen and filled a wine glass with water. She scurried up to the traumatized woman and threw the water in her face.

Stephanie held her breath. Lucidity sprang from her eyes. She gasped as if she'd been held under water for several minutes. Drake and Gabrielle braced for her reaction. Stephanie's face crumpled. She choked out hard bitter sobs.

Gabrielle fell to her knees and held the woman. "Oh, you poor thing."

Stephanie squeezed her fiercely.

"It's okay. I've got you," Gabrielle said hoping to sooth the woman. Gabrielle felt her shoulders bob and heard her soft whimpers. "There, there, now."

Drake stepped back and bit his knuckle. Stephanie was in bad shape. He knew she was suicidal. He looked at the row of prescription drugs a psychiatrist gave her. She was right. If she needed all those drugs just to get by, she'd be literally drugged out of her mind. Anger seized him. With all the impossible situations he'd lived through, this one he couldn't solve by just charging forward. He wanted to punch something. Although he killed ever last one of the bastards, they still won. They destroyed this woman's life.

Gabrielle looked at her watch—2:42 AM. "I think you should stay with me," she told Stephanie.

"No, No, I don't want to be a burden."

"Oh, no, you're not a burden. I have a bunch of leave stored up and I'm not doing much right now."

"You don't have to do this for me. I'll be all right," Stephanie sniveled.

"Honey, one thing you are not, is all right."

"But you shouldn't have to take care of me."

"Stephanie," Gabrielle said. "Drake needs to go to work in the morning and I think someone should be with you when you wake up. I'm not doing anything today."

"Gabrielle, you don't have to…" Drake protested.

"I've got this." Gabrielle replied. "You go back to sleep."

Drake looked at his watch. He probably wouldn't be able to get back to sleep. He looked at Stephanie sympathetically. "Are you going to be all right with her?"

Stephanie nodded.

"I'll just go in early and get a workout." He walked over to the door and opened it as Gabrielle helped Stephanie up and to the door.

At her apartment Gabrielle sat Stephanie down and looked at her. "I'm so sorry you have to go through this. Is there anything that I can do?"

Stephanie shook her head.

"I know you don't want to take all your pills, but I think you should at least take a Valium."

"No, just sit with me for a while."

"Okay, I'll put on a pot of coffee."

"Did you really have no plans for today?"

"I didn't, but now that I think about it, I think we," she pointed to Stephanie and then herself, "should do something today."

After a shower Drake strolled into the Company CO's office. When he saw his new boss in he stepped into his office and stood at attention, exaggerating the formality and bellowed, "SIR! FIRST LIEUTENANT SCOTT REPORTS AS ORDERED!"

Captain Jon Kim looked up and smiled. Then he shot up to attention also and saluted smartly. "This is where you return my salute," he said.

Confusion drooped over Drake's face.

"Mr. Congressional Medal of Honor," Jon said to clarify.

Drake smirked. "Do start giving me crap already. I don't have it yet." The two men approached each other and shared a bear hug.

"Oh, would you rather I call you Mongoose?"

Drake rolled his eyes.

Jon enjoyed his friend's discomfort. "Or just Goose."

"Who told you that?"

"I guess on the flight home they decided to give you a go-by."

"Yeah, whatever. I hate it."

Jon choked back his laughter, "But it stuck, man. You are the MONGOOOOOSE."

Drake picked at his ear with his middle finger and flashed it at his friend.

Jon laughed and then asked, "So, how are things going?"

Drake sat up in his chair. "Stephanie is messed up."

"Really?"

"Yeah, she showed up at my apartment strung out. Oh, and I called Gabrielle to tell her about Saunders." Jon Kim also spent Christmas with Drake, Gabrielle and Saunders. Drake laughed at himself. "I thought Gabrielle was going to rip apart Stephanie when she showed up. Her hackles said, 'no way bitch.'"

"Oh, I would have loved to have seen that," Jon laughed.

"Yeah, it was funny. Anyway, she calmed down when she realized who Stephanie was. As a matter of fact, I think they are out surfing together right now."

"Surfing?"

"Oh, it was freaky. Okay, so I've been in some sticky firefights, but nothing scared me as much as last night. Stephanie wakes up—actually she doesn't wake up—but she is screaming at the top of her lungs. And she's still asleep. I'm trying to calm her down and wake her up. Finally, Gabrielle uses they key I gave her last year to get into my place while I'm trying to control this screaming banshee. She gets a glass of water and throws it in her face to wake her up."

Jon's eyes grew.

Drake shrugged. "After that Gabrielle said she'd take care of her. I got a text not too long ago saying that they were going surfing."

"I hope she'll be okay," Jon said.

"She's not doing too well right now. We need to get her through the night without the nightmares." Drake shook his head again after recalling the evening. "Damn, she's messed up," he continued. "So how's it going with you…sir?"

"Oh, I'm just trying to put together my—our company."

"Our?"

"Yeah, do you want to be exec?"

"Oh, hell no." Drake wanted to be a life long lieutenant. He wanted to be a platoon leader and nothing more. Which also explained why he trained so intently.

"I didn't think so. So I'm brining in a guy to be the exec and I'm going to give you weapons." Weapons platoon was a special platoon in the company that had mortars, machine guns and SMAWs, a bazooka type gun. The platoon was usually parceled out to support the other platoons.

"Well, that is better than being an XO." Drake wasn't too thrilled about being the weapons leader because although it was technically a platoon leader position, it wasn't far from just being an advisor to the company CO.

"I think you'll like the way I'm going to put it together though. Since this isn't the invasion and we'll mostly patrol, I'm going to basically turn you into a fourth line platoon. Hopefully that will help with the patrol schedule once we get over there."

Jon picked up some personnel files. "Now talking about names, here's a kid I think you can help, a Sergeant Connelly. He had a tough time in Iraq. I guess he locked up once as a squad leader and they pulled him from the line."

"Hmm."

"You want him?"

"Yeah, I'll see what I can do."

"Well, that's good because you are the best platoon leader I got. I think that it is better that you try to work with him than having a butter bar try to square him away."

"So what you're saying is I really had not choice."

Jon smiled and handed him the file. "Consider yourself voluntold. Besides, I'm not too sure how good the new platoon leaders will be."

Drake flipped through the file.

"One guy," Jon continued, "thinks he's the best think since Second Lieutenant Drake Scott."

Drake continued to look through the file and replied without missing a beat, "No, nobody is that bad. I know Drake Scott and that guy is a complete asshole…at least that's what I've been told."

"You don't have to tell me. That Scott guy isn't worth a pimple on the ass of a dead jihadi."

Drake and cracked up. "Aw, man that is some funny shit. I'm gonna have to use that one myself."

"Nope, patented by me, all rights reserved. But I will need to you help me square away this LT."

Drake put down Connelly's file and looked concerned. "Why do I have to do all your dirty work?"

Jon leaned back and folded his fingers behind his head. "Because you are the biggest BAMF," Bad Assed Mother Fucker, "in the outfit. You have more street cred than anyone else. And I guess this guy, a Second Lieutenant William Houston, is some kind of hero badass wannabe. On top of that he's got an attitude."

"What is he, an Academy grad?"

"No, worse." Jon folded over the back of the personnel folder and held it out to Drake.

"Figures. Those guys all think they're John Wayne in *The Alamo*. So who is my platoon sergeant?"

Jon folded his fingers and laid his hands on his desk. "Well, that's another thing we need to work out."

"Do I get a choice?"

"Depends."

"On what."

"On whether I like your rationale or not. Who was a better squad leader, Alvarez or Jennings?"

"Who was better, or who do I want?"

"Who was better?"

"I have to admit they were both pretty good."

Jon realized he wasn't going to get a straight answer. "Let me ask you this. Would it be better if I put the best platoon sergeant with Houston, to take care of him, or should I give you the best one so you can better do all my dirty work?"

Drake focused. "That's not a fair question, sir. You need to make that decision."

"I will make that decision. But I want your input."

"Okay, I would say that Jennings has a tiny edge over Alvarez."

"So who do you want?"

Drake sat up agitated. "Well, I *want* Jennings, but not if rat bastard—"

"Houston"

"Whatever…rat bastard gets Alvarez."

"So Houston should get Jennings?"

"No!" Drake loved his guys. He hated that he had to give up any. What ate at him more was that Jon Kim was going to give whomever he didn't take to Houston. Drake ran his fingers through his hair and tugged at it. "I want Jennings."

"Okay, Houston gets Alvarez."

"One thing." Drake looked at Jon.

Jon could tell that the decision wounded Drake. "What is it?"

"Don't tell anyone that you asked me about this." A hint of anger trickled out of Drake's voice.

"I won't." Jon studied his friend. "But Drake, you're going to have to make these decisions eventually if you want to stay in the Corps."

"Yeah, I know."

"You can't always do it all by yourself."

"Yes, sir."

Gabrielle put her hands on Stephanie's hips and shifted them back and forth to show her how to steer her surfboard. "So this is how you seduced Drake?" Stephanie asked in her South African accent.

Gabrielle looked up and saw the smile on Stephanie. It was nice to see Stephanie smile. Gabrielle rolled her hair over her ear and looked down. She nodded. "Yeah, it is."

Stephanie giggled.

Gabrielle was glad the woman could laugh at something. "How much did he tell you?"

"Everything."

"Everything!"

"Yes, I'm afraid so."

Gabrielle buried her face in her hand. She sorted through their intimate moments and pulled out the most discreet one. "Did he tell you about us going to see *The Western Girl?*"

Stephanie nodded and giggled again.

"That bastard!"

"Yes, he is." Stephanie confirmed.

"He's such," Gabrielle held out her arms, clenched her fists and raised her eyes in frustration, "a guy!"

"Oh," Stephanie continued to giggle, "I thought you were going to say, asshole."

Gabrielle nodded her head off to the side and a smirk creased her lips. "Well, he's that too."

"You never told him did you?" Stephanie asked once her giggles subsided.

"Told him what?"

"That you're in love with him."

Gabrielle shot a defiant look back at Stephanie but knew from Stephanie's raised eyebrows she couldn't deny it. "Is it that obvious?"

Stephanie nodded.

"Please don't tell him," Gabrielle pleaded.

"Oh, no." Then Stephanie added, "I feel horrible though."

"Why's that?"

"Because I set him up with Grace."

Gabrielle looked down dejected. "He was never mine to begin with. Grace has always been there. I mean it was like she was in the bedroom with us the whole time. You know he never put a picture of me, but he had a picture of her in every room." Gabrielle's faced brightened as she reminisced about her conquest. "I have to say Grace was good for one thing."

"I know. I heard about the movie of Grace you used to, ah, how shall I say, set yourself up."

"He told you that too! Is there no discretion!" Gabrielle used a Grace Freemont movie to stoke Drake's libido before seducing him for the first time.

"I don't believe so. He's an open book. Besides, that is how I make my living—getting people to tell me their stories."

"Okay, so he doesn't know that I love him. I guess he doesn't know that you're in love with him either."

Stephanie's eyes darted around. "I...can't..." Stephanie could never have a normal relationship with a man. At least she didn't think so.

"I know, but that doesn't mean that you don't love him. There's a reason you turned to him when you needed someone." Gabrielle let Stephanie think about it and then dropped the subject. They both knew where they stood even if Stephanie tried to deny it. "But that doesn't matter because he has Grace now and we'd never be able to compete with her." Gabrielle said flipping her hand away.

"And they are very happy. Or at least they seem to be."

"How can you tell?"

Stephanie smiled at her work. "I know her real well and she talks to me. And he lights up whenever he talks to her or about her."

"Yeah, I know," Gabrielle said shaking her head. She didn't want to hear about it.

"I'm sorry. I saw how hurt you were last night—when I opened the door. I imagine you were hoping he was calling you for...for..."

"For a booty call? Well he didn't and that's probably a good thing. I probably need to move on."

"It's probably best for you if you do."

"Speaking of moving on." Gabrielle continued. "You can stay with me as long as you need."

"Thanks, I don't have a place to stay right now. I let my lease run out when I was in Iraq."

"Or did you want to stay with Drake."

"Actually, I asked him if he'd help me move into Grace's place on Saturday."

"Is he going to move in with you?"

"Oh, No! But I guess he could. I don't know. That might be a little strange."

"Its just that I—"

"You don't think I should be alone?"

"Yes, that's it." Gabrielle cemented a thought running through her head. "I'm looking for a place myself—something a little closer to LA. And I was thinking that you and I should get a place together." Gabrielle studied Stephanie's reaction. "At least until you're doing better." Gabrielle saw Stephanie's gears turning. "It's just a thought. I figured I'd offer since I had to move a little closer to work anyways."

"No, I like the idea. I think we should do it—at least temporarily," Stephanie giggled.

"What's so funny?"

"Nothing, I was just thinking about Drake's reaction when he hears that you and I are flatmates."

"Oh, you're not in love with the guy, you just think about him constantly." Gabrielle flashed her devilish smile.

"It doesn't matter. He would never go for a woman like you or I?"

Gabrielle looked stunned. The comment stung. "Why's that?"

"Grace is perfect for him. Don't get me wrong, he enjoyed his relationship with you, but in the end he would've never married you."

"Because I'm a barracks queen?" Gabrielle fought back her growing frustration.

Stephanie reached out and held her friend's hand to comfort her. "No, it's not that at all. You just have too much of an opinion."

"What's wrong with having an opinion?"

Stephanie swirled a thought in her head. "Nothing I guess. It is just that he doesn't want a woman who is…ah…well, it's not that he doesn't want a woman who is his intellectual equal. Heaven knows Grace is much more intelligent than I, but he's not the type of guy that wants a woman who is going to challenge him at every turn like you and I would. Don't misunderstand, Grace will challenge him and speak up when she needs…It's just that she has a certain softness, or vulnerability about her that incites his protective instincts." Stephanie was on a roll and looked Gabrielle straight in the eye. "Whenever I was in danger or vulnerable, he was so…ah…" Stephanie's eyes fluttered.

"Loving?" Gabrielle answered for her.

"Yes! Loving. But if I ever questioned something or had a thought or belief that crossed him, he lashed out at me. No, you and I weren't meant for Drake. Grace and he are perfect for each other."

"He's beautiful, she's beautiful, they'll have beautiful children." Gabrielle concluded and ran her hand through her hair knowing she had to move on.

"That's what I said."

"You know she's going to end up getting hurt."

"How's that?" The statement unnerved Stephanie. Gabrielle didn't mean it as a threat. She meant it as a warning.

Gabrielle squinted out towards the waves and thought of the past before she swilled in nagging sorrow. "I just know him."

"But you loved him right?"

"Yeah."

Stephanie couldn't follow her logic.

"How would you describe Drake?" Gabrielle asked.

"Ah…" Stephanie was still stumped.

"Did he, oh, how do I describe it, thrive in combat?"

Stephanie's face lit up when she recognized a coherent sentence. "Yes, as a matter of fact, he seemed to enjoy it."

Gabrielle looked down and ran her big toe through the sand.

"Yeah, he's going to crush her."

"How?" Stephanie didn't know where the logic would lead but she sensed the wisdom behind her new friend's words.

"Someday he isn't going to come home." Gabrielle's face didn't reveal any emotion, but the tear on her cheek did.

Stephanie reached a finger up to her friend's cheek. "You really loved him didn't you?"

Gabrielle pondered the question and then snapped. "Ah, oh…" she stammered. "Drake? Yes, but…" her thoughts raced so far ahead of the conversation she didn't what to answer. "I'm…it's…it's not Drake. I mean it is Drake that is going to break Grace's heart, but…well, you see…" She couldn't sidestep the inevitable. "I was married before."

Stephanie's eyebrows lifted. If Gabrielle didn't explain further she'd ask, but she knew what was coming.

"He was a SEAL."

"Seal?"

"Navy special forces."

"Oh." Sympathy filled Stephanie's voice.

"One day he just didn't come back."

Gabrielle's explanation didn't fully explain. Stephanie cringed, "Did he…" She paused hoping Gabrielle would clarify what happened to her former husband.

"It was a training accident."

"Oh, I'm so sorry."

Gabrielle explained how the Navy couldn't even produce a body and it probably wasn't a training accident either. She had no idea if he rested at the bottom of some ocean, or met some other dreadful fate in some foreign land. A worse scenario had him as a prisoner in some totalitarian state.

"So for you there wasn't any closure."

Gabrielle grimaced. She didn't want to relive this again. "It's actually best if I just don't think about it."

"That explains…"

"My reputation."

"Yes." Stephanie blushed.

"I don't know what I'm going to do. And I feel so bad because as bad as my situation may be, it doesn't compare to yours." Gabrielle shook her head. "Let's just surf and forget it all. How about that?" She smiled.

"Sounds good."

5

"Sergeant Connelly reports as ordered, sir!"

Drake returned his salute and smiled at his squad leader. This was a leadership challenge for Drake. The Marines who knew John Connelly didn't respect him. They considered him a coward that locked up in battle. Those who didn't know him would soon hear the story and then lose respect for him.

"Do you want to tell me about it?"

"No, sir."

"Fair enough. Will you tell me about it?"

Connelly pondered the question. Was it an order, or a request?

"Let me assure you, whatever happened in the past," Drake continued, "is in the past. If I'm worth anything as a platoon leader, I should be able to help you get over what it is that is holding you back. First of all, who was your platoon leader?" Then Drake quickly added, "No, don't answer that."

Connelly's eyes darted around Drake's office. How could he tell someone that charged a building full of jihadis about the time he locked up in battle? "Sir, it was right after Nasariyah. Remember when they tried to send all those regulars down to reinforce the hajjis in Nasariyah?"

"Yeah."

"Our platoon was on this road and these two big passenger busses rolled up nut to butt and came to a stop and all these regulars start pouring out." Connelly's eyes grew with excitement. He usually spoke with a slow Georgia drawl unless he got excited like now. He sat on the edge of his chair and started gesturing wildly. "Now it is just our platoon up against like two companies of regulars. We didn't know what was going on until we started taking fire. We shot at the windows, but they were all bullet proof. So the LT sends us in to try to take them out as they come off the bus. He splits up the platoon, one squad to each side and mine in between the two busses." Connelly sucked in a deep breath. The first since he started the story. "I try to direct my guys' fire but we are taking fire from both busses. I tell one fireteam to move out and the leader and SAW eat a face full of lead. So they're out in the open bleeding out. Another guy goes after them, and goes down too. I open my mouth, but I don't even know what to say. We were stacked up against the bus. A team behind me falls in, but a whole 'nother team rolls in and is put down. I can't even direct my guys' fire. Nothing is coordinated and my guys just keep dying—"

"Okay, okay," Drake said and held up his hands and waved them up and down. "Just calm down." He said in a soothing voice. "Get control of yourself right now. Control your brain and your actions."

By this time Connelly eyes bulged wild with excitement. He took in a couple breaths and slowed down. "Sir, I don't know how you did it?"

"What is that?"

"Run into a house with fifteen jihadis with just one other guy."

Drake chuckled. "Well it isn't like I planned it that way. We thought there were only two of them in the house itself."

"But still, sir, once you knew there were more than two, how did you just not freeze up?"

"I focused on what needed to be done, not on what my situation was. I know it doesn't sound like much, but that is what I did. As a matter of fact, when I read my AAR I thought to myself, 'are you nuts?' I mean, when you read it, like you did, it sounds crazy, but when I was in the middle of it, it was like doing the laundry. First you gotta do this, then this, then that, then the other, then you get to sit back and watch football on TV. It just felt like a task I had to do before moving on to whatever I needed to do next."

"Sir, it didn't feel like that for me. I just knew I was gonna die."

"Hmm." Drake thought back. "I had that feeling once when a couple RPGs came at me in Nasariyah, but I couldn't do anything about that anyway."

"Sir, what I'm saying is…I don't see how I could ever measure up to be in your platoon."

"But I think that is why Captain Kim put you in my platoon. Because he knows that you wouldn't want to let me down."

"No, sir."

Drake flipped through Connelly's file. "Do you smoke?" Most Marines smoked.

"Ah, yes, sir."

"Pull one out now."

"Sir?"

"Pull one out now."

"But sir," Connelly was confused. The government didn't allow smoking in doors.

"I didn't say to light it up." Drake put his elbows on his desk and pointed at Connelly. "Look, I need you to trust me and do whatever I tell you to do. If I tell you to take a crap in the middle of the hallway, I want you to ask me how runny it should be." His comedic tone belied his message. "If you trust me, then maybe you can trust yourself. Now pull one out and put in your lips without lighting up."

Connelly complied.

"So how does that make you feel? You wanna light it up?"

"Yes, sir."

"Is it going to drive you nuts if you can't?"

"Yes, sir."

"Good, I want to see you with a smoke in your lips all the time but never lit."

"Sir?"

"Connelly, as of right now, you are no longer a smoker. I want you to conquer this. I need you to be able to control your mind. You have to be stronger than your mind. And to help you, you and I are going to start PTing together. So plan on being here at 0400 tomorrow."

Connelly's eye's bulged. Drake's PT sessions were notoriously long and grueling. Scuttlebutt had it he once ran a whole fireteam into the ground until they all threw up.

"I also need you to train hard with your men. You've already been a squad leader, so I know you know your job, but I need you to be absolutely perfect in everything you do. You know that you have a reputation and the only way you can earn a squad's respect is if you know your stuff inside and out and never hesitate and always make the right call the first time. Otherwise when all hell breaks lose, your guys are going to doubt you and not follow you into a house full of jihadis. You have a head start because you've been a squad leader before, so I'm going to call on your squad first when I have a tough nut to crack."

"Yes, sir."

Drake's face softened. He leaned back and blew out a lungful of air. "So you're married?"

"Yes, sir."

"Kids?"

"Sir, I got a two year old."

"How long you been married?" Drake was going to keep asking questions until Connelly opened up.

"About four years."

"High school sweetheart?"

"Yes, sir."

"So she followed you?"

"Well…she got pregnant her—our senior year and her parents kicked her out."

"How old is she?"

"She's my age."

Drake cocked an eyebrow. It didn't add up.

"She lost the fist baby. Her daddy beat her real good and she ended up in the hospital. My folks took her in. We got married after I went into the Corps."

"How's she doing?"

"Oh, she's fine now. But SoCal is not her speed. We're from a small town and things here move just a bit fast for her."

Drake put down the file and looked at Connelly. "You let me know if there is anything I can do." He studied Connelly. "I mean it."

"Yes, sir. I know you do. And I really appreciate you giving me another shot."

"I don't mean just that. I mean for your family too. If your family needs anything let me know what I can do."

"Yes, sir."

"All right then, I'll see you in the mornin'."

Connelly reported out.

As Connelly stepped out of the room a second lieutenant walked in. Drake studied the nametag, HOUSTON. Drake stood up and offered a hand, "How ya doin'? I'm Drake Scott."

Houston shook Drake's hand, gave a nod and looked past him.

"You just report in?" Drake asked.

"Yeah, are the desks assigned?

"No, but that one is mine."

"Why is that?"

"Cause I was here first." Drake wondered about the question. He couldn't tell if Houston resolved that it was a first come first serve or a seniority issue.

Drake watched him put away gear and get situated. Curiosity picked at Drake. Houston didn't come out of TBS, The Basic School, and OIC, Officer Infantry Course, with high recommendations. Drake was openly cordial, but Houston continued to go about his way like Drake was in his way. "You got any questions?" Drake asked.

"No, not really?" Houston continued to put away manuals and other items.

Drake propped up his feet and watched. He thought about his first day in the company and how nervous he was and how much he wanted to talk to anybody who could offer him some direction.

Finally Houston said, "So I hear you played ball."

Drake smiled. "Yeah, I played a little."

"But that was in the Pac 10 right?" Houston meant it as an unveiled insult.

"If you don't count the Niners." Drake said referring to the NFL team that signed him as an undrafted free agent.

"Yeah, we play some serious competition in our conference."

"I know, I saw your guys get lit up in Norman seventy-seven nothing last week." Drake shot a stinger back at Houston. And then asked, "So you did OCS?" Drake knew that most ball players wouldn't be in the military via ROTC. They go to college on an athletic scholarship and then if they go into the military they go through OCS, Officer Candidate School. Drake knew Houston didn't go through OCS, so that meant that he was a walk on, and probably didn't even play all four years.

"No, I was ROTC."

"Oh." Point made.

A Staff Sergeant stepped into the office. "Alvarez!" Drake stood up. He was excited to see his old squad leader.

"Lieutenant Scott." Alvarez smiled and offered a hand. Drake shunned the hand and bear hugged his former Marine. The men broke. "I'll let you two talk." Drake still hated letting any of his guys go. He felt like he was abandoning them. He stepped outside the door to offer some privacy.

"Sergeant Alvarez, do you usually go around hugging lieutenants?" Houston said loud enough that Drake could hear it down the hall. Drake flaunted the affectionate greeting subconsciously to establish dominance. It said, *I'm the alpha. I know people. I know how things work.*

Drake stopped and considered what he was about to do. It could be bad, or could be beneficial. He pivoted and returned to the office. He interrupted the meeting. Houston scowled while relief washed over Alvarez's face. "Lieutenant Houston, I sent Staff Sergeant Alvarez into a city, filled with thousands of hostiles, with a handful of Marines and a lot of wounded that needed attention. It was nothing short of a suicide mission and he saluted smartly and moved out into enemy territory. At the time I thought I was never going to see him again. He and I," Drake pointed to Alvarez and then himself, "have been shot at and survived impossible odds. So I hug him whenever I see him. But I guess you wouldn't know jack shit about what I feel for this Marine because you don't have a jack shit of any experience in combat or what it means to be shot at with live rounds." Drake took in a long breath. "So if you got a problem with that, I suggest you shove it." Drake waited for a response. "You copy?"

Houston narrowed his eyes. Drake was out of line. He should have addressed Houston's behavior in private. Houston's leadership lacked any sensitivity, but Drake made things worse by calling him out in front of Alvarez.

On the other hand, seeing his old platoon leader back him up made Alvarez's image of Drake as a real leader flourish. Alvarez saw the passion and love of his men that defined Drake as a leader during his first Iraq tour.

"I said did you copy, Lieutenant?"

Houston rolled his eyes, "Yes, I copy."

Drake thought about other piece of advice he should offer, like listen to your platoon sergeant, but it would fall on deaf ears.

Drake walked into the apartment complex mailroom and froze. He couldn't believe the name he saw, W HOUSTON (304). He shook his head and opened his mailbox and immediately forgot everything else. He tossed aside the junk mail and opened the little box. "Some sweets for my sweets, Grace." She sent Swiss chocolates. He opened the box and flipped one into his mouth and started down the hall. He perused the first edition of his new *Hollywood Vine* subscription. One of the articles made him smile. It read *Beauty And The Beast: Grace And Her Marine* by Stephanie Chandler. He stepped to the side as someone approached.

"Howdy stranger?"

Drake looked up. "Oh, hi." Drake offered a feeble smile. It felt awkward. Pain slipped through the forced smile the woman wore as she passed Drake towards the mailroom.

"How is Stephanie?" he called back as her as she passed by.

"She's fine. I took her out and we worked at a Habitat for Humanity site today." Gabrielle, like Drake was a gym rat and used physical exertion and distraction to solve, or ignore problems.

"Good."

The conversation lacked investment. He talked to her to be polite not because he wanted to. She saw the card with the chocolates.

"Do you want one?" he asked without thinking.

She shook her head. "No, no thank you." It would have been odd. Would Grace appreciate it if she knew he was offering her chocolates to his former lover?

Gabrielle stepped into the mailroom and heaved heavy breaths. It used to be that when they saw each other, they'd light up and she'd feel so…loved. Yes, she used to feel loved. He never said it, but he showed it. She teased him that under his tough guy exterior was nothing but soft goo. She'd poke his belly and say, "nothin' but goo," whenever he allowed his softer side to percolate.

She lifted a finger to her eye and opened her mailbox when she felt the man next to her gazing at her. She pulled out her mail and allowed one letter to slip out of her hands so she had to lean over and pick it up. She offered him a nice view as she bent over. From the boots and trousers she could tell he was a Marine. *Yummy! Thank you, God! Just what I needed!*

She stood up and flipped through her mail slowly. She snuck a peek. He had his mail in front of him. He gazed over a letter appearing to read it, but his eyes were firmly planted on her chest.

Gabrielle ended the charade of looking at her mail and squared her shoulders to the young lieutenant. He still didn't catch on. She arched her back so he had less of her shirt in the way of her curves. He finally looked up. "Oh, I'm sorry."

Yeah, right. But he spun and scooted out. Fury raged in Gabrielle. She stormed up after him. He ducked into his room almost trying to avoid her. She stopped in front of his door and put her hands on her hips. So many thoughts raced through her head. They mostly revolved around how to get over Drake. She pounded on the door before she lost her nerve.

When he opened up the door she busted through the threshold. "What the hell, Marine. What happened to the Marine Corps and the Marines I knew and lusted?"

A dumb look occupied his face.

"What the hell!" Gabrielle continued. "You eye-fuck me in the mailroom and then don't even have the balls to ask me out and maybe get a chance at a real piece instead of just running back to your room like a scared little boy so you can jack off to the girl you just saw in the mailroom!"

"I…"

"What's your name, lieutenant?" Gabrielle barked.

"Houston, ma'am, Lieutenant William Houston."

Gabrielle smiled. Young naïve lieutenants melted her. She stuck out her hand, "Nice to meet you Lieutenant Houston. I'm Gabrielle." It was her first lieutenant since separating from active duty. The familiarity comforted her. "So, Lieutenant Houston, or may I call you William?"

"Bill, ma'am."

"Bill," she cooed. "My name is Gabrielle. You can call me Gabrielle."

"Ah, okay, Gabrielle."

"So, Bill. Is there something you'd like to ask me?" Her seductive tone deepened.

"Excuse me?"

"Is—there—anything—you'd—like—to—ask—me?" She breathed into his ear.

"Ah…"

"My God! I must be loosing it!" Gabrielle erupted.

"Losing what?"

"My touch," she said. It used to be that Marines would throw themselves at her. This guy displayed the libido of a eunuch. "Are you doing anything on Saturday?" She inspected his place as she moved through the small apartment. She looked for a picture with a girlfriend in it. That always made the chase more interesting. She eyed the DVDs next to the TV—all action thrillers. She turned her back on him allowing him to gaze at her well-toned backside without her eyes interfering. She slid a finger under the top of a pizza box—meat lovers.

"No." Houston said, still sporting a clueless stare.

"I'll pick you up at ten." Gabrielle made her way out to the door. "AM that is. Oh, and plan on getting wet and cold."

"Wha, What are we going to do?"

"You know how to surf, Bill?"

"No."

"You will by Saturday night," she said over her shoulder as she sauntered down the hall. An easy smile grew over her face. *That was fun.*

6

"Is that all there is?" Drake asked Stephanie after setting down the last box.

"That's all." Stephanie said referring to her last box. She and Drake stood in Grace's guest room. "I guess I didn't tell you, but Gabrielle and I are going to share a flat."

"Really!" Drake knew there was a friendship budding but it seemed quick.

"Yes, I need the company."

"That's fantastic."

"And what's better is that I was able to sleep through the night last night."

"That's wonderful. I'm so happy for you." A bright smile lit up Drake's face. He stepped forward to hug her and stopped. Stephanie was touchy about contact but she nodded and they shared a quick hug that was too short for Stephanie. She wanted more, much more.

Drake felt responsible for Stephanie. Sharing the burden with Gabrielle was a relief. "Then why are we moving stuff here?" he asked.

"A couple reasons. First, I wanted to store this stuff here while we looked for a flat instead of paying for a storage shed. Second, Grace wanted me to get a couple pictures of you in her house." A smile sneaked across her face. "Actually..." the smile grew mischievous, "she said, 'get me a picture of him taking a showing in my bathroom.'" Her eyebrows lifted and she reveled in the blush growing on

Drake's cheeks. When he recovered she asked, "You want to have a look around?"

Drake's eyes brightened. "Yeah," he said voice barely cracked a whisper. Drake's mind struggled to put everything together, that he was actually in Grace Freemont's house, strolling through her bedroom, inspecting her shower and sharing her intimate space.

"What is it?" Stephanie asked.

"I don't know. I just feel like I'm spying on her or something."

Stephanie studied Drake's reaction as they stepped into Grace's bedroom. A sly smirk creased her lips. "Do you want to take a look in here?" Stephanie teased as she laid her fingers on one of Grace's dresser drawers.

Drake's cheeks turned crimson again.

"She knows you're here. I told her you were going to help me. That's when she asked for the picture."

"I know."

"Did you talk to her?"

"We talked for a couple hours last night."

"And didn't you talk to her for a couple hours on Thursday night too?"

"Yeah."

"When do you sleep?"

Drake smiled wearily. "I get a couple hours here and there."

"What is it?" Stephanie said while delicately rolling the drawer out and peeking in. There wasn't anything she didn't know about Grace's house. She knew where everything was. It is just an act to taunt Drake. She still wanted to know what Drake hid behind his sneaking smile. "You sure you don't want to have a peek?"

"No…ah…I don't need to."

The knowing smile blossoming on Drake's face let her know something was going on and she wasn't privy to it. It used to be that she was the conduit between them. Now they were familiar enough that they didn't need her help to foster the relationship. Stephanie cocked a hip and put a hand on it. "And why don't you?"

Drake's face nearly cracked because he was working so hard to hold himself together. "I—can't—tell—you."

"Drake!" Stephanie's eyes widened. "What is it?"

"I'm not gonna tell."

"Fine," she huffed. She whipped out her phone. *At your house with Drake. He says he doesn't need to look in your panty drawers. What's he hiding?* "There," Stephanie declared. "I'll get to the bottom of his."

Drake busted out and doubled over in laughter.

"What is so funny, Lieutenant Scott?" He called her by her last name whenever he was upset with her. She thought she would try the last name address to indicate her frustration.

Drake held his belly and laughed shaking his head. He concentrated and spat out, "Bottom is the key word."

"Bottom?" Stephanie's phone buzzed.

"I'm gonna look around," Drake said.

Ask Drake why he doesn't need to look.

Stephanie reached for his arm and stopped him. "No, wait, she said, 'Ask Drake why he doesn't need to look.'"

"I'm still not telling," Drake said over his shoulder.

"But she said—"

"I'm still not telling."

He won't tell me, Stephanie texted while following Drake through the house. "Why won't you tell me?"

Stephanie's phone buzzed. *I'm a naughty girl.*

The secret drove Stephanie to madness. She was used to being on the inside of private jokes or getting people to spill. "Drake, would you please!"

"You said *bottom.*" Drake raised his eyebrows.

Stephanie looked back and thought about the situation. "She sent you panties!"

Drake smiled at her and turned away. "And I think they were covered in an expensive French perfume."

YOU ARE A NAUGHTY GIRL!!! Stephanie texted.

Yes I am ;-)

Stephanie's mind rolled on. She thought about pushing Drake for more information but realized he was too much of a gentleman even if he was a Marine. *So what do you two talk about every night for hours?*

All I can say is I'm a naughty girl ;-)

OMG. You are!

But we do spend a lot of time talking.

I hope so. Stephanie looked up and saw Drake was reading over her shoulder. She tucked away her phone. "Hey! This is private."

"Oh, okay," Drake laughed.

"Have you seen enough?" Stephanie hissed feigning disgust.

"Yep." Drake beamed at her expense. "Hey, I've got something for us to do."

"What is it?"

"I need to take you to the range."

"The range?" Stephanie asked as she locked up the front door.

"The shooting range."

"Oh."

"I meant to ask you. Do you plan on going back?" Drake asked.

"Back where?"

"Iraq."

"Iraq?"

"Yeah," Drake said softly. The intimacy in his voice belied the violence in the offer.

"Oh." Stephanie's voice faded.

"Oh, shit. I shouldn't have said that should I. Especially after your first night of sleep. I'm sorry I wasn't thinking."

"No," Stephanie reached out to Drake and placed a hand on his knee as he pulled out of the driveway to let him know she wasn't offended. "That's not it." Stephanie furrowed her brow. An eerie guilt swept through her. "I'll go back, but only with you." She felt like she just asked her best friend's boyfriend to sleep with her. Combat sealed an intimate bond, deeper than any lover could experience that only combat vets, military or otherwise, understood.

"Well," Drake said as he waited for the driveway gate to open. "I was thinking that I really needed to get you some time on the range. So I cleared it with PA—"

"PA?"

"Public Affairs."

"Oh, yes, that's who gets the press IDs."

"Yep. Anyway, I cleared it with PA so that this was an official interview by you."

"Oh, all right."

"It also means you get to shoot the weapons and use government ammo. Otherwise I couldn't let you shoot at all because we just can't let civilians shoot military weapons unless you brought your personal weapon."

Stephanie didn't fully understand all the legalities, but it sounded like Drake tied up any potential loose strings. At the range he handed Stephanie some hearing protection. On the line he drilled her on gun safety, how to load a clip and chamber a round. Then he slipped his arms around her to show her different grips.

"You're going to have to show me that again." Stephanie said. The warmth of his breath on the back of her neck distracted her. Not only did it distract her, it stirred a sensation she thought she'd lost. It threw into question the wisdom of returning to Iraq. Would Iraq raise specters she was trying to bury? Then, if she stayed in the states while Drake deployed could she ever forgive herself if he didn't come back. On top of this breaking into serious political reporting required her to go back into the line of fire. She shook her head clear and focused on Drake's instructions. These feelings shouldn't surface about Drake for other reasons too.

Drake slipped 9 mm rounds into clips as she unloaded rounds into a human silhouette. He filled clip after clip so that she could swap out clips like a vet. "Okay, now let me show you how to clean it and then I'll have you clean it."

Before calling it a day, Drake decided to run Stephanie ragged over hills.

"What if I don't want to go on a run with you?"

"Suit yourself, but it's not like you can go home, I drove remember?"

Drake watched Stephanie carefully and monitored her condition. They both checked their pulses after each hill. When Stephanie's reached a point that her body wasn't recovering by the time she got to the bottom of the hill, he said, "You about ready to give?"

Stephanie shot an, *are you kidding me,* look. "You are honestly going to allow me the option?"

"Why wouldn't I?"

"Because you are a sadistic bastard when it comes to running me ragged."

Drake smiled easily. "C'mon, I'll buy us some Chinese and we can pull out one of Grace's movies."

"Chinese? Does it always have to be Chinese? How about Italian for a change?"

"If you're paying."

Stephanie pouted.

"Fine." Drake sounded exacerbated. "I'll buy you Italian."

"Wonderful," Stephanie chirped. She could still wield her femininity even after enduring Iraq.

Drake and Stephanie pulled plates out of Gabrielle's cabinets and piled their meals onto them. "If Gabrielle was out apartment hunting, shouldn't you have gone with?"

"Oh, she didn't go looking at flats," Stephanie said as she clicked the remote to start the movie. She sat down next to Drake. "She went surfing."

"Hmm, surfing, eh?"

Stephanie studied Drake for a reaction. "Yeah, with some Marine."

He didn't react. He seemed more interested in the movie. Stephanie wondered if he wasn't listening or if he was just concentrating on the move. She decided against repeating herself to make sure he understood the situation. Instead she begged the question. "It's about time."

"What's about time?"

"It's about time she started seeing someone again."

Drake struggled to digest what Stephanie said and watch the movie. "What are you talking about?"

"She hasn't seen anyone since you left for Iraq."

Drake put his pasta-loaded fork down on his plate. "You mean to tell me she hasn't…"

Stephanie treaded on thin ice. She could be opening the door to something that could crush Grace. Loyalties tugged at Stephanie since her flourishing friendship with Gabrielle fostered sympathy for Gabrielle's feelings also. "No, she hasn't."

Drake cocked his head in a question. "I guess we all deployed and she didn't have anybody to play with," Drake said ignorant of the insult he just lobbed at Gabrielle.

"No, that's not it."

Drake put his fork down without taking a bite, still loaded with pasta. "What was she doing?" From what Drake knew of Stephanie, or what he thought he knew of Stephanie, she wasn't the type to beat around the bush.

"You honestly don't know?"

Drake's eyes darted to the corners of the room searching for a feasible scenario.

"You don't know how—"

"I need an extra large meat lovers supreme." Gabrielle stormed through the door with her phone pinned to her ear, her keys and a DVD in one hand and her shorty in the other. "Yeah." She gave her address and phone number. She looked over at Drake and Stephanie and smiled *hello* at them. She scooted into the bedroom to get a change of clothes and then back out into the hall and to the bathroom to take a shower.

Stephanie looked over at Drake. His eyes studied the TV and the movie. Stephanie huffed, but not loud enough. Drake didn't react. He didn't even ask about what Stephanie was going to say. Stephanie wondered what to make of it. Was he that into Grace? Did he not care about what Stephanie thought or why Gabrielle didn't see anyone?

Drake paused the movie when the bell rang announcing the arrival of Gabrielle's pizza. Gabrielle trotted out of her bedroom in a robe drying her hair and grabbed her wallet. She pulled out a twenty, opened the door and smiled sweetly, "Here you go. Keep what's left over." She shot a smile to Drake and Stephanie as she put her pizza down. "I'll be out of your hair soon." She yearned for a reaction from Drake. Drake promptly disappointed her when he hit PLAY again.

Stephanie hurt for her friend. When Gabrielle came out in a loose T and swim bottoms on Stephanie asked, "So who are you spending your evening with?"

"A Lieutenant Bill Houston."

"Houston!" Drake protested. He slammed his plate down and stared down Gabrielle.

Stephanie and Gabrielle shared a look. Drake surprised both of them. He seemed so uninterested and now was zeroed in on the conversation.

Drake stood up. "Houston?"

"Yeah," Gabrielle smiled coyly. "He's a really sweet boy."

"He's an ass. You can't..." Drake stopped himself.

Gabrielle's eyes lit up. She poked him in the chest. "You don't get to tell me who I do or don't do. I do whatever I please with whoever I please."

"I'm telling you he is an jackwad. I'm telling you as a friend."

"As a *friend?* Because you sound like a jealous boyfriend."

"Like I was ever your boyfriend. I was just another stop along the line."

Stephanie gasped.

Gabrielle's face fired up. "No, Drake, you're the ass here, not Bill." Gabrielle grabbed her pizza and DVD and stormed out of the room.

Stephanie sat quietly. She knew the darker side of Drake and didn't want to upset him anymore. But she ached to give Drake the full story, the story he seemed uninterested in.

Gabrielle knocked at the door and thought to herself that she forgot to bring something to drink. Houston possessed little, if any, sophistication. She figured he'd only have beer and probably domestic at that.

"Hi, I didn't know…" Houston stammered. He didn't expect her so soon. She must have needed it in bad way.

"That I was coming over?" Gabrielle flashed a charming smile. "I thought that a big tough Marine like you would be a little hungry after today."

Houston's eyes feasted on the box.

"Meat lovers," Gabrielle said.

"Meat Lovers!" Houston's eyes grew as he took the pizza from Gabrielle.

"I thought you'd like that." Gabrielle made her way to the DVD player and put in the movie while Houston set the pizza down and pulled out a slice. He bent over backwards and slid a wedge of pizza down this throat. "Mmm hmm. That's good," he mumbled through his full mouth. Tomato sauce seeped out of the corner of his mouth.

Gabrielle took in the sight and sighed. No sophistication to speak of. *Drake wasn't this raw was he? Dammit, why do I have to think of him now?* "Do you have any wine?"

"Wine?" Houston grimaced as he quickly spun his head around the room looking for a bottle he knew wasn't there. "Uh, no."

"Just beer?"

"I have beer and some Cokes…and water."

Gabrielle tried to avoid sighing again. "I'll have a beer."

Houston popped the tops off two beers. He handed one to Gabrielle.

Gabrielle walked into the small kitchen and stood by the pizza. She stared at the pizza. She couldn't do it. *Haven't I grown out of this yet?* She had played this routine so many times before that she had memorized the script. But if she went back to her room now Drake would see her and know that nothing happened. *Why should I care what he thinks?* But she did care what he thought even though he was gone for good. She still wanted to retain some dignity. Sleeping with Houston didn't build dignity though. *Oh, I can't do this.* Gabrielle turned around. "What the hell are you thinking!"

"What?" Houston had ripped off his shirt and was tugging at his belt. "I know why you came over."

"You do?"

"Oh, yeah, I've heard all about you."

A cold shiver shook Gabrielle's spine. Her reputation haunted her once again. "Ah, I don't think so." Gabrielle stepped toward the door.

"Oh, I do think so." Houston cut her off.

Gabrielle saw fire burning in Houston's eyes. "Bill, I'm going to leave."

"I don't think so." A sick calmness overtook Houston's voice.

"Bill…" Gabrielle said in a careful measured tone, "I'm-going-to-leave." She reached for the door.

Houston grabbed her arm.

"You're hurting me, Bill." Gabrielle tried to stifle the fear seeping through her voice.

"Then don't be a tease. Is this how you play your game? You play hard to get?" He tightened his grip and pulled her in.

My game? Gabrielle shuddered. The legal system would condemn her. She couldn't threaten him with reporting him. She would have to list in detail her long sordid past conquests. The married ones would suffer along with her. Too many officers would go down. Some of the higher-ranking ones would have painted her as an evil vixen out to seduce every man she fancied. Unfortunately for Gabrielle their testimony wouldn't be a lie. She prowled Pendleton for prey with reckless abandon. "Bill, you're scaring me." Gabrielle shielded him off with her free arm. Houston grabbed her other arm and leaned in to kiss her. Gabrielle turned and he landed on her cheek. Gabrielle's stomach churned. Houston wrapped his arms around her and pinned her against his his with one arm and ripped at her T-shirt with the other. Gabrielle fell limp. She knew she wasn't strong enough to overpower Houston. She had to think. Houston's hands violated her. "Bill..." she cried too hard to continue her sentence.

Houston savored the sight. She submitted. The hesitation cost him though.

Gabrielle focused. She had one shot. Otherwise Houston would go from ugly to frightful. She closed her eyes then flashed them open. In a single motion she pounced on him. She sank her teeth into his cheeks, slammed her heel into his foot and rammed her fist into his groin. Houston's nervous system choked with pain and Houston fell to the ground. His hand clamped around her T-shirt and tore the back half off as she slipped out the door.

She sprinted down to her apartment and stopped short of it. She stared at her hand as it reached for the handle. She heard herself heaving sobs. Her chest pumped air into her lungs as she tried to recover. She looked back down the hall to make sure Houston didn't follow her. She didn't want to go in and face Drake though. The indignity mortified her. She reached for her car keys. She considered going somewhere to get away. But she didn't have a full shirt on and she needed people. She needed people who cared about her. She needed the old Drake, the one before Iraq. She leaned against the door and slid down to a crouch. Sobs bubbled over. *Go ahead and cry. Get it all out. Let it go. You need to cry and let it out.* Debilitating grief wasn't a stranger to Gabrielle.

7

"Do you hear that?"

"What?" Drake didn't hear anything but the seductive Britanic accent purring from the blonde in the movie.

"It sounded like something thumped against the door." Stephanie failed to break through Drake's fixation on the exquisite figure on the TV. Drake still had to pinch himself. The cyber love affair fostered an odd sense of connectedness and unfamiliarity at the same time. If Drake closed his eyes he could see her in their conversations. However, they never had a conversation in person. It was all a dream. But it wasn't a dream. He built a relationship with and enigma that existed somewhere out there. "You didn't hear that?"

"No," Drake answered without giving serious thought to the question.

Stephanie's senses teased her. She swore she heard what sounded like sobs at the door. Stephanie wanted an answer. She picked up the remote and looked at Drake. She snickered to herself. Drake sat on the edge of his seat with his elbows on his knees as he studied the girl in the movie. Stephanie worried what would happen if she turned off the TV. The TV held the center of Drake's consciousness. If Stephanie turned it off Drake would probably fall into such disarray mentally that he might forget to breath.

Stephanie tiptoed to the door and listened. She definitely heard sobs. She turned to look at Drake but he couldn't focus on anything but the TV. Besides Stephanie wanted to stay quiet to catch whatever was going on outside the door before whoever was there realized someone heard the sobbing. She turned the handle and opened the door to find a half naked Gabrielle curled up on the floor. "Gabrielle! What happened?"

Gabrielle covered her face mortified. Her shoulders bobbed in rhythm to her sobs.

Drake broke his lock from the TV. "What is going on?" Drake stood up. He didn't expect to see Gabrielle until tomorrow. Then he saw the torn T-shirt. "What the hell is going on!"

"Drake!" Stephanie chided Drake. She tried to get a hold of the situation and Drake's anger wasn't helping.

"Oh, hell no!" He broke into a sprint down the hall.

"Drake!" Gabrielle screamed down the hall. She looked around. Some neighbors were opening their doors to gawk at the spectacle. "Shit!" Gabrielle stood up and took a step after Drake and stopped. She had to go back and get a new shirt. "Go stop him," she told Stephanie and ran to her room and threw open her closet.

Drake pounded on the door.

Houston knew that Gabrielle would be back. He prepped his line about her reputation for this moment when she came back to confront him. When he opened the door and saw Drake he couldn't line up the logic of why Drake stood at his door. Before Houston's mind resolved itself, Drake's fist smacked Houston's jaw.

"You piece of shit!" Drake barked and cocked his fist for a re-attack. Houston flew into a counteroffensive and launched a fist at Drake's face. Drake slid his head to the side slightly and used an open hand to guide Houston's blow off to the side. Drake stepped forward and caught Houston's throat in the crook of his elbow. Drake wrapped his arm all the way around Houston's neck. Drake grabbed his own shirt as he tightened his arm around Houston's throat. He slid his other forearm behind Houston's neck and squeezed Houston in a figure four choke hold. Houston tried to turn his neck to the side to open his airway. Drake flexed his shoulder, biceps, forearms and hand allowing Houston no quarter. Houston pulled at Drake's arm to try to open some breathing room to no avail. Drake's arms tightened in a vice grip. Houston tried to gasp. If he could gasp that meant some air traveled in and out, but nothing came out. Houston made an effort to kick Drake in the shins. Drake rotated his hips behind Houston and lifted him off the ground so his back hyperextended backwards. Houston's fingers fell away from Drake's arms. Houston's sight turned gray and then black as his eyes rolled backwards.

"Stop! Drake, Stop!" Gabrielle shrieked as she rushed through the door. Gabrielle's mind raced through legal scenarios. "You're going to kill him!" She banged on Drake's shoulder with closed fists. Then she saw a look on his face she'd never seen before. She'd been his lover for nearly a year and knew everything about him. At least she thought she did. She'd never seen anger like this in anyone. His face snarled inhumanly. She couldn't break through his focus. "DRAKE! STOP!" Gabrielle balled up her fist and pounded his face in a hammer strike.

Stephanie stood back. She had seen Drake under every condition. But like Gabrielle she'd never seen him like this. In a firefight he looked clinical, devoid of any emotion. If she saw had seen any emotion in combat, he looked like he was enjoying being a master at his job.

Gabrielle's blow broke through. His face twitched and it registered his surroundings. He relaxed his arms and Houston dropped to the floor.

"You...you ASSHOLE!" Gabrielle shook violently. Drake saw the frustration in her face but didn't understand it.

"What the hell is your problem!" Drake yelled.

Gabrielle froze. Drake still looked like a predator in search of prey. His flexed shoulders frightened Gabrielle. She didn't want to push him too much. He'd been through combat. There were stories of veterans snapping and going on rampages.

Stephanie dropped to her knees and placed her fingertips on Houston's wrist. She felt light bumps and saw his chest rise and fall. "He's breathing," she said but Drake and Gabrielle stood locked in a faceoff.

"What did I do?" Drake asked.

"You idiot—"

"How am I the idiot?"

"Now, I can't do anything to him legally without getting you in trouble." Gabrielle fumed for a minute while Drake processed the information.

"Yeah, but," he couldn't justify his reaction anymore. In Iraq he killed Stephanie's attackers. He wanted to kill Houston too although he wasn't going to. If he was going to kill Houston he would have twisted his neck, not just cut off his air.

Gabrielle's face burned red. "Aaahh!" she screamed in frustration, then turned and stormed off.

Stephanie stood up and studied Drake. She offered her most disapproving glare.

Drake returned the look. "What? What did I do?"

Stephanie backed up to the hallway and Drake followed her. "You don't understand do you?"

"Understand what? He's," Drake pointed at Houston who started to stir, "He's the one who tried to rape her," Drake closed Houston's door and followed Stephanie down the hall. "What did I do?" Drake continued following Stephanie. "Hey, would you stop and talk to me?" Stephanie continued towards Gabrielle's door. "What did I do to you? Why won't *you* talk to me?" Drake grabbed her shoulder.

Stephanie spun on him in front of Gabrielle's door. "Get your bloody hand off of me!"

"Sorry," Drake forgot for the moment about Stephanie's delicate nature.

She bore holes through him with her eyes. Sobs echoed through the door. "You really don't know what you did?"

"No, I don't." Drake considered pushing his situation. He wanted to vent, but he also wanted Stephanie to talk to him. He took a chance. "And I'm pretty sick and tired of this game you two are playing!"

"Game! You think this is a game! You pompous ass!"

Drake reevaluated his situation. "You know what," he said calmly and turned away. "This ain't worth it." He waved a hand over his shoulder. "I'm outta here."

"That's it. Walk off like you don't care because you never did."

Drake pivoted. "I DON'T CARE? How can you say I don't care! I nearly killed a guy because I care."

"That's not it." Stephanie shook her head. "You're such a guy."

"Oh, that's bullshit! What the fuck does that mean?"

"Let me ask you this. Do you care about Gabrielle?"

Drake waved his hand toward Houston's room. "Yeah, I think that is pretty obvious."

"Do you love her?"

Drake twitched his nose and shook his head trying to understand the logic.

Stephanie continued, "Because a man doesn't go killing another man over a woman unless he's in love with her?"

"What?" Drake asked indignantly.

"I told you, you wouldn't get it."

"Of course I don't get it. That's nonsense."

"Do you love her?"

"Who?"

"Gabrielle!"

"No!" Drake's face scrunched revealing the idea's absurdity.

"You had a relationship with her and you felt absolutely nothing for her?"

"Look, I don't know why you are pissed at me, but all we had between us was sex and nothing more."

"It was just sex?"

"Yes!"

"Really?"

"Yes! She slept with half of Pendleton. I was just another notch in her bedpost." Drake shook his head, waved in disgust and turned away for his room.

"She deserves better than you."

Drake froze. He was finished with the conversation, but that statement left too many questions. "Who?"

"Who do you think I'm talking about?"

"Chandler, I don't know what type of sick game you're playing, but I'm getting pretty sick and tired of it."

"You don't deserve either of them."

"Gabrielle or Grace?"

"Yes, you don't deserve either of them. You know she loves you?"

"Grace?"

"No, you bloody sod, Gabrielle!"

"You've lost your mind, Chandler." Drake turned away. This time he wasn't going to turn back because Gabrielle didn't do love, she did sex.

"She told me herself."

Drake froze again and then turned. "What?"

"She still loves you."

Drake held his arms out in a quandary. He half laughed and half cried. "What am I suppose to do with that?"

"Feel like the ass that you are."

"Fine, I'm an ass." He turned and left for a third time. This time Stephanie failed to pull another arrow out of her quiver. Drake opened his door and slipped inside. He looked at watch as he plopped on the couch. He flipped open his phone and sent out a call. "Good mornin' sunshine. Did I wake you?"

"I love it when you call me that," a Britanic voice said on the other end.

"What?"

"Sunshine. And no, I've been up awhile."

"I'm glad you like it."

"That and when you call me, Gracie."

Drake laughed and released some tension. "So what do you want me to call you, sunshine or Gracie?"

"Whatever you want, darling."

Drake sank into his couch. "Well I like it when you call me that."

"What, darling?" she asked.

"Yes. Well, I'm glad I can at least make you happy."

"Did you have a bad day?"

"Yes, but we don't have to talk about it. How are you doing? Do you have to work today?"

"No, but you aren't going to get off that easy. What is bothering you?"

Drake's body shuddered. He felt something. "Thank you."

"I'm sorry, I don't understand."

"Thank you…for caring."

"Now, Drake, I'm sure I'm not the first girl that ever cared about you."

"I'm sure you're right. Maybe you're just the first person that I noticed it from."

Grace giggled. "Maybe you're just growing up."

"Or maybe…" Drake stopped himself. "Well, right now nobody likes me."

"Nobody?" Grace said with mock sympathy.

"Not around here at least."

"So, tell me…"

Grace already knew Drake's history with Houston. She listened to Drake describe the night's events. Grace listened attentively. He concluded, "And now everyone is pissed at me."

"Drake," Grace's tone unnerved Drake. She didn't sound right. She sounded insecure. "I understand if you still have feelings for Gabrielle."

"But I don't—I never did."

"You never did?" Grace's tone soured more.

"Well, nothing significant. She's always just been a good friend—a friend with benefits once."

"I believe you Drake if you say so. I'm sorry I've made you defensive but I have to agree with Stephanie. Usually beating up another man is reserved for a husband or boyfriend."

"Grace you gotta believe me when I say I don't feel that way about Gabrielle."

"I know, and I'm glad. But that doesn't make her feel any better."

"I guess so. It's just that I didn't like the guy to start with. He's a little punk."

"I know…I wish I was there."

"So do I."

"I would just hug you and make it all better."

"That'd be nice."

"I am jealous of her though."

"Who?"

"Gabrielle."

"Why's that?"

"She has someone to watch over her and protect her. I imagine I'm just as jealous of Stephanie. As a matter of fact I'm very jealous of Stephanie for going through all what you did together. I would do anything to have had that experience with you…except for…of course."

"Grace, in a way you were with me. When I need to go to my happy place I always pull out a picture of you and imagined us together."

"Hmmm?"

"No, not like that. I mean just sitting down and having a coffee. I lived for the times we talked and your emails. I swear I was the happiest guy in Iraq because of the thought of coming home to you."

"But you didn't come home to me."

"I know but someday we'll get together."

"I hope I'm not a disappointment to you."

"How could you ever be a disappointment?"

"Have you ever heard the term airbrush? I don't look exactly like I do in the magazines and movies."

Drake chuckled, "Grace, when we're eighty, none of us are exceedingly attractive. At the end of the day it is the person that you care about, not their looks."

"I must say…"

"What?"

"I've never, I could never imagine a man saying something so…insightful."

"Oh, I'm sorry, let me drag my knuckles back on the ground for you."

"Oh…" Grace giggled to herself. "Did I hurt your feelings?"

"I've never," Drake mocked. "I could never imagine a woman saying something so…insensitive."

Grace laughed, "That's me, one crass cranky lass."

"Oh, so I should just be in this for your fine piece of ass."

"Well," Grace heaved in a deep breath. She hungered for him. If he were on the same side of the planet she would find him and satiate her desires. "Right now, I would mind being your piece of ass."

"Well, that isn't gonna happen right now with you an ocean away."

"Aw, poor baby." Grace teased. A thought sparked in her head. A naughty thought about what she needed to do after she'd bedded him. And she was going to bed him. They'd had months of foreplay over the phone. She was ready any time for him. She crossed her legs and squeezed. "Maybe if you're a real good boy, later on when I get back we'll have one of our special talks."

"You're awesome, you know that?"

"Well, that disappoints me."

"How does that disappoint you?"

"That it took you this long to figure that out."

"You're right I should've known."

8

"Sir," Drake said with a halfhearted half sarcastic salute.

Jon Kim looked up and returned the salute and looked outside. Not even a glimmer of light crested the eastern sky. He looked at his clock. "You back already?"

"Yeah, I wanted to take it easy on him today," Drake said referring to Connelly.

A chuckled ticked out of Jon's teeth. "That'll be the day."

"He's doing well. I like him."

Jon put down his pen. "That's good. Do you think he'll be effective?"

Drake sat up in his chair and gestured with his hands rolling them around as if they were trying to pull the words out of him. "You know what is great about him." His hands kept rolling, "He doesn't complain...at all. He didn't even ask about how long we were going to go or when we'd stop."

"That is good. Most gomers would just bitch the whole way through."

"It is like he is paying some penance."

"He is."

Drake looked off to the side and nodded conceding the point. "Yeah."

Changing the subject slightly Jon asked, "How do you sleep at night? He knew the answer. He and Drake were best friends now that Doug English wasn't around.

"Fine."

"Cause you did some twisted stuff down range that would've messed up some people's minds."

"No, I sleep okay. I don't have any problems." Drake accentuated his voice in a scholarly manner. "I have no morale dilemma with wasting a bunch of dirt bags in Iraq."

"How well do you think he sleeps at night?" Jon said, again referring to Connelly.

Drake sat back, "Oh, I never thought about that."

"Yeah, well, that's why I make the big bucks and I'm sitting here," he said referring to the company CO desk.

Drake smiled. "You know what takes care of sleeping problems?"

"Yeah, I know, more PT. Stephanie called me and told me about you trying to kill her."

"Really? Oh, man, it was just a little run. What a cry baby."

"How is she? Is she sleeping through the night yet?"

"She's been staying with Noccionni—"

"Gabrielle? How the hell did that happen?"

"Long story. But their not talking to me right now."

"Now what did you do?"

Drake told him the whole story of Gabrielle's day with Houston.

Jon's laughter grew as the story went on. Then he concluded, "So Houston is going to show up today with a shiner?"

"Yeah, I guess so."

"It must be nice."

"What?"

"To have a CMH coming your way. You can't get in trouble for doing anything."

"Watch I'll be the first Marine ever to be awarded the CMH at my court martial."

"So how is Doug doing?" Jon asked.

"I haven't heard from him much. He wants to go back and get with a platoon, but right now he can't even walk."

"That's going to be tough."

"He should be getting in the pool anytime now to start working on it though." Drake stood up. "Well, sir, I didn't mean to take up your time. I'll let you go."

"Oh, one last thing. You are going to have a commander's call this Friday, right?" Drake's commander's calls brought in a crowd beyond its intended audience. Before leaving for Iraq, even some of the battalion staff showed up at his commander's calls. They usually centered around a military or leadership movie. Drake started them on Friday afternoons after punishing his platoon with long physically demanding days all week. He wanted them to limp into the weekend dead tired. Tired enough that they couldn't muster the energy to cause trouble.

"You betcha!" Drake said as he whipped off a salute to his boss and friend.

"You gonna start off like last year?"

"Yepper!"

Jon Kim grinned and rubbed his hands together in anticipation. He tapped CNTL-ALT-DEL on his keyboard to wake it back up. In outlook he opened up his calendar and scheduled a meeting. He titled it LT Scott Commander's Call. Location: Base Theater. Date/Time-Friday 1630. He considered the addressees. For those under his command above the rank of sergeant he made the meeting mandatory, optional for everyone else. He included the Battalion staff. Jon looked through his contact list and hovered over one name. He decided to include her, but she wasn't going to read the email anyway. He pulled out his phone and looked at his watch. It was way too early to call the girl so he texted, *drake cc call fri 1630 theater.*

"What the hell!" Houston protested.

Drake stopped short of the door. He didn't know why Houston was erupting, but he figured he'd learn more if he let the situation develop before walking in.

"Frank, did you read this?" Houston asked another platoon leader, Second Lieutenant Frank Willis, that Drake hadn't met yet. Willis graduated from Nebraska. He didn't possess innate intelligence, but he kept his mouth shut and followed direction with enthusiasm. While his academic marks suffered barely kept his ROTC scholarship, his military marks rated in the top percentile.

Willis shrugged his shoulders. "If the CO wants us to be there I'm sure he has a good reason."

"Maybe I have something I want to do with my platoon! What if I want to have a commander's call?"

"Scott's been there, done that. Maybe the boss just wants us to see how it's done before we have our own."

"He isn't all that impressive," Houston said.

"I dunno, it looks like he's going to get the CMH. If that isn't all that impressive, I'm not sure what is."

"Have you met him? I've met him and he's an egotistical maniac. That whole Farmhouse Shootout thing was a total ego trip stunt. I heard the two star chewed his ass for going into the farmhouse. From what I've read he actually screwed up big time, but got off because he got lucky and came out alive and now they are going to give him a CMH."

Unlike Houston, Willis avoided confrontation unless the situation called for it. He usually made his point, listened to the opposing view and moved on. "All I know is the guy has been shot at and led Marines in combat under fire. I can't say I've done that and it looks like we're headed that direction. I think I could learn something from him."

"Have you met him though? He's an arrogant prick!"

Drake plastered on a warm smile and walked in. "Lieutenant Willis?"

Willis snapped up to attention. Not only did Drake's reputation loom large, Drake himself swallowed up any room. He walked in at 6'4" and 215 pounds. His square shoulders accentuated his overbearing size. Awe filled Willis' eyes.

"No, we haven't met," Drake said as he stuck out a hand.

Willis took his but still couldn't close his gaping mouth.

"Sorry, did I interrupt anything?" Drake asked.

"No," Houston said and got up to leave.

Drake sat down. "Have a seat—tell me about yourself." Drake said. Willis eventually overcame the initial shock and the two peers shared their life stories. "…and now their both pissed at me." Drake concluded as Staff Sergeant Jennings walked in.

"Sir!" Jennings saluted with an oversized grin.

"Sergeant Jennings!" Drake grinned back and threw him a salute. "How the hell are you!"

"Couldn't be better, sir!"

"Why? Did you finally lose your virginity?" Drake teased.

"Hey, sir, why don't you go play a game of pin your dick in the squid," Jennings said referring to the stigma attached to the Navy.

"No, I won't steal any of your boyfriends. You can keep them all to yourself."

"Fuck you, sir."

"Ya see, Willis. As long as they tag a 'sir' on it, they think they can say anything," Drake said.

Willis smiled nervously and took it all in.

"So you wanna work for someone else?" Drake asked Jennings.

"Oh, hell no!" Jennings said. "No offense, sir," he said to Willis. "But the LT here," he said pointing to Drake, "has got his shit wired tight. I fuckin' won the jackpot. I feel for Alvarez."

"He's stuck with a guy that needs some seasoning," Drake said. "We'll have to watch out for him," Drake said flipping his hand to the side.

Willis nodded conceding the point.

"But don't worry though," Jennings continued. "You just follow the LT's lead," he nodded towards Drake, "and he'll square you away. Oh, that and listen to your platoon sergeant."

"That's what I hear," Willis said.

"But don't think you have to have all the answers right off the bat. Why," Jennings laughed and then censored himself, "the LT here, got so jacked up in the beginning—"

"Yeah, but we don't have to talk about that. We might go through that again. So don't spoil any surprises," Drake said.

"Oh, okay. Sir, don't worry," Jennings continued. "We'll get you hooked up."

"Room ATTEN-TION!" Jennings bellowed on Friday afternoon as Drake trotted down the aisle to the stage. At the stage he leapt from ten feet out bypassing the stairs to land on center stage.

"All right! You ready to rock-n-roll!" Drake clapped his hands together hard and rubbed them like a fat man sitting at a feast. He planned this commander's call to mimic the first one he gave a year ago. Jennings and Jon Kim begged him to replay the last one. All the old salts wanted a replay. Drake swore them to secrecy because knowing the punch line defeated the effect. But even the vets who knew the punch line wanted to see the act again.

"Mon-Goose, Mon-Goose," started floating through the crowd.

Drake smiled and waved his hands to quiet them down. He hoped that didn't give away the punch line. He surveyed the crowd. Jon Kim sat in the crowd with the other platoon leaders. Jon had texted Gabrielle to tell her Drake planned the same commander's call as last year. Gabrielle was still pissed at Drake, but she wanted Stephanie to see the spectacle and sat near Jon with Stephanie. Drake surveyed the crowd then Drake saw his target—Houston.

Drake gave his command philosophy about training and proceeded to start his theatrics. He strolled to the podium where a computer sat that controlled the display on the screen. "Other than that, we are all Marines and we…being Marines…are visual." Drake tapped the computer and a seductive picture of Grace Freemont popped on the screen. Heavy grunting and howling proceeded. A wave of loneliness rushed over Drake. He missed Grace. *How the hell could I miss someone I've never met?* He wished she could see him in front of his men. He looked up at the screen. Yep, she was all his.

Drake tapped the computer again and the image disappeared. Playful boos and hisses peppered Drake. He smiled in return. "Okay, now that we've established our dominate sense, I'll use that dominate sense to see if I can get a point or two across." Drake wheeled out a box draped in a drop cloth. "So who here thinks they are a badass?" The old salts raised their hands just enough to get the boots, to raise theirs. Drake spotted Houston with his hand up. "Okay, so in this fight…" Drake lifted a drop cloth draped over a box. The box was a Plexiglas container with two halves slip by a partition, one with a mouse, the other a cobra. "Who here is the mouse?" No reply. "Who here is the snake?"

Most of the boots raised their hands. The one hand Drake wanted to see go up stood in the air. "Lieutenant Houston, so you're the snake?"

"You have to believe that you're the best," Houston replied.

Drake paced back and forth. "That's a good philosophy. It is good to have confidence." Drake stopped. "So I think we have a new call sign. Captain Kim, should we dub Lieutenant Houston here, Snake?"

Kim swallowed a chuckle as he visualized how the scene would play out. Houston sat up in his chair. He relished the idea of earning a call sign.

"Or perhaps, Cobra…as in Cobra II, the operation he wasn't part of?"

Jon struggled to control his chortles. From a leadership perspective he shouldn't engage is demeaning one of his lieutenants, but Houston deserved what was coming.

"Okay, so Cobra it is." Drake's devilish smile returned.

Houston sank back down in his chair. He knew he'd been had now. Drake was too nice about it and the smile gave it away.

Drake reached into the container and pulled out the mouse and stuffed it away in a box and placed it under the container. He pulled a larger box out and placed it in the side of the container that had housed the mouse. He slid off one of the sides and out popped a mongoose.

Houston groaned. The Marines roared. Chants of "Mongoose, Mon-goose," rippled through the auditorium once again.

Drake pulled the box out of the mongoose's side. "You see the problem with being confident, or rather overconfident, is that there is always a bigger badass that is bigger, stronger and faster. So, as we train, think about that bigger badass and how much more he's training. You've earned your EGA," eagle, globe and anchor, "but that and three-fifty will get you a Starbucks. You need to maintain—no—build on the Marine that the Corps has made of you so far. So! Without further adieu…let's see who is the bigger badass, the mongoose or the cobra?" Drake lifted the center divider and the predators sized each other up. After a few feints by both contestants the mongoose pounced on the neck of the cobra. The mongoose snapped its head back and forth to whip the body around. When it paused the cobra hung motionless in his jaws. The mongoose snapped it back and forth a couple more times to make sure the serpent expired. "And we have a winner!" Drake declared. "So, what is the moral of the story?" He paused for effect. "Train, train and train some more because when it comes to a fight second place is the first loser. And in our business, as it is with the snake and mongoose," Drake waved a hand at the victorious mongoose with its prize in its mouth, "second place is fatal."

Drake followed up his commander's call with a movie that highlighted leadership as he did every Friday before his last deployment. After the movie and his closing remarks. He packed up his laptop.

"As good as ever," Jon said as he walked up to Drake.

"Thanks, sir," Drake looked over his shoulder to see if any of his guys were around and he could drop the "sir." "What happened to the girls?"

"Gabrielle and Stephanie?" Jon asked.

"Yeah."

"They didn't stick around. They are still pissed at you. What the hell happened?"

"You want to go get a beer. I'll tell you the whole story."

Jon looked at his watch. It was still very early on a Friday night. "Sure."

"No place loud though. It's a long story."

"Whatever, I'm game."

9

"You in place?" Jon Kim called to Drake over the radio.

"That's affirmative." Drake replied. He looked over the area and imagined where his platoon laid in ambush. He felt sorry for Houston. Jon Kim right now was delivering him a scenario he'd never engage in. He forced Houston into a situation that required dynamic leadership and a flexible response. Drake stood on the other end of the scenario where he'd ambush the unsuspecting newly minted platoon leader.

Drake, for his part acted as if he was in Iraq or Afghanistan. He meticulously staged the platoon into an L-shaped ambush within the border of the assigned range. Drake called Connelly on the radio and instructed him to send out a team to walk the approach into the ambush and to patrol the area for enemy, that didn't really exist, but that is how it would be in reality—train the way you fight. They would point out any telltale signs Drake needed to address.

Local vegetation allowed Drake to set up a near ambush, within fifty meters. A near ambush creates more shock as Drake had learned previously when he was the new lieutenant walking into the trap. He knew too well how a unit could evaporate in seconds. He twitched at the memory of his previous company Captain Wilmington, walking up and saying in a slow drawl, "What…the fuck…are you doing?" A seasoned platoon leader now, Drake had sectors of fire assigned to optimize chaos in the enemy. Although the main objective for the ambush was to see Houston's reaction, Drake tried to squeeze every ounce of training opportunity for his platoon. Even the waiting was critical. Drake continued to scan his men to see if they controlled themselves and didn't grow restless. Because Captain Kim offered up the prey on a platter, Drake wanted to make sure his platoon executed the ambush flawlessly. Even if they botched the ambush, they would most likely destroy Houston's unit.

Houston was a cancer. Drake turned it to his advantage and drove himself to exercise more precision in his leadership. He wouldn't dare to allow Houston to find the slightest crack in Drake's execution. Drake's platoon would hit him and disappear before Houston ever knew what happened to him.

In the distance Drake finally saw a green glimmer bouncing along the road. Kim gave Houston's platoon a bogus, time critical, mission. More and more men appeared running to their pseudo death. Drake looked left and right to picture in his mind one last time where the fields of fire laid. He judged the length of the staggered column racing at him. He eyed the point man and mentally drew a line of where Drake would initiate the ambush when the point man crossed it. Normally the attackers blew Claymores into enemy to initiate the ambush, but Drake's advantage was so overwhelming already that Jon had Drake forgo the Claymores. Drake sat in a position to oversee his formation. When the point man crossed the line Drake's M-16 cracked, a closed bolt weapon, to initiate the ambush. Automatic weapons, M249s and M240s saturated the killzone. Grenadiers and riflemen attacked any area not already laid to waste from the hundreds of simulated rounds pouring into the formation. Drake's senses heightened. The game "slowed" for him. He'd master his craft to the point he could soak in every data point of the onslaught that ended before Houston realized it began.

The first rifle crack puzzled Houston's brain. Who the hell was shooting and why was one of his guys shooting? The ensuing small arms cacophony fried Houston's wit. He first tried to understand why his entire platoon started shooting at once. Then he realized the fire was incoming. Somebody fucked up big time. He wasn't supposed to engage here. The engagement zone was still down range. Some other unit somehow engaged the wrong unit, his unit. "Cease fire! Cease fire!" Houston called out to the aggressors. And with everyone in Houston's platoon's MILES gear squealing like a stuck pig, Drake's ordered his platoon to disengage and melt away to the rally point.

"Goddammit Moore!" Houston barked. Sergeant Moore, a squad leader, took over as platoon sergeant since Jon simulated that Alvarez was wounded in action. Alvarez knew the scenario from the previous deployment when Wilmington unleashed it on Drake so Jon didn't want him to participate. "What the hell are you doing!" Houston continued to dress down Moore, a transfer from another company. He accused Moore of everything from subversion to sabotage.

"Houston!...What...the fuck...are you doing!" Jon called out in the slow drawl manner reminiscent of the previous company CO, Captain Wilmington. Beneath the harsh tone, Kim wore a smile. The scenario worked just as Wilmington described. Not only did it work, Houston's reaction offered a major teaching point. "You just got Sergeant Moore's killed...along with everyone else," Jon said. "Now, Sergeant Moore's mama is gonna be awfully mad at me. What am I gonna tell her?"

"Sir, what the hell? Who was that?" Houston said. "Who the fuck hijacked our range?" Houston's confusion continued. "Sir, there is no way we are going to make the objective on time now.

"So what are you doing do?"

"Sir, we got to reset the MILES gear first."

"Yeah, we'll get that reset."

"Sir I don't see how we're gonna make the objective now." Houston continued, "Do you know who that was? They need to have their range card pulled for this."

"No, I don't think they need to have their range card pulled."

"Why not?"

"Because I put them there."

"What? Who was that?"

"Looks like the Mongoose got the better part of the Cobra again."

Houston shook his head. "You mean that was Scott!"

"Yeah, Lieutenant Scott can set up a pretty good ambush can't he?"

"Oh, that's bullshit, we didn't have a chance."

Jon smiled to himself. Houston fell into the trap. "Where exactly does it say in the jihadi handbook that they need to give you a chance or fight fair?"

"But sir, in the real fight, we will have to make that objective. We're going to have to accomplish the mission. People will be depending on us to get the job done."

"That's right you're going to have to get the job done and you're going to have to fight your way there. In school they laid out the scenarios so that you could tell what was going to come. Here we're not going to afford you that luxury." Jon continued, "This is real life and a real war we are going to have fight. I can't let you think you think you know it all when you don't."

Houston huffed. He wanted to ask a question, but didn't know how so he just blurted it out. "I'm guessin' Scott doesn't have to go through the same scenario?" Houston wanted to be the one to ambush Scott if the situation allowed. Vindictiveness boiled in his veins.

"Nope."

"Why's that?" Houston pouted without thinking. What was left of his military bearing vanished.

"Lieutenant Houston," Jon's voice turned on Houston. Amusement time ended. "Not that it is any of your business, but Lieutenant Scott authored this training scenario. I think he could probably master it. It isn't like he hasn't seen his time in combat and dealt with jihadis up close and personal." Jon thought back to the time Drake interrogated two young jihadis. Drake's intuition of human nature far exceeded the average man. Somehow Drake knew exactly what buttons to push to create an effect. "What you need to do is worry more about Lieutenant Houston and not Lieutenant Scott. You need to debrief your men and show me you can execute an ambush. The next platoon should be by in," Jon looked at his watch, "a little over an hour."

"Yes, sir," Houston fumed. "Do I get Alvarez back?" he asked referring to his platoon sergeant.

"Yep,"

"Staff Sergeant Alvarez!" Houston called over to Alvarez who was leaning up against Jon's humvee chatting with the first sergeant.

Houston set up his ambush and when it looked like the platoon was settled in, Jon asked, "You good to go, Bill?"

"Yes, sir."

"All right, make it happen." Jon settled back into his humvee with his gunny, the first sergeant, and drove back to the starting point where he briefed Second Lieutenant Colt Larsen on the scenario that would run him into ambush unsuspectingly. When he finished Jon asked, "You got it?"

"Yes, sir," Colt nodded and then turned to his platoon sergeant Charlie Johnson. "Charlie this is how I would like to tackle this." Colt briefed him on the idea and then asked. "Does that sound workable?" Colt wanted to get his platoon sergeant's buy in before proceeding.

"Yes, sir," Charlie replied.

"Well, all right then. Squad leaders!" Colt smiled confidently. He briefed the basics of the field exercise and then got to the meat. "Novak, you take your squad out first. Sergeant Johnson will go with you." Jon let Johnson go on the exercise since he came in from a different company. "I'll be in the second wave." He pointed to the other two squad leaders. "We'll, follow you up by about two hundred yards." Colt surveyed his leadership team. "If we run into trouble along the way, and I think there is a good chance we might, this is how we'll handle it." Colt continued to brief likely scenarios.

Jon watched the Colt's platoon head out and rolled in behind them in his humvee. "Gunny, you believe this?"

The company first sergeant Gunny McElroy shook his head, "Houston's fucked. Larsen has his shit wired."

"Yeah, I think you're right." Jon worried about how Houston was going to react. Drake just pummeled him, and now it looked like Larsen was going to give him more than he could handle.

Houston tapped the Indiglo on his watch to illuminate the time in the dark. The next platoon should appear around the bend in the next few moments. He scanned the kill zone and imagined where he would commence the attack. Then he saw the leading enemy targets, tangos. He settled into his position and fingered the safety on his M16. He licked his lips in anticipation. The force seemed small. His guys would cut them up in seconds. He smiled in anticipation. The smile dissipated quickly though when he saw a second force trailing the original. He sized up the leading force again and realized it was only a squad and it was approaching the kill zone now. His head locked up. He needed to act quickly. He wanted to ask Johnson what he thought, but he didn't want to look week and he didn't have time for Johnson to mull it over in his mind. The leading force was leaving the kill zone now. Houston had to act now. He looked at the trailing force one last time and then opened fire on the trailing man of the leading formation who was already out of the kill zone. The hasty shot tailed off and missed his mark. The rest of his platoon opened fire as briefed, but without any coordination. With neither enemy force in the kill zone some of his platoon shot at the leading unit and some at the trailing unit. The leading unit dropped and opened fire on Houston's platoon.

The battle for fire superiority ratcheted up instantly. At the same time the leading portion of the rear unit quickly gained fire superiority over the flank of Houston's platoon whose fires were mostly focused at the lead unit.

"Move! Move! Move!" Colt called to his third squad. His squad leader took the back half of the trailing force sprinted into the woods under the cover of the superior firepower. Once in position the squad continued to attack the flank of the ambush and rolled into the formation with thirteen weapons, four of them fully automatic, shredding the fixed ambush position. The ambush was still trying to pin down the lead formation before focusing on the trailing formation when a third formation pounced on them from the flank.

"Cease fire, Cease fire," Colt called out to second squad. Charlie did the same for the leading squad. They didn't want any friendly fire incidents. Third squad rolled into the ambush site and was getting too close for the other two squads to continue. It was all on them now. The way the counterattack was heading, it didn't look like first or second squad fires were needed. Third squad had everything in hand.

Houston's platoon didn't have any fires left to rotate over to the flanking squad. MILES gear lit up throughout the Houston's platoon indicating they were out of the fight.

"Sonuvabitch!" Houston screamed when his MILES gear lit up.

"Cease fire, Cease fire!" Jon called on the company net. The leadership echoed the command and soon the woods returned to its quiet darkness.

"Sir, I don't get it," Houston fumed as Jon walked up.

Jon put a hand on his shoulder. "Don't worry about it, Bill. Go home get some sleep and we'll talk about it on Monday.

Drake pulled out of range control and flipped open his phone. The clock read 0427. He calculated the time in London, it was too late, she'd be filming. He considered his schedule for the day, back to the apartment for a little rest, then back to base for some unit PT and then another commander's call. He hadn't talked to Gabrielle or Stephanie in weeks. He wondered if they would show again this week and if they'd stay long enough to talk to him or were they still that pissed at him. Sadness overwhelmed Drake. He called her anyway and left a message. "Just wishing I could talk to you." He hung with Jon quite a bit, but had to temper it because Jon was his direct boss now. He felt like he was on an island between what used to be, before redeployment and what will be with Grace. The bonds he formed with his previous platoon and even Stephanie, Gabrielle and Jon outmatched what he felt for his new guys. Although he was fond of Connelly who was a good shit, it wasn't the same as Ramirez. He thanked God for having Lincoln, Jennings and some of the other old salts from his previous platoon in the unit.

Who the hell do you think you are that you can say you'll have a life with Grace Freemont. You need to get your act together, Scott, he scolded himself. He needed to immerse himself in the present. What he did was in the past. *Maybe this is a good thing. Maybe I'll focus on doctrine more instead of the seat of the pants crap I pulled off last time.* He smiled. His ambush was textbook.

He glanced at his phone once again as he drove out the gate, 0432. He realized the time difference between California and Washington DC.

"You're up a little early," First Lieutenant Doug English said as he answered his cell. Although he wasn't surprised, He spent many early mornings with Drake. "I wish I was there with you."

"You'll be before you know it." Suddenly Drake understood how small his frustrations compared to real problems.

"I hope so." Doug waited on the line. Usually his friend didn't call this early, something was up.

"So how's it going…your rehab that is?"

"Well," Doug laughed to himself. "I've certainly had a strange turn of events. But before I get into that, tell me what is on your mind."

"Ah, nothing really," Drake said sheepishly. "I just miss the old times when…"

"Yeah, me too." Doug's bright mood softened a little. He missed the old times even more than Drake. But recent events overpowered his reminisce. "So, anyways, you'll never believe this…"

10

Erika Hess sprinted out to her BMW M5. She unlocked the trunk with her fob from a hundred yards away. When she reached the car she threw up the trunk, snatched her gym bag and ran back to the rehab facility. "Damn him!" she cursed. She threw open a locker and shed her clothes. She slid her tall slender athletic frame into a bikini, grabbed a towel. She didn't have time for this. Her four star boss needed her back at the Pentagon. She looked at her watch and realized she wouldn't get back to the puzzle palace.

She couldn't get Doug English to smile the first time she saw him and it challenged her. For personal and professional reasons Erika visited the wounded warriors when they returned. All of them were happy to see her and her homemade brownies, until she met Lieutenant English. Her figure belied her age and knowing Marines as intimately as she did, she offered some eye candy in addition to brownies. They could never know her status was the only caveat to her morale calls. Even the worst off smiled at the seductive blonde, all except Lieutenant English. Erika pried at him until he spoke to her. He never offered a smile but when she asked, "What can I do for you?" He growled, "Get my gun back in the fight!" Since then she took on Lieutenant English as a personal challenge. She continued to see as many wounded as possible, but she checked up on English almost daily. She was the first to see him after each of his surgeries to rebuild his leg and assisted with many of his physical therapy sessions. She grew fond of the young Marine desperate to go back to Iraq where he nearly lost his leg to three 7.62 millimeter rounds that turned his leg into hamburger. She enjoyed seeing the smile on his face as he made remarkable progress. His therapist continued to warn him that not every day would be a good day. "Oh, no, every day is a good day," he protested. "We'll see about that," the therapist repeated her warning. After watching him suffer his first significant setback, Erika knew he would try something stupid.

"Just go back and rest. This will happen time to time." The therapist continued. "Take tomorrow off and we'll have another go at it on Monday, okay?"

Doug's eyes narrowed, not menacingly but determined, enough for Erika to notice. "Sure that'll be good," he lied.

Erika stood silently and watched Doug walk towards the locker room. She shifted her eyes back to the therapist who documented Drake's progress on a clipboard as she spun around and leaned up against a swinging door to backpedal into a hallway. Erika's eyes darted back to Doug who opened a locker room door while looking over his shoulder at the therapist to make sure she vacated the pool area. "What are you doing?" Erika chided.

"Oh, nothin'," Doug said sheepishly.

"Nothing?"

"No, nothing and it's none of your business what I do."

Erika bit her lip. She couldn't unleash on the insolent lieutenant because she never offered the foggiest inkling who she really was. Instead she bolted out to her car.

When she returned in her bikini she found Doug attempting a hybrid squat using the edge of the pool for leverage the way the therapist showed him. "What the hell are you doing!"

"None of your God damn business," Doug grunted without looking at his accuser as he tried to raise himself from a squat. He thought it was Erika, but it could have been the therapist in which case it would have been her business.

He cranked around his neck and saw a sight that rewired his brain.

Doug spent every ounce of energy and focus on getting his gun back in the fight for months. He read physical therapy journals and everything he could about the war. Seeing the tall slender blonde with sharp athletic curves stunned him. But the sight of the enticing blonde sparked a dormant ember in his brain. His hand slipped on the side of the pool and he smacked his head on the edge of the pool.

Erika jumped into the pool and grabbed the large Marine and lifted his slumped head out of the water. "Help!" she cried. She tried to see if he was coming to. "Help!"

The swinging door flew open. "What is going on! Why is he in the pool!" The therapist scolded Erika as she burst through the door. The therapist ran over to grab Doug's arms to pull him out of the water.

"He thought he would try to exercise on his own."

"Why did you let him do that! Do you know how dangerous it is for him to do this on his own! He isn't supposed to do this on your own!"

Erika shook her head. The accusations grew old. "Look, he jumped in on his own. I just happened to be here."

The therapist looked at Erika in her bikini and raised her eyebrows.

Erika shook her head and said, "Just help me get him out.

The two women heaved the Marine out of the water and onto his back.

"Ah, fuck!" Doug said as he came to and reached for his head. He looked up and saw the two girls and braced for a tongue lashing.

"What are you trying to prove," the therapist asked. "That Marines really are that stupid."

Erika wanted to protest. She was a Marine, earned a Masters of Journalism from Columbia and considered herself somewhat intelligent. But the evidence laid before the therapist proved overwhelmingly against Marines possessing any intelligence.

"No, I was just…" Doug unlocked his jaw to release a grizzly bear moan.

"Yeah, well, now you aren't. Go home and don't come back 'til Monday," the therapist said. "And no overdoing it. You're doing more harm than good."

Doug nodded, conceding his faults.

"Do you have any muscle relaxants left, Motrin?"

"Yeah, I still have some thousand milligrams."

"You'll want to take one of those before that leg cramps up on you."

Erika kept quite. Admiration tempered her anger. Seeing Doug laid out, wounded and frustrated stirred her admiration for her pet project. She had poured a significant emotional investment into his recovery. Doug's parents were poor Oklahoma farmers and couldn't afford to leave the farm to watch over their oldest child. Erika wondered how many other Marines suffered alone. She shook her head trying to clear it before any other emotions percolated. Having been abandoned by her first husband for another woman she couldn't fight her natural urge to please men. Deep in her psyche she wondered what she could have done more to make the marriage work, notwithstanding her ex-husband's lack of moral character. She blamed herself. She must've driven him away. Sure she was angry with him. But she still bore more than her share of the blame.

"Can you get him home?" the therapist asked Erika.

Erika looked at her watch. "Yes, I can get him home."

The two girls lifted the Marine to his feet and helped him to the locker room door. "Don't let him back in the pool," the therapist admonished one last time.

Erika nodded and watched the therapist leave. After a few moments Doug emerged from the locker room with his brace and cane.

"I guess I'm going to have to babysit you," Erika said with a smile. She couldn't stay angry with the Marine. She understood his desire to get back into the fight although not on a personal level. She hadn't been to Afghanistan or Iraq yet. She made a mental note to put herself in a position to deploy so she might understand what made Marines like Doug tick.

"I'm sorry," Doug said sheepishly. "Just get me home and I'll be good."

"Wait here while I get changed." Erika sat Doug down in the waiting room then turned to the receptionist. "Don't let him move."

Doug drank in a long lustful examination of the bikini clad figure that precipitated his decline. *So that is why everyone was also so excited to see her, because it wasn't her brownies.*

When Erika returned she smiled at Doug. "Are you ready to go?"

"Yep."

Erika slipped Doug's arm over her shoulder and bent with her knees to help him up. "Did you take your Motrin yet?"

"No, I have some at home."

"I have some in the car that you can have."

"Okay."

Erika asked for directions to his billet and proceeded to get jammed up in rush hour traffic in DC. "Are you all right?" Erika asked after a long awkward silence. She stole a glance at him and saw him tightening his shoulders and running his hand over his pained face.

"I'll be fine."

"You don't look too good."

"I'll be fine."

Erika dropped the conversation. She saw the discomfort in his face. After another shorter awkward silence, Doug's mind failed to control his nerves. His brain wired signals to the nerves in his legs to lock up and tear against each other. He growled through gritted teeth. He slammed his head back against the headrest and his arms flailed. One pounded the passenger window the other landed on Erika's knee.

Erika's back arched. Her eyelids fluttered and her toe slammed the accelerator forward. Erika instantly filtered out

Doug's groan and gyrations to control the car. The skin on her inner knee popped, shooting stimuli throughout neglected wastelands in her body. She'd sworn off men when she learned an old playmate replaced her with someone more than twenty years her junior. *Men ARE pigs.* Nerve endings blossomed with sensitivity. Hot blood pulsed to hinterlands long forgotten. Her chin fell and quivered. A delicate moan drifted from her lungs. Her fingers squeezed the steering wheel.

When Doug regained his situational awareness, he immediate snatched his hand from its inappropriate location. But before he could Erika's hand flew down from the steering wheel and slammed it back onto her thigh slightly north of its previous locale. Doug turned away. Opiatic sensations stifled the pain and erupted surging desires. Nevertheless, he slid his hand off her thigh at a glacial pace. Erika's hand bounced from the steering wheel to his hand again securing it closer to her inner thigh and frustratingly near the objective. Doug stole a glance at her and saw her chest straining against her blouse with heaves. Pronounced nipples declared their need. Erika's breath filtered out of her lungs in short eager puffs. Doug didn't move while she fought through traffic. She looked over her shoulder through him and to her blind spot as her left foot hammered the clutch and she downshifted. The engine roared to life as she punched the accelerator shooting the car through the right lane and onto the off ramp. Her body refused to wait, she would take her chances on the side streets. "Damn!" The light on the off ramp blinked form yellow to red. "Fuck it!" Her foot tried to punch the accelerator through the floorboard.

"Oh, is that what you want?" Doug giggled and inched his pinky higher up her inner thigh. The gap between Erika's knees broadened invitingly. Erika's jaw stretched open but nothing came out. Task saturation overloaded the priorities in her brain. Doug noticed the red light and cringed. She wasn't stopping As he braced for impact his hand tightened on

Erika's thigh and pushed a yelp from her throat. Erika jammed both feet on the clutch and brake to avoid slamming into the car on the other side of the intersection. "Fuck!" she squealed. The M5 stalled. Erika's hands and feet gyrated and she cranked the starter—nothing. She forced herself to focus. She didn't have her foot on the clutch. She tried again and slid the gear knob into first and ran her hand back up her thigh to move along his hand that wasn't progressing fast enough for her. Then she ran her hand up to her temple to wipe away a bead of sweat. She thrust her hips forward to try to accelerate the process. Doug brushed his pinky against her silky panties then immediately withdrew his advance. At first he thought she was still wearing her bikini bottoms they were so damp with desire. Then he assimilated the stimulus and response. He felt his chest heaving and out of the corner of eye saw Erika whimper. Her fingers dug into the steering wheel. She turned the wheel and darkness covered them. Doug looked out the window without seeing. It took him a second to realize they were in a parking garage. Erika's hand bounced from the steering wheel to Doug's hand and slid it into position. She held his hand there and pressed on the back of his fingers. Doug relented and massaged her. Erika slid her car into a slot and released in a wave of barks. She cried and moaned for over a half minute. Her hands squeezed her breasts. Her head bobbed back and forth. Then she arched back with her chin high in the air where it quivered out a throaty moan. When it was over she stepped out of the car without a word. Doug chuckled to himself and shook his head. His door opened. Erika reached in and grabbed his cane. "This isn't my billet," he said.

"Ah, no," she said stating the obvious.

"I guess I'm not going to make it home tonight?"

"Ah, no."

Doug looked up at her with raised eyebrows.

"Just get out," she demanded.

"Okay." Doug put his hand on the seat and pushed himself up and out of the car. Erika grabbed his free hand

and pulled him along. In the elevator he built the courage to steal a glance at her. Erika stared straight ahead. Her chin set in determination. *If Buckhorn can do an 18 year old, I can do a…*Erika turned her head and ran her eyes over Doug to try to calculate…*25 year old.* Erika surveyed Doug again. He was handsome. She had never looked at him that way. All she saw before was a ripped up leg. He also looked young. A lusty moan rolled up her throat. *A 25 year old!* Even with the bum leg he would have capabilities that far surpassed her recent playmates.

The elevator dinged and the door opened. Erika stepped out and blocked the door so Doug had time to exit. She scurried to her door ahead of Doug and dug for her keys. She flipped through them and they fell through her fingers. She grabbed her doorknob to steady herself. Her chest heaved pumping air in and out. She could feel her heartbeat all the way to her temples. A steamy sauna boiled between her legs. Slowly she lowered herself to her keys when Doug's hand slipped in just before it and snatched them for her. She looked at him. He looked confident and at ease. A tinge of anger throttled her. *Who does he think he is—all cocky?* Then she remembered that he's been through combat. This probably wasn't that stressful for him.

"That one." She pointed to a key. Doug jimmied the door and opened it for her. Erika stepped in and pulled the keys out and put them in her purse that she dropped to the floor. She reached for the lights and hesitated. She kept herself in good shape and she had spent a lot of time with Doug over the past weeks, but she also hid her age well. Now was not the time to reveal how old she really was. She pulled her hand back from the light switch and grabbed his hand. She pinned him to the wall and planted her lips on his. She pressed her chest up against his and ran his hand up between her thighs. She settled onto him and moaned from the bottom of her chest.

Doug dropped his cane and wobbled. Erika pulled back and steadied him. She needed to get him to the bed. She leaned over and picked up his cane for him and took his other hand and led him to the bedroom. Instinctively she reached for the light switch again and again stopped short. She wheeled Doug around and pushed him down onto the bed.

The muscles in Doug's legs protested and he groaned.

"Are you in pain?" Erika asked.

"A little."

"Well," Erika worried about how the pain might affect him. "I really don't give a damn." She ran her hand down his pants. "And it appears you don't either."

Erika studied his face for the first time. An innocent smile glowed on his face from the night city lights that beamed through her sheer curtain. The smile warmed her. She smiled back but it wasn't the same smile. Her smile came from seeing someone who wasn't as jaded as she. Abandoned not only by her first husband but other lovers for younger girls. It wrecked havoc on her view of men and love.

"Are you okay with this?" Doug asked hesitantly.

A giggle slipped through Erika's lips.

"I mean…I don't want you to think…"

"Oh, you're precious." Erika laughed. She drew in a slow breath and calmed herself. She held his face and kissed him softly on the lips.

"What's so funny?" Doug sounded hurt. "I don't get it. I—"

"I just think it is cute how you think you are taking advantage of me."

"Huh?"

"It's been a long while…" she ran her hands under his shirt and lifted it off of him. She straddled him and ran her fingers up his abs to his chest. His tight skin felt dreamy. "Since anyone worried about whether I was 'okay' with this." She ran a tongue up his torso and purred while unbuckling his pants.

"Anyone? How many 'anyones' are there?" Although Doug enjoyed Erika's illicit behavior his mind whirled.

"Let's me make this clear. I'm not the one being taken advantage of here." She tugged at his trousers. "Damn!" She forgot to get his shoes off. Her lack of recency left some gaps in her bedroom rhythm.

"I'm getting that feeling." Doug watched as the woman worked on him. A surreal haze clouded his mind. This didn't happen to him—ever. Drake came to his mind. *This happens to Drake—not me.*

"What?" Erika wasn't really listening to him.

"I'm getting the feeling I'm not really taking advantage of you."

"No." Erika smiled. She dismounted her prey and slid off her skirt, panties and blouse. "You're not." She saddled back up on his naked body and ran her finger over her ear to slide her short blonde hair behind her ear as she leaned over to kiss him. She purred again. She leaned back and guided his hands up to her breasts. He squeezed.

"No, softly." She trained his hands to lightly tease the sensitive skin around her breast. Her hips rocked back and forth on him, pressing herself onto him. She savored his youthfulness. *Younger is better* she thought to herself.

"That's better," she huffed through stifled breaths. *Don't go crazy, he's got a bad leg,* she reminded herself. She grabbed his hands and pinned them down. As she lowered her chest she offered her breast to his lips. He lurched his neck forward and struck on his prey.

"Not so hard," she instructed. "Use your tongue."

Doug swirled his tongue around her nipple.

"No, flick it back and forth." Doug's tongue tickled her, but not enough.

"No faster," she panted.

Doug's tongue flittered back and forth.

"Oh, God! That's it!" she cried. She ran her hands up to his and intertwined their fingers. Her muscles tightened and she curled her hands forward, bending his wrist backward. She struggled to hold on. "Oh, baby, I need you to blow."

Doug stopped his tongue and blew softly on her breast.

Erika's throat choked up so bad she could barely eek out, "That's not what I meant..." a heavy groan shot out of her. "But it works, baby." *Young men—hard bodies—pliable minds—why the fuck didn't I think of this before.*

Erika's hip grinded on him. She watched his chest swell, his pecks tight and hard. She felt him grow and jerk. He growled through his teeth. She popped through convulsions of ecstasy. She belted out a sharp high-pitched moan. Her legs braced. She ran her hands down to his chest and felt it bulge.

The rolling euphoric wave subsided and muscles released from their lock. Erika panted heavily and fell off of him. Her head swam in opiatic endorphins. She let her chest heave to draw in oxygen to deliver to her strapped muscles. Her eyelids slid closed and she heard her lover breathing next to her. She raised a finger to brush up against his good thigh. She just wanted to have the connection.

"Are you okay?" Doug asked.

The question startled Erika. She leaned over onto her side and propped her head up with her palm. She ran her other fingertips in lazy circles over the smooth skin of his chest. "I'm sorry, what?"

"Are you okay?"

"What? Are you worried about me?"

"Well, ah, yeah."

Erika giggled, "Oh, you're precious. I'm going to have to keep you around." She leaned over and let her chest fall on his and kissed him.

"So you are okay?"

"Yes, I'm fine," Erika said with faux dignity.

"Did you..."

"Did I what?" Erika knew perfectly well what he was asking. She toyed with him. It had been a very long time since a man worried about her. Most men she frequented either didn't care or thought enough of themselves to assume they satisfied her every need. She found Doug's concern charming.

"You know…"

"No, I don't know."

"I mean, was it good for you?"

"Was it good for me?" Erika chortled. "Really, you're worried about whether I enjoyed it or not?"

"Well…yeah."

Erika placed her hands on his cheeks and kissed him. "It is wonderful to be young and unjaded."

"Huh?"

"Uh," Erika treaded into a topic she wanted to avoid. "Nothing. But I did."

"Did what?"

"You know."

"No I don't know." Doug grinned.

"Oh…you!" Erika kissed him hard on the lips. She reached to see if he was ready for seconds and then helped herself to dessert.

11

Erika cracked an eye open and read 0556 on her clock. She leaned to get out of bed and heard the frame creak. She pulled the sheets up over her chest and looked back to see if the noise stirred Doug. She needed to get to work and wanted to sneak out without revealing too much. Doug's arm reached for her and Erika slipped back into bed. Her body treated her well. Ocean of lotions and potions in her bathroom fostered a picture of youthfulness. Her chest was a different story. Not exercise, creams nor diet could give her an eighteen-year-old bosom. Only surgery could work that magic. And while a significant portion of women her age chose this direction, Erika didn't.

A satiated smile slithered across Doug's lips. Erika resisted the urge to kiss them again. She needed to get to work and didn't have time for that. "Good morning," she said.

"Mmmm. Good morning."

"You look like a happy boy." Erika cringed. He could be her boy. He was young enough. This cougar thing took some getting used to.

Doug reached up his arm and stretched and groaned a morning growl. "I am a happy boy."

Erika's mind searched for a solution. "Would you be a dear and get me my robe?"

Doug cocked an eye. "Now you're modest?" The question appeared strange, but getting laid was worth the eccentricity.

Erika rolled her eyes not knowing how else to react and motioned toward her closet. Doug propped himself up on his elbows and threw his good leg over the side of the bed. He looked back at Erika. He played up his bum leg for sympathy.

Erika motioned to the closet again.

Doug huffed with exaggerated effort when he stood up. He opened to closet and a familiar sight overtook him. It reminded him of his own closet. The closet held brightly colored distinctly feminine clothes. But it also sported a section of drab colored clothes that matched the clothes in his closet. They were uniforms. Panic flushed his body. They were Marine uniforms! And if she was enlisted, he could be put in jail. His eyes darted to the sleeves, but they were slick. The panic subsided. She was an officer. His eyes rolled up to the collars. He expected to see a yellow or silver bar, perhaps even silver railroad tracks. They resembled railroad tracks, but as they came into focus he saw a menacing eagle with its wings spread and its talons clutching deadly arrows. The panic returned ten fold. She had to be married and the shirts had to be her husband's. But the shirts were too small. "Holy shit!"

"What is it?" Erika forgot about the uniforms.

Doug turned with his jaw dragging on the floor. "You're a…"

"A what?" Erika smiled and enjoyed the look on Doug's face. A strange pride seeped into her soul. Her secret escaped. She might as well enjoy the moment.

"You're a fucking Colonel!"

Erika giggled to herself and put her fingers to her lips to control her laugh over the irony. "Well, I am a Colonel…and as for the fucking part, I thought we established that last night."

Doug's eyes bulged. "What…who the fuck are you?"

Erika's giggle grew. She knew whatever she had last night was over now that Doug knew her secret, so she might as well enjoyed the ride as long as it lasted. She fluttered her eyelids. "If you're asking me who I was fucking, I thought that would have been self evident."

Doug shook his head trying to wrap his head around the moment. She could be a regimental commander. "What do you do? Who do you work for?"

Erika slowed her speech and spoke methodically as if addressing a kindergartner. "I'm the Marine Corps Chief of Public Affairs and I work for General Steinmark."

Doug's eyes rolled, "Oh, Steinmark." His shoulders bobbed in disbelief as he chuckled at his predicament. "Do you have lunch with the Commandant too?"

Erika played along with the sarcastic question. "Not today, but often."

"Ha," Doug cried in disbelief and fell onto the bed. He yelped in pain as his leg bent over the side of the bed. "Sonuvabitch! That hurts!"

"Aww, Erika lean over him and placed a hand on his chest. "Poor, baby." Doug shot a look at Erika just as a thought struck them both. "Yeah, I should probably cool it on the 'baby' thing, huh?" Erika offered.

Doug shrugged. "I guess so."

Erika saw there was more to the statement. "What is it?"

"I dunno. I guess I always wanted to be a mother fucker."

"You are such a boy." Erika leaned in to kiss him. "I have to take a shower." Erika stood up and lowered the sheet. She braced for his reaction, but it never came. She'd seen young breasts in women's locker rooms for years and felt sensitive about how she aged. The fact her husband left her for a younger woman didn't help. Erika sighed with relief. Having a young man lust after her felt empowering. "Now, I'm supposed to watch you. So you don't do something foolish and hurt yourself. But I have to go to work. So, please stay here, at least until I get back from work."

"I'm not going anywhere." Doug folded his fingers behind his head as he laid back taking in the sight of his conquest. His eyes feasted over the woman's body.

Erika playfully shook her hips. "I'll make the wait worth your while."

Doug propped himself up on his elbows. "You will!"

Erika stopped dancing. "Yes, why is that so hard to believe? I like sex."

"Well, uh, so do I!"

Erika's mood continued to darken. "We need to talk though."

"Uh, oh."

"No, it's not like that."

"Oh."

"Well, it is a little like that."

"Uh."

Erika kneeled onto the bed and placed a hand on his chest. "Doug, I'm considerably older than you."

"Sure." He didn't understand Erika's point—yet.

"We can't…"

"We can't what?"

"This isn't going to last." She tried to remember what it was like to be a twenty something year old. In her twenties nearly everyone she slept with was a potential life long mate. It wasn't like now deep into her forties and avoiding emotional ties like the plague.

"Why not?"

Erika sighed in frustration. "We can't ever be a normal couple." The argument worked for her.

"So…we'll be an unnormal couple."

"Doug, I'm probably the same age as your parents."

"So."

Erika worried about perceptions and the relationship's potential. Even though lovers came and went without a second thought in her life, Doug was different. He was younger and probably looking for something different.

"Doug, you deserve someone younger. You deserve to have a chance at a family."

"Why do I need a family?"

Erika sighed. "You do. You'd feel empty without one. Besides, can't this just be a cheap lay you can brag about to your friends and we end on a good note like normal people?"

"How do you know how I'd feel?" An edge slipped into Doug's tone. He thought she was overly presumptive.

"Because I don't have one."

"So, it seems to work for you. And if this is going to be a cheap tawdry affair why can't we just roll with it?"

"I…" Erika choked on her emotions. "I didn't choose this life," she said sweeping her hand across her room.

"I don't understand. You wanted to have children?"

Erika shook her head. The conversation confused her. "No, I didn't want children, at least I didn't think so." When she was honest with herself, the first Christmas card with her ex, new wife and child crushed her more than her divorce. Her maternal pangs stung much harder than she imagined.

"I don't get it."

"What don't you get?" Erika asked although she knew her logic skipped a step.

"You don't…didn't want children, and yet you assume I do?"

"I didn't think I did, but eventually I think I did. And you will one day."

Doug shook his head trying to follow her. "How do you know that I'll want to have children?"

Erika hung her head. The young man peeled away her hard shell with a shrewdness no one else matched, or cared to match. She looked up and focused her eyes squarely on Doug's. "Because my husband left me for someone to have his children with." Erika sighed. "He's now married to the girl who is a decade younger than me—and still considerably older than you I might add. They have four kids. He flies to Paris every other week in the triple seven he flies for Delta. They have a Mansion in Peachtree City, Georgia. And to top it all off, if I remember correctly, she was named Volunteer of the Year for this kids' school." Erika hung her gaze on Doug trying to register any cognitive synthesis.

"So?"

"So," exacerbation crawled all over Erika's speech. "When you get tired of me, you'll find someone to have a family with and leave me for her. I'm not going to be part of that. You need to go find your…" Erika tried to control her tongue and failed, "young little breeding bitch now before someone gets hurt. I deserve better than this." Erika stared at Doug's slack jaw. Before he could mount a re-attack she added, "And now I need to take a shower."

"I know why he left you," Doug said just before she closed the door. Her fingers tightened on the door. She fought the urge to pursue the conversation. She wondered what Doug could possibly have reasoned even though the answer might eat at her. She lost that internal fight. "You do?" she asked peaking her head back out.

"Yes. He left you because you are cold and selfish."

Erika stepped towards Doug and cocked a hand back. She unleashed it with all the fury she wanted to unleash on the life that she felt was stolen from her. For his part, Doug left his jaw out. "I'm cold and selfish! You…" Erika's brain short-circuited. She didn't know whether to call him judgmental, arrogant or cruel. "HOW CAN YOU CALL ME COLD AND SELFISH. HE'S THE ONE WHO LEFT ME!"

"Because you only care about yourself."

"How can you say that! You don't even know me!"

"You fucked me last night because you wanted to. Today you say you want no part of a relationship with me because you're afraid I might leave you. Did you *ever*, for one second, consider my feelings in this? From what I've seen you only care about yourself."

"Look, I'm not going to play these childish games with an adolescent." Erika stormed back into the bathroom.

"Yeah, run away from a serious conversation. That's the mark of true maturity." Doug said through the door. "I should also add that you are a coward." Doug listened for a response. He didn't get any reply. Instead if he listened carefully he could hear muffled sobs. *Oh, shit.* Doug crawled along the floor to the door and swung it open. "I'm sorry," he said before she had a chance to say anything.

Erika looked at the pathetic mess of a man on the floor and softened.

"I shouldn't have said those things," he said.

Erika slumped to the floor and cradled him. "No, you shouldn't have." Then she added, "But it's true."

"What part was true?" Doug offered a feeble smile. "That you're immature?"

"No—well—yeah, but more about me not thinking about your feelings at all."

"Well, you didn't, did you?"

"No, but you don't have to say it."

"Oh, yes, I do."

Erika smiled and kissed him softly.

"Why do we have to have a conclusion to…this? Why do we have to know how it ends up? Can't we just enjoy what it is for now?" he asked.

"Cheap sex?"

"Yes!" Doug beamed. "Just good old fashioned cheap sex. I make you feel good. You make me feel good—"

"And then you'll leave me for someone else?"

Doug hissed and shook his head. "Now, why do you have to go and ruin this wonderful cheap sex thing that I'm imagining? You're really harshing my mellow. And besides, how do I know that you won't leave me for someone who is more…" Doug swallowed, "mature." He said *mature* as if it was an insult.

Erika ran her fingers through his short hair. "You are adorable and irresistible." Erika cringed. The second adjective tied her too closely to him. "Maybe I should keep you around. You know, I'll keep putting food at my door and I'll keep seeing if you keep showing up."

A satisfied grin grew over Doug. "I'll keep coming back if you keep serving what you fed me last night."

"What was that? Cheap sex?"

"Yeah, what is wrong with cheap sex?"

"Nothing, I guess." Erika smiled. "But I need to be just a little selfish here. I need to go to work. And I need to take a shower to go to work." Erika got to her knees and helped Doug up.

"Fine. I'll let you go to work. But I'm going to wait for you right here," Doug said pointing to the bed.

"Okay, but you can watch TV in the living room and get some food from the fridge. I'm sorry there isn't a lot in there—"

"Yeah, I wouldn't expect there to be too much in there. I'm guessing guys buy you lunch and dinner just about every day and they probably even come around in the morning offering to take you out for coffee."

A confident smile sprouted on Erika's lips. "So," she said over her shoulder as she walked back into the bathroom, "what if they do?" It was true, a nice little bolster for her ego.

Doug folded his fingers behind his head looking like the king of the court. "Ask for a double order to bring some home to me."

"Oh…you…what am I going to do with you!"

"I'm sorry I guess have haven't been perfectly clear on that. I expect you to feed me, then fuck me."

Erika pursed her lips in mock anger and threw a hand towel at him.

Erika thought about the possibilities in the shower and grew more comfortable with the idea of spending time, she couldn't commit to the word *date*, with the young Marine. She finished her shower, threw on a towel and wrapped another one around her hair. She stepped out of the bathroom.

"…I've got to go. I'll talk to you later." Doug tapped END on his phone.

"Who was that?" Erika said with some jealously. "Did you have to give your other girl this address so she could come over while I'm at work?"

"Wow, you *really* don't know me. I can't even get a collie to come—"

"I disagree, you got me to cum."

Doug's mouth hung open. A charge lit into his body. "You keep talking like that and you'll have to take another shower."

"No," Erika turned serious. "I don't have time for that." She returned to her original question. "So who was that?"

"It was my mom, I wanted to know what her exact birthdate was. I wanted to know if she was younger than you."

Erika rolled her eyes. "No, really who was that?"

"Just a friend."

Erika huffed. "Whatever, fine. Act like a two year old."

Doug realized he played the coy game one hand too long. "Just a guy that was in my company."

"Oh. Now was that so hard?"

"No, not really. I've never had a jealous girlfriend before."

Erika gasped out a laugh. "Girlfriend? What? Are we going to prom or something?"

"What is so funny about that?"

"Nothing." Erika lifted her eyes. "You have no idea how different our worlds are."

"Why's that?"

"Look, I don't have time right now. I've got to get dressed." Erika marched over to her closet and sorted through a uniform to put on.

"You might have heard of him, Drake Scott," Doug said making conversation.

Erika paused. "Who?" The name rang a bell.

"Drake Scott, you know, the CMH guy."

"Yeah, yeah. I know him." Erika's mind churned and her face showed it.

"Oh, no."

What?" she asked. Doug's reaction broke the spell. "

"Not you too," he said

"Me too?"

"Yeah, I swear that every girl that guy meets ends up throwing her panties at him."

Erika continued to paw through her clothes. "No, that's not my interest in him, but here." She tossed a pair of panties at Doug. "I'm officially throwing my panties at you." She peaked a look at Doug. Doug lit up like a five year old on Christmas morning. Erika smiled. *Simple pleasures.* Doug raised them to his nose and Erika smirked waiting on his reaction.

"Hey! That's! Ah, that's, ah, what is it!"

"It's lavender. I don't know what it is called, but it's Lady's Burberry."

Doug lowered the undergarment and flashed a confused look. "Do you have a pair of these lying around to throw at every guy you drag home?"

"No," Erika chuckled. "I spritz them."

"Spritz them?"

"Yes, I spritz them for when I have a," she adopted a voice fit for a TV commercial, "not so fresh day."

Doug looked at the panties and then back at her. "Does it work?"

Erika cocked her head off to the side for a second in a half shrug. "I don't know. But it makes me less self-conscious. So it works for me."

"Where did you ever get such an idea?"

"Cosmo," she said snapping her nylon stockings into a garter belt.

"Cosmo? You read that?" Doug imagined that Cosmo was for girls his age, not a Marine Corps Colonel.

"Yeah, I read it when I'm on the bike." Erika took spinning classes back-to-back five days out of the week. "I can't concentrate enough to read anything work related when I'm spinning."

"Erika, did you hear me?" General Steinmark said.

"Hmm, I'm sorry, sir, what?"

"I said, have you got the plans for Lieutenant Scott's movie release all planned out?"

"Ah, sir…I," Erika stammered. The topic of Lieutenant Scott whipped around in Erika's mind. *Sir, I'm finishing the last touches on Lieutenant Scott's movie release. And, oh, by the way, I fucked the living hell out of his friend last night. Totally blew away his mind. Had him whimpering like a puppy dog.*

"Erika?"

Erika shook her head to clear it. "Yes, sir."

"Are you okay?" Steinmark asked. It wasn't the usual boss—subordinate inquiry. Steinmark pulled Erika along with his career. She worked as his Public Affairs Officer ever since she was a captain. Steinmark saw her husband destroy her the day he separated from the Corps and left Erika on the same day. Steinmark felt a small thorn of guilt for the way he worked her when she was married. Erika dedicated a minimum sixty, usually eighty, hours a week to the Corps. Steinmark felt that if he had made her go home occasionally, she might have kept her husband. As far as Steinmark could tell she had no life outside of the military. When TDY, she woke before Steinmark and went to bed after him. He heard stories about the string of momentary lovers she collected, but she never put together a real relationship he knew of. She never showed up at a social event with the same man twice. In short he felt more like an overbearing father than a boss.

"I'm fine, sir. I just need to—"

"Go home, Erika," Steinmark smiled. He looked at his watch—1432. It was plenty late for her to go.

"Sir?" Erika sounded hurt. Her inability to concentrate disappointed her because she felt she was disappointing the general.

Steinmark's smile broadened and he laid a hand on her shoulder. "Go home. You've earned it."

"I'm sorry, sir."

"No need to be sorry." Steinmark skirted around saying anything more. He didn't want to get too close to her personal life.

"But sir, I need to—"

"Erika, I'm fully capable of running the Corps without you."

A feeble smile creased her lips. She grabbed her bag, loaded some folders in it and stood up.

"Are you happy?" Steinmark asked as he stood up to walk her to his office door. He didn't know exactly why he asked. He saw a secret behind the smile on her face though.

Erika stopped and turned to face him. "I'm having fun, sir."

Steinmark beamed. "That's good. I'm happy for you."

12

The Division Commander on Camp Pendleton assembled his staff for the weekly staff meeting at 0800 on Monday. The staff hated it because that meant either coming in at 0600 on Monday to update slides that needed to be into the Chief of Staff's office by 0730, or coming in on Sunday to update PowerPoint slides. The General didn't believe anyone should work on the Lord's Day and frequently roamed offices sending Marines home on Sunday. But he also wanted current and accurate slides on Monday at 0800. He wanted to start the week off up to speed on the division's activities. After two grueling hours that rivaled survival training in its tortuous mind games, the General released his staff. By 1030 the Regimental commanders took seats at their own staff meetings where they passed on information from the Division staff meeting. Around 1300 Battalion commanders sat with their Company Commanders. By 1500 Jon Kim walked into his office where his XO and three platoon commanders, sat at a small table for his staff meeting while the NCOs worked the platoons.

"Stay down," Jon said as they began to get up. Jon went over notes passed down from Division to Regiment through Battalion to him. Then he sat back and tried to come up with a way to prop up the ego of one of his platoon leaders. "Bill," he said to Houston. "Don't worry about Friday morning. That exercise is supposed to fry your brain." He gestured with hands. "Look, the Battalion XO started pulling that stunt long ago. I got lit up when I was a platoon leader." He pointed to Drake, "Even hero boy here—"

"Hero boy?" Drake protested and scrunched his face with disapproval.

Jon chuckled. "Yeah—hero boy—here even got lit up. Everyone has gotten lit up in that drill." Jon shook his head realizing that fact wasn't true anymore. "Except for Colt—"

"Yeah," Drake piped in, "how the hell did you know what was coming. I mean…how…"

Colt Larsen hid his type A personality well. He was competitive, but mostly with himself. He didn't need anyone else to keep score. Because of that he appeared to be a type B personality. "Oh, it was just so obvious," he said rocking back in his chair and folding his fingers behind his head.

Drake leaned forward. Unlike Colt, he was openly competitive. He also was a professional and if there was something he thought he needed to know to make him a better leader he was going to ask. "How the hell was it so obvious?"

"Yeah, Colt," Jon asked. "How did you know that was coming?"

Colt chuckled and then twisted his face into character. He looked at Drake. "Scott! You magnificent bastard!" he growled channeling George C. Scott as George S. Patton. "I read your God damned book!"

"Oh…fuck!" Drake groaned slapping his forehead. "You asswipe," Drake teased and slugged Colt so that he would fall off balance.

Everyone cracked up. Jon had lost control of the meeting momentarily and let it go. It was the end of the day and their schedule was free for the rest of the day. He looked at his watch. It was still a little early to crack open the fridge and pull out some cold ones.

"What? You think you have to be a Stanford grad to read—no offense, sir," Colt side barred to Jon, "You know we read at Northwestern too. That 'N' on the helmets was for Knowledge. Cuz we be smart at Northwestern also too."

"I thought the 'N' on Nebraska's helmet was for Knowledge," Drake said

"Hey, now. Go easy on Big Red," Willis chimed in. Willis graduated from the University of Nebraska and wasn't going to be a Rhodes Scholar anytime soon. What he may have lacked in cerebral capacity though, he made up with by sheer effort and dedication.

"Okay, Okay." Jon took control of the meeting. "Let's stop this for now and we can pick it up on Friday at Maggies," he said referring to Maggie Maes, the college meat market and hangout. He looked across his guys. "Everyone in? Hero boy, here is buying the first round."

"Again with the hero boy?" Drake groaned.

Jon smiled. "Yeah, I kinda like it."

"Oh, fine," he said and then swatted at Colt. "But asswipe buys every other round."

"Yeah, cause I made a shitload of money off of my published book," Colt said sarcastically. "Oh, that's right it was hero boy that made all the Benjamins."

"Hey, he can call me hero boy because he outranks me. You, ya little pissant two LT, I out rank—"

"Yes, sir!" Colt interrupted throwing Drake a sarcastic salute.

"So you don't get to call me hero boy." Drake struggled to contain his laughter.

"Yes, sir, hero, sir, boy." Colt replied.

"Asswipe." Drake slugged Colt again.

"Ma!" Colt cried to Jon. "Hero Boy keeps punching me."

Jon choked down his laughter and said, "Am I going to have to send you boys to your rooms?" The room exploded in laughter. "Hero Boy, Asswipe, now stop it!"

When the laughter subsided Colt asked. "Hey, when did I get stuck with Asswipe as a call sign?"

"When I gave it to you just now, Asswipe," Drake replied.

Another explosion of laughter rocked the room. Drake grew fonder of Colt by the minute. He was the little brother he never had. Colt's dedication to his profession by going out and reading impressed Drake. He underestimated Colt—that bothered Drake. Never, ever underestimate someone. That will get you killed.

"Okay, I give up," Jon said. "Here are the rest of the notes from the staff meeting if you guys want to read them." He got up and walked over to a small fridge, reached in and pulled out some Heinekens. "I say it is time to crack'em."

On Friday Drake walked out of his apartment and walked down the hall. When he found Colt's room he pounded on the door.

"I'm coming. Hold onto your skirt," Colt said to the knock at the door as he did a final check—keys, wallet, phone. He opened the door and said to Drake, "Dude, you gotta get me a better call sign than Asswipe. Houston's starting to call me Asswipe now."

Drake laughed. "Houston?"

"Yeah." Colt said. "Are we going to get him too?"

"Yeah."

"I guess we moved in too late to get the warm welcome to the neighborhood that you got though, cause I never learned to, ah...what was it...surf."

"Shit, I keep forgetting you read that." Drake shook his head. "I shouldn't have let Chandler see my whole journal and tell her every God damn piece of my life. I didn't think anyone would really care about my life."

"Are you kidding me? Hero boy? I only wish I had your life!"

Drake laughed.

"What's so funny?"

"Nothing, it is just that Houston had a shot at her and jacked it up royally."

"Noccionni? Really?" Colt asked.

"Yeah."

"From the book, it sounded like if anything was a sure bet, she was."

"She pretty much is—or was."

"How did he blow that opportunity?"

"I don't know. It got kinda ugly." Drake explained the details.

"That dude needs to get laid in the worst way."

"Yeah, he does."

"He's so wound up, it is killing him. We got to get him laid tonight."

"Okay," Drake said as he knocked on Houston's door.

The band in the basement at Maggie's played classic rock while the band upstairs played progressive. Both were loud, so the Marines sat at a table in the bar.

"You played football at Northwestern?" Drake asked Colt starting off the conversation. He remembered the comment about the 'N' on the helmet. He didn't know if Colt meant 'our helmet,' as in our team's that he was a member of, or our university's.

"No, baseball. A gentleman's game, not a knuckle dragger's."

"Fuck you." Drake rolled his eyes at the insult. He waved over the waitress. He leaned over and said, "Start a tab," as he handed her a credit card. Kidding aside, Drake possessed much more wealth than the other Marines.

"Sure, what would you like?" the waitress asked. She continued around the table.

When she reached Colt he turned and asked Drake, "You're paying for this right?"

"Everyone except you, Asswipe."

"Okay, Colt protested, if you're going to call me Asswipe, can we at least say Alpha Whiskey?"

"Or, how about Whiskey Sour," Willis interjected.

"How about just Sour," Houston said.

"Sour puss," Jon teased.

Drake laughed and then said, "How about just Pussy."

Colt rolled his eyes. "Whatever, you guys call me whatever you want."

"Now that sounds like Sour Grapes," Willis continued.

"Grape Ape!" Houston cheered.

"Magilla Gorilla," Jon continued.

"No," Drake said adopting an official tone. "Just Magilla." He looked at Colt. "That fine with you?"

"If it makes you happy, Hero Boy." Colt turned on his chair to look at the waitress. He felt bad for making her wait, but she smiled at him demurely nonetheless. "I'm sorry, we haven't grown up yet. But since he," Colt pointed at Drake, "is paying for it I'll have a Guinness."

"Yes, sir," she replied and started to turn away.

Colt touched her arm to stop her. He noticed the name and the gray eyes. Her also noticed the cheek bones and curiosity finally seized him. He possessed a curious mind, which drove him to read *Storming Baghdad*. It also tickled his mind about their waitress. Her Eastern European accent broke the dam. "Nika," he leaned over. "Where are you from?"

"Russia." She smiled politely and turned away to fetch their drinks.

Dennis Redding, Jon's XO, asked, "You already hitting on the waitress?"

"No," Colt replied. But he did admire her derrière as it sauntered through the crowd.

"You wouldn't tap that?" Dennis asked.

"Nah, I did enough college girls to last a lifetime. I would like to think I've moved on from that," Colt replied.

"Okay, I got it. Whiskey Delta!" Dennis exclaimed.

The table roared with laughter. But the name could never stick. Weak Dick, or Whiskey Delta was too common throughout the military for one Marine to claim the title.

"How about just Asswipe," Colt concluded.

"Aww, don't be a sour puss, Sour Puss?"

Colt rolled his eyes again and discreetly searched for the waitress. He enjoyed looking at her, but he also wanted his beer. The conversation grew tiresome. Colt didn't answer. Any answer was going to charge another attack on him.

When the conversation died down some he asked, "Hey, Hero Boy, since you are such a reader yourself, where can I read about a fire and what the fuck team?" Colt picked at an open scar from Drake's past. When charging into the farmhouse to save Stephanie he only took one other man for various reasons. When the division commander asked him why he only took one other man, he said he read about a fire and maneuver team that is used in other countries. The general replied, "A fire and what the hell?"

"He said, 'fire and what the hell,' Ass—"

"Is that why you got lit up by the general?" Houston asked.

"Dude—relax," Drake shot back. "This isn't about me, it is about getting Asswipe an appropriate call sign."

"He just needs to get laid," Colt replied. "And yes, this is about you, Hero Boy."

"Hey, I get laid!" Houston protested as Nika walked up to the table. She set beers on the table. Houston turned away to hide his flush cheeks.

"By yourself doesn't count," Redding said.

Colt chuckled at Houston's embarrassment and watched Nika walk away again. When she was out of earshot he said to Houston. "Oh, bullshit, you haven't had pussy since pussy had you."

The table broke into hysteria. Jon choked on his beer he laughed so hard. Drake raised his bottle up to Colt who tapped it with his. When the table subsided and a pregnant pause grew over the table the Marines each looked across the roomful of co-eds. Drake was already spoken for, so he ended his search first. "So why aren't you playing for the Yankees?" he asked Colt.

"Tommy John surgery my sophomore year—"

"You were a pitcher?" Drake asked.

"Yeah, and a torn—"

"I gotta take a piss," Houston declared.

"I'll alert the fucking press," Drake replied.

"Torn rotator cuff, my senior year," Colt finished. Then he continued, "Hey, we should ask that waitress to hit on Bill."

"Her?" Drake asked. "I thought you would've liked to have her to yourself."

"Don't get me wrong. I wouldn't kick her out of bed. Well, actually, I would, there's a lot more room on the floor. But we need to get Bill laid."

Drake raised a finger and searched for Nika. When she showed up Drake pulled out a hundred dollar bill and said, "Would you mind going out on a date with my friend?"

Nika saw the hundred dollar bill and tried to remember what president was pictured on the note. She had never seen a hundred dollar bill. College students didn't tip well, if at all. Her mother made minimum wage as a motel maid and her father made just over minimum wage as a school custodian. When they took asylum in the US, they left everything back in Russia. She thought of what a hundred dollars could do for her family.

"Drake don't do that to her," Colt protested.

"Do what?"

"She's not a hooker."

"What's the matter? You want me to pay her to go out with you?"

"Man! How did you ever land something like Grace Freemont?"

Drake glanced down below the table. "When you have the goods…"

Colt rolled his eyes.

"How about this," he said to Colt and then looked back at Nika. "Tell my friend," Drake pointed at the empty seat and then the bathroom, "that he has a nice smile and if he asks you out I will pay for the dinner with this here hundred dollar bill that I will give to you, okay?"

Nika didn't know what to make of it. She's been approached in every crude manner dreamt up by an assortment of drunk college boys, but they rarely tossed around hundred dollar bills. She didn't remember what the friend in the bathroom looked like, but the one who asked where she was from has nice caring eyes. "Do I get the money if I just say he has nice eyes?"

"Sure," Drake said. He looked over and saw Houston coming out of the bathroom He stuffed the bill in her apron and flashed her a wink.

Nika reached in and felt the bill in her hand. She stepped back and inventoried her appointed date as he got back on his bar stool. Nika looked over at Colt and saw the disappointment in his face. She couldn't do it. Betrayal tugged at her. She leaned in to Drake's ear while looking into Colt's eyes and whispered. "Tell you friend he has nice eyes."

Drake leaned over to Houston and said. "She says you have nice eyes. She's been waiting for you to get back so you could ask her out."

Colt's eyelids drifted closed. It was a car wreck.

"Really!" Houston bellowed. "You want to go out with me?"

Nika couldn't say anything so she nodded. Drake pulled a pen from Nika's apron. Things happened so quickly Nika didn't know how to protest. Drake wrote down Houston's phone number on a napkin and handed it to her. "Here is his phone number."

"Thank you," Nika said and walked away quickly. She felt dirty.

Drake watched her walk away. She did have a nice ass. The he hammered his open hand onto Houston's chest. He grabbed a handful of shirt and pulled him in close. "Look, jackwad, you treat her like she's my sister, you copy, over?"

"Yes, sir," Houston stammered.

"I don't want to have to fuck you up again, you copy?"

"Yes, sir."

"Cool," Drake growled and shoved him back in his place.

Silence fell over the table. Not everyone knew the full story behind Drake's actions. The Marines all lifted their beer to their lips to end the awkward moment.

"Forty-Five," Jon said.

Colt slapped the table, "It's about time one of you guys caught the clue."

"What? I don't get it?" Drake asked.

"Knuckle dragger," Colt replied. "Hell, everyone I've met throughout my entire life has called me Forty-Five from the moment they met me. You couldn't have figured that out if I shot you with a forty-five."

"Oh, is that a pitcher thing?" Drake asked.

"Ya think?" Colt chided.

Drake chuckled and sipped his beer. Then he asked, "So were you a fastballer is that why everyone called you Forty-Five?"

"I could bring it."

"How hard did you throw?"

"I hit ninety-six consistently. My top was one oh one."

Drake took another slug of beer. "That's brining it. It's too bad you blew out your arm."

Colt smiled and said, "Hey, I'm living the dream now buddy."

"Damn straight," Drake replied.

"But I don't have a Grace Freemont on the hook."

"No you don't," Drake smiled his Cheshire cat grin. "Don't worry. Well get you laid next time."

"Don't bother. I can get my own hookers," Colt jested then realized he needed to keep that part of the evening quiet. Luckily, Houston was too lost in a fantasy to catch the remark.

13

Nadia's screen flickered. Her chest gripped her heart and it stopped beating. The computer rebooted. She instinctively hit the red light on the power strip and watched the light die. She pulled the cord from the wall and got up. "Hana, love, we need to go to the store," she said in British English with a heavy Arabic accent. She spoke to her five-year-old girl in English. Nadia dreamed to be a Westerner and was well on her way at an English college when her Iraqi husband coerced her back to Iraq. Maybe her daughter could live the dream she had for herself. Nadia leveraged her CompSci degree into a job that paid the Sunni—Shia mixed couple enough to rent a modest home in Nasariyah before the war. She hadn't been paid since the war started. She continued to sell household items and furniture for food.

She also leveraged her degree to help the West. She hid her cyber tracks very well. Only the US Air Force knew who she was and what she was doing. Stephanie Chandler didn't even know how deep Nadia dove into the cyber world.

Through her husband's family's tie to the Ba'athist Party she snuck through an email account and ripped emails and data off of the regime's servers. From there she delivered them to the US. She applied some intricate scripts and jimmied the locks to almost any US agency, FBI, CIA, and NSA to name a few. None of the agencies knew what to do with the intruder. They simply shut everything down and cleaned her out of their systems. The problem was they destroyed any cyber forensics that could have helped them. When she tried a US Air Force server, she got a pop up stating, "NICE WORK. LOVE WHAT YOU'RE DOING—JUST NOT HERE. STAND BY FOR INSTRUCTIONS." An elite Air Force Cyber Ranger Team, CRT, named so because they conduct missions similar to Army Rangers. They infiltrated and exfiltrated enemy networks, conducted raids, direct attack operations, and recover cyber data. The CRT had tracked her since she first started infiltrating Saddam's network. They wanted the data she collected, but on their terms. Because Nadia wasn't US service personnel, she could conduct operations US law prohibited the CRT from conducting. Most of the time the CRT skirted and outright ignored US law. But with a semi-trusted agent on the outside, they could keep their digital fingerprints off the dirty work. As much as CRT was interested in Iraq, they wanted Nadia to focus on Iran. With the US preoccupied with post 9/11 events, Iran accelerated their nuclear weapons program. And although they condemned the 9/11 attacks, a Sunni lunatic lead it after all, they still hated America and the West. Their activities didn't escape the CRT.

Nadia's cyber trail traveled the world over, but now it seemed the Iranians had her. "But mama, we don't have any money." Hana said trying to understand the concept of going to the store without money.

"I know, love." An inventory shot through her mind. She had a half loaf of bread without mold and a small block of cheese she and Hana had been eating as fast as they could because she had to slice off a small strip of mold each time they ate. And there was about a half gallon of clean water left. "Maybe the Americans have some water for us."

"Mama, they didn't last time."

"Love, we need to try."

Hana didn't understand her mother's urgency. She watched her mother franticly scurry about the house. Nadia pulled out an old hard drive that was in her husband's computer and pulled her hard drive out and then swapped out the modem. Then she plugged the system back in. It looked like she was never there.

She didn't have time to debate with herself about who cracked her. She couldn't stop her mind though. The Russians could have easily snooped her out. They hacked better than anyone, except for the US Air Force. The restart was sloppy though. It screamed HERE I AM! I HAVE ACCESS TO YOUR SYSTEM! It looked more like the Chinese who were just starting to dabble in cyber warfare. But the Chinese didn't have a reason to go after her—neither did the Russians for the matter. Iran on the other hand didn't hack as well as the Russians, but were fairly clean. The restart seemed bush league. It didn't have to be professionals though. As much as the Iranian government tried to force its will on its people, Iran contained several different groups with different agendas. Nadia had read email traffic and stayed in the background. She watched and aided an array of people in Iran who were trying to destroy the Iranian government, which included scientists that worked in Iran's nuclear weapons program.

The CRT had monitored Nadia's work. After long debates and arguments that ended at the squadron commander level—if the conversation progressed any higher it would have been nixed, it was too close to being over the line—a package of scripts fell into Nadia's hands courtesy of the CRT. She in turn worked with agents she trusted in Iran.

The next day a Supervisory Control and Data Acquisition (SCADA) attack failed a boiler regulator in an Iranian nuclear site. Thirty-four people died in an underground explosion that leveled the complex. Nadia hacked into DIA's satellite feeds to watch the smoke billow out of the underground vents. She sat back and smiled.

Right now though, she needed to assume the Iranians knew exactly who she was and where she lived.

"Hurry, love." She motioned to Hana. She wrapped her arm around the girl to protect her from the dangers approaching. They stepped outside the backdoor into an alley. Nadia scanned the area wondering where to go and where they, whoever "they" were, could be coming from. Iranian agents and sympathizers ran rampant though southern Iraq where the Shia dominated the landscape. Nadia lowered her head and started walking to create space between her and her computer. A speeding van squealed to a stop within inches of her. This was it. She knew how it would go down. She had seen the ugly videos on the Internet. The door slammed open and bearded men stormed out.

Nadia wrapped her arms around Hana and bent over and smelled her beautiful daughter's hair one last time. She wondered if thoughts flooded her husband's mind just after he foolishly, her husband was a fool, stepped out of the house with an old Russian SKS to take on the Americans trying to earn his family's respect once again. Did thousands of images flood his mind as he stepped out and ran into the muzzle of Jamal Lincoln's M-16. When Pfc Lincoln's finger twitched a couple times ending his life did he have the regrets that Nadia experienced now? Why did she do any of this? Why did she tangle with the Iranians? Noble intentions or not, this began the ugliest time of her existence. Her friend Stephanie Chandler experienced what she was about to endure. But Stephanie didn't have a five year old. No matter how bad it was for Stephanie, it wasn't as bad as it was for the family in Basra that had to watch family members beaten, tortured and raped. She saw the video on an enemy website she hacked into before the video went public. Stephanie said she wanted to die—Nadia could not only sympathize, but empathize. When her screen flickered, should she have gotten her husband's rifle? Did the American's take the rifle when they searched her house? What would she have done even if she had the rifle? Would she have turned it on herself? What about Hana? Would she have to have taken her life too? Yes. That sequel to a branch in history was much more desirable that the limb they hung from now.

Nadia relaxed her body for the last time. She soaked up the feeling of her baby in her arms. Her eyelids slipped over her pupils and she tried to freeze time in her mind. Large meaty paws pounced on her. Her body shook to the core and ripped her and Hana off the street and into the van.

"Mommy!" Hana shriek. The first of many Nadia thought. She wondered how long she would have to endure her daughter's torture.

"Shhh…ma'am."

Nadia's brain tumbled into disorientation.

"Sir, we got it. Get some sleep."

"I'll be good," Air Force Captain Barry Horton said as he poured himself another cup of coffee. He looked at his watch. He'd been up for over twenty hours, but something was in the works, he just didn't know what it was. Heavy traffic passed in the area. Horton sat back down at his command consol. He sipped the black coffee and let his eyes scan the monitors in the trailer set up just outside of Nasariyah. A flicker caught his eye. "What's going on with her?"

"I don't know, sir."

"That's not her." Edginess grew on Horton's voice. Horton put the coffee down and leaned forward. He watched a screen that mirrored Nadia's display flicker off.

"Tell me what's going on?"

"It's rebooting."

"Hostile?"

"Don't know yet." An operator frantically tapped on his keyboard trying to diagnose what happened to the computer they monitored.

The screen blacked out. "She's gone. It ain't gonna come back," Horton said. He tapped on a tuffbook and sent a message to an address in a chat room. EXECUTE FALLEN ANGEL.

Navy Lieutenant Jake Netaceretachuvski's tablet came to life. "Guys, we got a redirect." The SEAL squad sat in place on a Strategic Reconnaissance, SR, mission, with an alternate for a rescue if required. They watched a house on the north side of Nasiriyah that was home to an insurgent leader that hadn't been home in a week. Air Force Captain Horton had sorted through the FRAGOs to see who was in the area. When he saw the SR mission he contacted the mission's OIC and requested assistance if circumstances dictated.

"Do we have eyes on target, Foxy?" a team member asked.

When Netaceretachuvski arrived at his first team the Senior Chief laughed and then scratched his head. Labeling the new Lieutenant with a call sign would be too fun. The dilemma of which one to choose stuck in the Chief's craw. Right off the bat he wanted to call him Fucking-Too-Long. However this presented two problems. One—the call sign was too long itself, two—it gave the Lieutenant too much credit on a personal level that the Chief wasn't willing to award. He tried the phonetic option of Foxtrot-Tango-Lima, which was too long also. Then Fucking-Long presented a problem he already addressed. He settled on Foxy or Fox. When the occasion fit, sometimes Foxtrot Lima was converted to Foxy Lady. So Jake Netaceratachuvski answered to Foxy, Fox or Foxy Lady.

On cue, he received a mIRC, Microsoft Internet Relay Chat, message: STANDBY FOR VIDEO FEED. "Working it," Foxy replied.

Horton pinged Nadia's phone and pulled the lat and long. He sent that to a friend from ROTC stationed at Indian Springs who operated Predators. NEED EYES ON... He listed a request stating he needed to track a target that was at that location at the time listed, signed General Mills, a joke on rank and cereal the two shared since college. The jump in chain of command was ridiculous and the joke bought the operator enough leeway to play to direct the sensor operator in that direction for a short time. The predator operator rolled back feed until he saw the target and then ran it forward to real time and sent the feed to Horton who matched up the cell phone with the video just before he watched the target toss the phone into a neighbor's courtyard knowing that not only would the American's be following her, but perhaps the Iranians too.

Foxy had briefed the four man team about the redirect long before. "We got eyes," Foxy said as they loaded into the van. He directed them to the target and bolted out into the street, snatched the target while the driver waited to punch the accelerator and the other two members looked for trouble. "Ma'am I have instructions to start you on your way to the US."

Nadia's mind skidded to a halt. She prepped her mind around what she expected to hear in Farsi. The words the man spoke jumbled her head. She understood them a lot better than she imagined. It wasn't Farsi. The man looked too big to be Iranian, or what she imagined an Iranian to look like. She continued cringing, but a blow never landed on her. Something was wrong. Or, if not wrong, not what she expected. It was English she realized. Why were they speaking English? It made no sense. Hope tried to sprout from her breast, but she beat it down. She couldn't take the disappointment. She cracked open an eye to investigate. The bearded man had fair skin! Was he Chechen? Why would a Chechen speak English? The man wore a smile—a genuine smile, not an evil smile.

"Lieutenant Netaceratachuvski, US Navy," Foxy said holding out a hand to Nadia.

Nadia couldn't hold back her hope anymore. Joy bounded down her spine. She held out a hand to the Navy Lieutenant and clutched Hana with the other and savored the smell of her girl's hair. She wept for joy.

"Mama, what is wrong?"

"Nothing, everything is wonderful."

Horton had briefed his boss on the Nasariyan agent he used to get into the Iranian nuclear program and not much else. His boss didn't want to know too much. One item he mentioned was that Horton liked her being in Nasariyah so he could leverage her ability to skirt US law, but it was personally dangerous for the agent. If the operation blew up and the agent needed to be recovered Horton wanted to be able to relocate the agent to the US. His boss agreed. Horton planned out all the details to include a position at a US bank and a part-time position she could perform anywhere in the country assigned to a classified unit at Camp Parks, California. He even had identification including a new last name for her on American passports. He had decided her new last name would be Martinez. Her olive skin could pull off the Hispanic background. O'Malley or Peterson wouldn't have worked. He had contacted an office in the green zone that could make anyone an American citizen. The operation paralleled the witness relocation program.

The van rolled into a FOB, Forward Operating Base, and pulled up to a helicopter.

Foxy opened the door and helped the young mother and her child out and looked around. A humvee sped into view. Out hopped an air force captain.

"Thanks, Foxy." The captain smiled at the lieutenant and shook his hand.

"No problem," he said. "Have a good trip ma'am," he said to Nadia.

Nadia leaped forward and wrapped her free arm around the operator's neck. "Thank you!" She kissed him on the cheek. It was a Western custom she had picked up in England that she hadn't been able to express in years. "Thank you, so much!"

"You're blushing, Lieutenant," Horton giggled.

Foxy stood dumbfounded for a second trying to reply with a zinger, but fell speechless. He simply nodded with rosy cheeks and ran off to the van to return to his original mission.

"Nice to meet you, Nadia."

Nadia looked with a question mark. She didn't even get to know the navy lieutenant and now she was in the presence of an air force captain who she didn't know, but seemed to know her. She saw the helicopter and understood it was for her, but the captain wasn't making a move towards the helicopter.

"Nice work. Love what you're doing."

Nadia lit up. "You're the one!"

"Yes, ma'am." Horton beamed. "If you'd like, we have a plan for you to relocate to the US?"

"Oh, yes!" Nadia cried and wrapped her free arm around the captain. Hana couldn't follow the events, but mama was happy so she smiled.

An American lawyer, Fawn Hollings traveled to Iraq just after the invasion to aid with women's rights issues and was turned onto Nadia's case by *Hollywood Vine* reporter, Stephanie Chandler. Hollings pushed for Nadia's departure to the US, but the military squashed the possibility. Hollings pried her resources and found out the air force held up the process, she stormed into every staff meeting with the air force and demanded to know why Nadia wasn't on her way to the US. The air force finally relented to the miniscule blonde and offered up Barry Horton. Horton and Hollings scratched at each other viciously over whether Nadia should be relocated to the US under political asylum or used in Iraq to do Horton's dirty work. In the end, Horton promised to put an evacuation plan in place if Hollings relented. She didn't have any leverage to move anyone out of the country without military assistance so she agreed to the plan.

"You'll need this," Horton said holding out a package that contained documentation to create a new life for Nadia and Hana Martinez.

"Thank you! Thank you!"

Horton smiled. "Okay, now, you need to get on board so we can get you out of here."

Nadia trotted up to the helicopter where a door gunner helped her up and into a seat.

Horton waived and then flipped open his phone. *She's on her way stateside.* He texted.

Thank you. Fawn Hollings replied.

We still need to talk. Horton replied.

I'll see what I can do. Hollings texted back.

Horton shook his head.

14

Thirty-six hours later Nadia and Hana Martinez opened the door to their new condominium in Southern California. Nadia didn't sleep for the first few nights. Elation boiled an adrenaline rush she couldn't restrain. She wanted to take it all in. She loved every second of every moment. In a small way she also feared that if she fell asleep she'd wake up and the dream would be over and she'd be back in Nasariyah. She set up her cable and other utilities. She dove into her two jobs. She settled Hana into a school and went grocery shopping with the advance on her salary. She wandered the grocery store's aisles and relished the experience. She decided to cook a meal. But the bounty she now enjoyed would be more exquisite if she could share it with someone. She pulled out a business card and her new cell phone.

"Hello?"

"Hello, Stephanie? This is Nadia."

"Nadia!"

"Yes."

"Where are you!"

"I'm in the states," Nadia replied.

"You are!"

"Yes, Yes, I live in Southern California now!"

"Oh!" Stephanie squealed in her South African accent. "That is so wonderful to hear." It had been so long since she'd heard good news that emotions overwhelmed her. "I just can't…" She couldn't think what to say.

"Well, Stephanie, I would like to thank you."

"You're so very welcome, my dear."

"No, I mean I would like to cook dinner for you tonight to say thank you," Nadia offered.

"Oh, all right. That'd be lovely."

"I would like to thank all of you. Could you bring Lieutenant Scott too?"

"Oh..." Stephanie's voice trailed off.

"Are you not..." Nadia didn't know how to broach the subject. What she wanted to ask was very inappropriate in her native culture. In the US though, it didn't feel too out of line. "...friendly?"

"Oh, we're still friends."

"Just not lovers."

Stephanie smiled to herself. Just the consideration of the subject warmed her. "No, we were never lovers."

"Honestly?" Nadia asked.

"Yes, honestly."

"But you looked...so...so...intimate." Nadia's vocabulary failed her.

Stephanie's eyelids fluttered. An ache cracked her chest. "No, we were never intimate."

"Oh, that is such a shame. You two looked so..."

"I know," Stephanie said cutting off Nadia's stammer. "But we were never."

"Is there any chance..."

"No," Stephanie cut her off again. "He's in love with a wonderful friend of mine."

"You mean that actress?"

"Yes."

"I couldn't imagine she could ever hold a candle to you."

"That is sweet of you to say, but he's in love with her and she's in love with him and you'd believe it too if you saw the two of them together." The irony struck Stephanie. Nobody had seen Drake Scott and Grace Freemont together. They had never been together.

"Well, then…" Nadia had spent sufficient time skirting the issue. "Do you think you could invite Jamal Lincoln then?"

"Jamal?" Stephanie smirked. She saw the sparkle in Nadia's eye when she looked over the 6'5" former basketball player when the unit fought through Nasariyah. The smirk didn't stem from Nadia's affection towards the tall black man, but the irony behind it. Jamal Lincoln held the M-16 Nadia's husband pressed up against when he stepped out of their house. Jamal's finger twitched a couple times and made Nadia a widow. "Yes," Stephanie drew the word out. "I could get Jamal to come tonight."

"Wonderful."

Stephanie pulled up along side the barracks and out bounded a handsome Marine. "Hello, Jamal," Stephanie said through the open passenger window.

"Hi, ma'am," Jamal said as he folded himself into the car.

"Jamal," Stephanie hissed as she threw her car in gear and sped off. "If you call me 'ma'am' one more time," she leered over towards his lap, "I'll cut your balls off."

Jamal's body squirmed. He'd seen her handy work with a knife.

Stephanie smiled at herself. She liked having weight behind the threat. From now on whenever she threatened a man, he had to think twice about his actions. "I've done it before and I'll do it again."

"Okay, okay, I'm sorry, Ms. Chandler."

"Dammit, Jamal!"

"What? What is it?" Jamal shook in fear.

Stephanie bolstered an evil grin. "Call me Stephanie." She looked back down at his lap. "Or else."

"Yes, Stephanie it is!" Jamal said holding his palms up in submission.

Stephanie purred with satisfaction. She hadn't felt this good in a long while. A frightening thought crossed her mind. Why did she gain so much satisfaction out of the fear she could cause? The nightmares had tapered off. They still occurred on a regular occasion, but they weren't relentless every night like they were in the past. More than ever she concluded she served justice as best she could and her mind seemed to be satisfied. Any relationship with a man, besides Drake, was still out of the question. And right now she hated him. She didn't fully understand why she hated him, she just did. It must be because he broke Gabrielle's heart. On the other hand if he didn't break Gabrielle's heart, he'd break the heart of Stephanie's closer friend, Grace. *Damned if he does, damned if he doesn't. Poor guy. To hell with him though. He's still a guy and still deserves my scorn.* "So how is your boss?" she asked.

"LT? He's good."

Stephanie analyzed Jamal's reaction. "No, really. How is your boss?"

Jamal leaned his head to the side as he organized his words. "He's...he's not the same."

"Oh," Stephanie sounded heartened.

"Yeah."

"How is he not the same?"

"I dunno. It is hard to put a finger on it." A silence hung indicating Stephanie would wait out the answer. "He doesn't smile as much. He looks...I don't know...not as happy." Another silence begged for details. "He doesn't have Lieutenant English to hang out with and he can't hang with Captain Kim like he did before and he..." This time Jamal stopped he was just on the edge of being out of bounds.

"And?" Stephanie wouldn't relent.

"Well, I think he liked Lieutenant Noccionni being around. Actually, we all did. Oh, don't get me wrong," Jamal pressed quickly knowing Stephanie's ties to Grace Freemont. "He would never pass on, or do Miss Freemont wrong. I think he likes having her." Jamal cocked his head. It sounded wrong or inappropriate because at the heart of it, she was just a pen pal.

Stephanie made a mental note to call Grace and see how she was. "I think this is it," Stephanie said looking at a condominium complex.

Jamal followed her up a flight of stairs. When they reached the condo, Stephanie looked at the number and then back at Jamal with a question hanging over her.

"What is it?" he asked.

Stephanie pointed to a nameplate stating MARTINEZ.

"Could be who lived here before," Jamal said with raised eyebrows.

Stephanie lifted her eyebrows also. "Could be." She knocked.

Nadia opened the door wearing American skintight jeans and T-shirt in her quest to become Americanized. Delight flushed over her face. "Jamal! Stephanie!" She reached out and grabbed their hands and pulled them into her condo.

Stephanie watched Jamal's eyes wash over the attractive figure of the young mother. *If that is what she was after, she hit a homerun.* Stephanie thought to herself.

"Hana, our friends are here!" Hana sat in front of the TV watching ESPN.

Jamal did a double take. "Is she watching Sports Center?"

"Yes, she is." Nadia said proudly. "I think it will Americanize her. I think it is better than those MTV channels.

"Oh, yeah!" Jamal agreed and stepped over toward Hana and sat on the couch. He felt a little out of place but Sports Center was something he could relate to.

The precocious child climbed onto the man's lap and squeezed his cheek. "Your skin is black."

Jamal snickered and looked at the adorable girl. "Yes, it is."

"And really tall. Are you a basketball player?"

"No." He smiled. "But I know one."

"Really?"

"Yep."

"What team does he play for?"

"The Lakers."

The girl looked back at the TV while her mind worked. Then she spun back around on his lap. "Could you take me and mommy to a game sometime?"

Jamal smiled. The little girl stole his heart in a matter of seconds. How could he answer anyway other than, "Sure, I'll take you and your mommy to a game."

"Yay!" she squealed and lifted her arms in triumph. Then she whirled around again and focused back on Sports Center and leaned back into her newest best friend.

Stephanie saw Nadia beam and knew the score. Her role was chaperone. She leaned back outside and tapped the nameplate. "For a second I thought we had the wrong place."

"Oh, that is my new last name."

"Oh?"

"Yes, I'll tell you all about it, but first let's eat." Nadia entertained her new friends with her life story that spanned from Iraq to Jordan, England, back to Iraq and now the US. She explained in detail what she did, but didn't talk much about her husband.

Stephanie felt the white elephant in the room. She agonized about asking Nadia about her husband, the man who killed her husband sat right there with them. In the end the reporter in her overpowered her sense of decency. "What about your husband?"

"Amir? Oh, he was a fool," Nadia said waving her fork to the side. "I never loved him. He tricked me into marriage. He tricked me into going back to Iraq. I'm—we're much better off without him." She smiled at Jamal who buried his eyes in his lamb kabob.

You are one cold bitch, Stephanie thought. Then she considered Nadia's history and her own actions. *Well, men really are scum, so who am I to judge.*

Nadia continued to describe in detail what she did with her computer before the war and after she started working as Captain Horton's agent and the double life that she led now.

Stephanie couldn't stop it. The reporter in her wanted to hear more. On occasion she glanced over at Jamal and saw his face awash in awe.

"And that is where we are today," Nadia concluded with a smile.

Stephanie reached out and held her new friend's hand.

"What is it?" Nadia couldn't miss the concern on Stephanie's face.

"Nadia," Stephanie said. "Don't ever tell *anyone* this story." Stephanie considered how the success of a book about what Nadia revealed to her would compare with *Storming Baghdad,* which alone made her a wealthy woman. Nadia's story would put in the company of Bob Woodward.

"But that is what I did before I worked for my new job at Camp Parks. I can't talk about that?"

Stephanie eyes drew shut and she shook her head. Then she opened her eyes and laid them squarely on Nadia. "Nadia, you can't ever talk about this again." Stephanie didn't know every military secret, but she looked to the window. With a laser an agent from any nation, or from a non-state for that matter, could paint the window and recreate every last word Nadia just said. What Stephanie knew, and Nadia didn't, was that if her story got out, she could be just as vulnerable in the US as she would be in Iraq.

Nadia cocked her head in a question mark.

"You can't tell people what you did," Stephanie continued.

"But that was before I got this new secret job. They told me I couldn't talk about what I did for this job."

"And that is another thing." Urgency filled Stephanie's words. "You can't talk about your *secret* job. To everyone else you don't have a secret job. You only have one job and that is at the bank. You have to remember that." Stephanie turned to Jamal. "You can't speak a word of this to anyone, understood."

"Yes, ma'am." Jamal's eyes bulged in disbelief. He knew more about what was happening in parts of the world than the Commandant of the Marine Corps.

The "ma'am" didn't register with Stephanie. She had a crisis on her hands if she couldn't explain the tenuous situation her friend was in. "Nadia, if anyone ever asks, you are a simple Latino girl with a small job at a bank and that is it. You don't do anything else. You work with computers, but you don't know much about computers." Stephanie considered how to explain that she was Nadia's worst enemy in a way by being a reporter, but that might too far of a stretch to comprehend. She stuck to the basics. "Those people that were after you in Iraq can come after you here too. Our borders," *Our borders? Listen to me talking like a right wing American zealot.* "Are much too easy to permeate. These people..." Stephanie stopped. She had to change course. She didn't want to terrify her too much. Nadia didn't need to be paranoid, just short of it. "If they wanted to come after you. You have to make it so they can't find you. So don't tell anyone what you do." Stephanie wanted to also convey the need to keep state secrets but she didn't want to confuse the subject. If she just kept it simple, that Nadia could talk about anything she did for her own personal security, that would suffice.

Jamal bounded up the steps to Nadia's condo. Nadia watched from the inside and opened the door before he could knock. "Hello, Jamal."

"Hi."

She wrapped her arms around him and reached up on her tippy toes. She kissed him on the cheek the way she thought a Westerner would and then she thought that at the end of the night she'd give him a real kiss like in American movies.

"You ready to go?" Jamal asked.

"Yes, we are," Nadia said.

"Yep!" Hana squeaked and ran up to Jamal and leaped at him with her arms up in the air indicating he needed to catch her.

Jamal lifted the little girl up in the air and lowered her to kiss her on the top of her head. She giggled.

"Here, let's take my car. I just got it today," Nadia said holding out her keys.

"A Lexus?" Jamal looked incredulous.

"Yes, I had to turn in my rental car today, so I bought this one. Is it not a good car?"

"Oh, it's a good car all right." Jamal looked at Hana. "Are we ready to go see the Lakers beat the Knicks?"

"Yep!" the little girl squeaked and crawled over Jamal's shoulder to his back so he could give her a piggyback.

They piled in and Jamal backed the seat up to get comfortable. Nadia put Hana in her car seat. On the way Hana sang a song she had learned at school. On the freeway Jamal felt the car lurch to the side when a car brushed up against them from behind. "Damn, oh, sorry," he said. *A brand new Lexus and it already has a ding.* Jamal put on his blinker to pull off to the side of the road.

"What is it?" Nadia asked.

"Oh," Jamal censored his words. "Bad LA drivers." He looked over his shoulder at Hana. "Is everyone okay?"

When the car pulled to a stop Jamal stepped out and knew he was in trouble. Two hooded Latinos stepped out of the other car. Jamal wondered if he should run. It was too late though. The driver lifted his hoodie to reveal his handgun.

Jamal held up the keys so they knew he wouldn't pose a threat. "Just let me get my family out of the car." He thought he could get more sympathy if it looked like he was just a family man.

"What you got there, a seniorita, mi amgo?" the driver said indicating his displeasure at a black man stealing a Latino woman.

"Uh—"

"We need to get out of here," the accomplice said cutting off Jamal.

Jamal looked and thought he recognized the man's gait as he walked away.

"What? ¿Estás loco?" the driver asked.

"C'mon let's just get out of here," the accomplice demanded.

The driver started to backpedal but leered at Jamal one last time and tapped his pistol. "Get you next time, mi amigo."

Jamal stood and watched the car speed off. The passenger looked away so Jamal couldn't see him. Jamal noted the license plate for insurance purposes. He'd have to report it as a hit and run. He slid back into the driver's seat.

"What happened?" Nadia asked. "Are LA drivers that bad?"

Jamal thought about how to answer. "No, they weren't bad drivers."

"I don't understand."

"They wanted to steal your car."

Nadia tried to imagine how Jamal negotiated his way out of her car getting stolen. "Why didn't they?"

"I really don't know."

"Is it because you are a Marine? Did you scare them off?"

"No, I don't think so."

Nadia ran her hand up and down Jamal's shoulder. "I think it is because you are a Marine and they didn't want you to bring them trouble."

Jamal didn't know what to say so he answered, "Maybe," and hoped that would be the end of it.

The Lakers beat the Knicks by twenty-four and Jamal's friend got to play some during garbage time at the end of the game when New York had no chance. Jamal watched Hana more than the game. She loved sitting up close to the players and cheered herself horse. Nadia, in turn, watched Jamal mostly.

After the team showered Jamal met up with his friend and introduced him to Nadia and Hana. Hana was on her last legs but she let out one last cheer for Jamal's friend. Nadia took Hana from Jamal and said, "I'll start towards the car so you two can talk for a minute."

Jamal's friend leered at Nadia's tight ass in the skintight jeans. "Mmmm Mmm, you tap that yet, bro?"

Jamal smiled. "It's not like that."

"It aint? MILF, bro—I'd tap that shit."

"Hey, it was good to see you get some PT," Playing Time, Jamal said changing the subject.

"Yeah, I gotta take it when I can."

"Well, I better get going," Jamal said as he watched Nadia make a turn and walk off in the wrong direction.

"Good to see ya, bro."

"Yeah, you too," Jamal said over his shoulder.

Jamal and Nadia drove home in silence as Hana drifted off. After parking the car Jamal lifted the sleeping girl out of her car seat and carried her up to the condo and laid her in bed as Nadia pulled back the sheets. Before Jamal could turn towards the door Nadia pressed herself up against him and locked her lips onto his. When they broke for air, without a word, she took his hand and led him to her bedroom.

15

"Baby, I mean it this time. It's over." The words kept rolling through Miguel Ramirez' head. It was all he could remember from the night before, hearing Teresa end their engagement once and for all. He lifted his hand to his head to try to subdue the pounding. He lowered one foot from his mother's couch and steadied it on the floor. An empty beer can clinked when his foot knocked it over. He felt his chest rise and fall a few times. Then his brain stirred enough to demand a cigarette. His fingers fumbled over his pockets, and the side table next to the couch that had become his bed. When he couldn't find any he sat up and looked around. Eight empties dotted the floor in his immediate vicinity. That sum didn't include the collection on the front porch and in the kitchen. How long would his mother put up with him? The *war hero* label lasted only so long. Teresa, his fiancée finally gave up when she had a black eye and a cast on her wrist. She lied, even though everyone else knew the truth, because she still cared about him. And she would take him back in a heartbeat if found a direction. Right now though Ramirez oozed toxicity and he knew it. He watched his fingers tremble because he lacked a rudder. Who was next, his mother, his sister, who? Who would he levy his anger upon next. He left the Corps hoping the nightmares and anger would subside, but it didn't. He tried getting high, but hated sneaking around his mother and high school sister. Teresa also called it off the first time she discovered he smoked weed. Alcohol worked, so he drank himself numb. He looked into his wallet. Soon the money would all be gone. He needed a job, he needed direction, but first he needed a cigarette—and maybe a beer.

He stumbled out of the house and down the street. Maybe he'd ask for a job at the corner market. *Oh, that sounds like a plan, "Hey, gimme a pack a Marlboros, a six pack of Bud, and how about a job?" Maybe tomorrow I could look for a job. Who the hell am I kidding, tomorrow is not going to be any different than today or yesterday.* He thought about the jobs he could possibly apply for. Maybe he needed to move to another state and just start all over. He made a mental note to go to the VA and see if they could help. At least if he was in another state he wouldn't hurt anyone he loved.

"Que Pasa?"

Ramirez looked over to the street. It was the 1967 Impala that had been rolling along next to him for the last half block. If he had his wits about him his training during gang life and the military would have built his situational awareness and he would have paid more attention. "Hey, man!" Ramirez cheered. Ramon Gutierrez was an old friend he hadn't seen since he left for the Corps.

Gutierrez opened the passenger door and Ramirez slid in. It was good to see a friendly face. "Where's Teresa?" Gutierrez asked.

"Gone."

"Sorry to hear that." Gutierrez handed Ramirez a flask and Ramirez tipped it up to his lips for a shot. Gutierrez tapped the accelerator and they cruised down the boulevard and onto the highway. "I heard you got out of the Army."

"The Corps," Ramirez corrected him.

"Yeah."

"So what are you into?" Ramirez asked.

Gutierrez explained that he stayed in the gang Ramirez left. Ramirez squirmed in his seat. Leaving a gang was dangerous business. "So you learned a lot in the Army?"

"Yeah, I did."

"That's good."

Ramirez breathed a sigh of relief. Gutierrez explained that he'd moved up in the gang and that other gangs were moving in on their territory and their operations. One gang in particular was in with the police and working with them to destroy Ramirez' old gang. "So, I was wondering if you could help me?" Gutierrez asked.

Ramirez' head cleared. He felt blood pulsing in his veins, for the first time since leaving Iraq. "I'm listening." It had been too long since someone asked him for help. It made him feel needed, a part of something possibly.

Gutierrez explained that he wanted Ramirez to knock down, if not out, his rivals and get the police off of him.

"¿Tienes dinero para este?" Ramirez asked if he had money for this.

"We got a stash."

"How are you…" Ramirez thought better of asking the question wandering in his mind.

"Cree esto? Do you believe this? A brother driving a new Lexus?" Gutierrez said pointing to a Lexus with a black man driving with an olive skinned woman in the passenger seat.

Ramirez jerked in his seat as the Impala tapped the Lexus.

"This is how we are making some of our stash." After the Impala pulled up behind the Lexus, Gutierrez opened his door and waved for Ramirez to come with him. Gutierrez eyed the passenger and then the tall black man in front of him. "What you got there, a seniorita, mi amgo?" Gutierrez said indicating his displeasure at a black man stealing a Mexican woman.

"Uh…"

Ramirez narrowed his eyes and focused. The black man looked familiar. "We need to get out of here," he said cutting off the black man.

"What? ¿Estás loco? Gutierrez said.

"C'mon let's just get out of here," Ramirez demanded.

Gutierrez backpedaled and leered at the black man one last time and tapped his pistol. "Get you next time, mi amigo."

Inside the car, Gutierrez slammed the steering wheel as he watched a potential $25,000 drive off. "What the hell was that?" He looked over at Ramirez who had his head tucked deep inside his hood. "Hey, what happened?" Gutierrez's tone changed.

Ramirez shook his head. "Nothing,"

"Did you know him?"

"Yeah."

"Oh," Gutierrez tempered his anger. Ramirez still might provide a benefit. "So do you want to help me or not?"

"Yeah, I'm sorry. It's just…"

"Está bien. It's cool."

Ramirez raised a finger to his temple trying to clear his mind. He needed to think clearly. "Your contacts south of the border good?"

"Sí."

"And you got money?"

"Sí."

"Okay, lets go somewhere we can talk."

Gutierrez drove through a neighborhood and into an open lot where he and Ramirez could speak openly in Spanish without the threat of the authorities.

"Get out a piece of paper," Ramirez demanded. He thought about writing out the list himself, but then decided against it. He wanted as much distance from what he had planned in his mind as possible. "Take this down. This is what we are going to need." Ramirez dictated a detailed shopping list that included sanitized weapons, explosives, timers, untraceable cars and an army of talented men willing to leave the country for a long period for a healthy sum of money.

Over the next few days a car rolled up to a bank of mailboxes just after they were filled. A man jimmied the lock of a specific address each day and left. When he found the credit card offer, he stopped for a few days and then continued until the credit card application returned with a credit card. When the card came in he handed the card to a man with an ID created for someone who resembled the man who lived at the address, Tyrone Griffin. The fake Tyrone Griffin walked into a local hunting store with a credit card and all the credentials to buy a Weatherby Vanguard rifle and NightForce tactical riflescope. The trace on this weapon left a definite trail.

A week later US Customs stopped a truck with a false front wall in Del Rio, Texas. Behind the wall someone stockpiled a treasure of drugs. In Nuevo Laredo, the Border Patrol stopped a similar truck with over a dozen illegals confined in the compartment. While the US authorities scrambled their forces to investigate the two feint attacks devised by Ramirez, a fishing boat launched from the US side of Lake Amistad and ventured up the Rio Grande. Beyond Comstock it married up with a Jon boat that floated down a Mexican tributary into the Rio Grande. In less than a minute the boats separated. The fishing boat continued up the Rio Grande to the Pecos and approached a launch where the Dodge Ram that dropped it off in Lake Amistad waited for it. The pickup pulled out onto Highway 90 and sped a short distance toward El Paso. When a white van showed up in it rear view mirror, the pickup pulled over and the van slid in behind it. In less than a minute both vehicles continued on their way.

The driver inhaled against his cigarette one last time and looked at his watch. Then he looked towards the west. Yes, it was sufficiently dark. He stepped out of the car and popped open the trunk. He scanned the area to look to see if anyone paid any particular attention as he unfastened the brake light. He slid back into the driver seat, dropped the car into DRIVE and looked over his shoulder as he pulled out into traffic on the main thoroughfare. At the second light he rolled into the left hand turn lane and stopped at a red light. When the traffic cleared he pressed onto the accelerator and turned against the red light. He rolled into a residential neighborhood and looked into the rear view mirror. Nothing. He stopped at stop sign on the first corner and turned left, drove a block, turned left again and then made another left onto the main thoroughfare where he pulled up to the same red light. He repeated the same sequence of events again and again. He looked at his watch. He knew it wouldn't take all night, but he didn't think it would take over an hour. At an hour and fifteen minutes flashing lights alerted him that his task was just about over. He rolled to a stop, pulled out a cigarette and waited as the officer ran a check on his bogus plates.

The shooter watched the sun dip below the horizon. When the last rays disappeared he looked at his watch and waited. When a thin red crust slit the horizon he watched a car make a left hand turn against a red light. The shooter scanned the area behind the car and saw nothing following it. From his rooftop he watched the car circle the block and repeat the process. Eventually the initial rush slowed and he was able to control his heart rate. He breathed deep and evenly trying to lower his heart rate as much as possible. He anticipated another rush when the car did get pulled over. He imagined it in his mind and played mental gymnastics visualizing the moment he would see the flashing lights. All the calculations, the distance, angle down to the target area, and even Coriolis effect. The first shot would be a cold bore shot and he shot about a dozen cold bore shots over the past few weeks to know how the rifle would shoot. All he had to do now was put a bullet on target, collect his fee and flee the country.

Flashing lights shocked his system and he sucked in a lungful of air to calm his heart rate. The bait car stopped right where it was planned to stop and the police car stopped exactly where it was expected to stop. The shooter scanned the passenger seat of the patrol car for a partner and waited patiently for several minutes while they ran the plates. A dim outline indicated a partner sat in the passenger seat. The shooter made a quick calculation about how much he would have to hold the cross hairs off the target to adjust for the bullet traveling through the glass if the partner didn't get out of the car. He anticipated the next rush and quickly calmed down when the door opened and the officers emerged from the car. A wash of relief flooded the shooter's system. A shot through the glass would've been tricky, but with the two officers in the clear the difficulty dropped drastically. He gentle moved his finger off the trigger guard to the trigger. He had played with the trigger when he customized the rifle and took most of the resistance off. The passenger side officer stood up in between the door and the car with his hand near his holster. The shooter took in a breath and let half of it out. A soft squeeze caused the rifle to belch. He chambered another round and prepared for a second shot that wouldn't be cold bore and might be on a moving target. The round entered the passenger side officer's face just below his eye and instantly killed the target as it traveled down and in towards the base of the skull. The other officer heard a shot in the distance and then moments later, his partner fall to the ground. He turned his head to look at his partner just in time to catch a round slightly below his ear that traveled through the base of his skull separating his spine from his brain.

The shooter packed up and slipped out of sight while the bait driver stepped out of his car. The shooter wiped down the rifle and drove to a dumpster near Mr. Griffin's residence where he dumped the rifle.

The bait driver searched the officers with latex gloves and removed their wallets. On the way back he reattached his taillight. Before he left the scene he texted two addresses to separate numbers in code. He reversed the street address and looked at a map to send the street just to the north or east of the target street, 123 4th became 321 5th. With this task accomplished he pulled the chip from the phone, drove over to a storm drain and dropped the chip in the drain. From there he traveled to Mr. Griffin' residence where he placed in Mr. Griffin's trash can the latex gloves he used to handle the cyclotrimethylene-trinitramine, C4, he planted along the road. Then he drove to a chop shop that would disassemble the car to the point no one would ever be able to piece it together. From there someone drove him to a dock where he boarded a boat that would head south.

The first team received their text, checked a map and drove off to a destination. Disappointment crushed them when they saw the target. They'd still get a cut, but not as large. The address belonged to an apartment complex. Their orders were to leave no evidence. They wouldn't be able to dispatch the officer's residence without blowing up the entire apartment complex and causing too much collateral damage.

The second team rolled up to an address and exited their vehicles. Some provided security, others planted explosives and another crew broke in the house.

"Honey?" the woman asked not expecting her husband to be home anytime soon. She shuffled out of the bedroom in the dark and reached for the light switch when a club smacked against her head and she dropped to the floor. Two other men traveled through the house looking for anyone else. One man saw a girl about three years old in her bed. Calmly and efficiently he placed a chloroform soaked rag over the girls nose and mouth and left it there. Another man found an infant and performed the same operation. The man who clubbed the woman lifted her up and taped her to a dinning room chair. "Is everything in place?" he called to his teammates. One of his men stepped outside where he got a couple nods and he nodded back to the man who steadied the woman in the chair. He pulled out some smelling salts while the other man grabbed the phone and a third brandished a suppressed pistol. The man with the smelling salts waved it under the woman's nose. Her head bobbed and then twitched. When she opened her eyes horror raced through her soul. The man with the phone dialed 911. "We are calling 911 right now. We are going to kill you." The man said without emotion. He sounded like he was simply asking to make a withdrawal at the bank.

"NO!" The woman screamed.

"Nine-one-one, what is your emergency?" The man with the phone held it up for the woman to hear and speak into the receiver.

"There's a man here," the woman's voice quivered, "and," her chest heaved with anxiety, "he's going to kill me!"

"What is your location?"

The man with the gun answered with two thuds from the suppressed pistol to the woman's face. The man with the phone placed the receiver on the floor and the three moved out the front door. The last man strung eight-pound fishing line across the front door at shin level. The man with the gun wiped it clean and placed it in a paper bag. Eventually he would drop it from a boat into the Pacific Ocean.

A man listening to a scanner raised his head and cocked it to the side when he heard that police were responding to a shooting involving at least one police officer. He fondled the phone in his hand and told himself to be patient.

Then he heard police responding to a shooting at an address that matched his information.

A patrol car drove up to the house that called 911. Both officers scanned the entire block. One was a member of the California National Guard and an Iraq War veteran. His time down range heightened his senses. When he approached a situation, he saw everything. He scanned rooftops, bushes cars, everything. Both men circled the house and saw nothing out of place. The veteran's partner knocked on the door and didn't get an answer. The veteran continued scanning the street trying to understand what he was missing. He had breached so many doorways in Iraq he half expected to come face to face with an AK-47. But it was one thing to see and anticipate everything and another to see it in time to do something about it. "STOP!" The light from inside the house reflected off a wire just above his partner's ankle as his partner entered the house. The partner turned and looked at the veteran. The partner didn't understand the terror flushed on the veteran's face. Then his face reflected a bright orange and everything fell quiet.

Neighbors called 911 to tell them a house just blew up. The man listening to the scanner looked at his watch. He noted the time and added fifteen minutes for his target. He listened as more and more first responders reacted. When the fifteen minutes elapsed he called the first number where the shooter assassinated the police. A line of C4 sparked and blew open a four-foot ditch that ran half a city block. Two police vehicles blew fifty feet into the air. A third one in the rear flipped two and a half times and landed on a car driving along the boulevard killing a 19-year-old woman. No first responder survived.

The man listening to the scanner called a second number and got the same results at the exploded house location. He separated the phone from the chip and disposed the chip before heading south of the border.

Ramirez sat on his mother's couch alone in the house. He rocked back and forth nervously. He fondled a Miller Genuine Draft in his hands. He fingered the twist off top. He had twisted off so many. The release of pressure and the popping hiss associated with it could calm him. He settled the bottle in the webbing between his thumb and forefinger. He squeezed and then let go. He played with the pressure between his finger and thumb wondering how much pressure would cause enough friction to hear the popping hiss. He was going to cave and he hated it. He hated himself.

A knock at the door broke his concentration. It was Gutierrez. "Hola ¿cómo estás amigo?"

Ramirez opened the door without a word.

Gutierrez stuck an envelope at Ramirez. "That was beautiful!"

Ramirez took the money and stuffed it in his back pocket and waved Gutierrez in.

"There's more if Griffin gets convicted."

"I know."

"Did you see it?" Gutierrez slapped at Ramirez with the back of his hand in a joyful manner.

"Yeah, I saw it."

"You don't look to excited. Man, we can really use you." Gutierrez couldn't understand Ramirez's melancholy.

"I don't feel too well." Ramirez lied. He saw too much. He saw men die and a family destroyed including a baby and a toddler. He left the Marines to get away from death and he landed in a lifestyle where an old man was thirty. Death wove itself into the very fabric of this society. Bullets ricocheted throughout the neighborhood on occasion. Indiscriminately they found their mark in gang members. That is how Gutierrez rose to the top, through attrition. They would also strike *noncombatants,* non-gang members including children and even babies. But Ramirez calculated last night's operation. He planned every last detail of it. He didn't tell Gutierrez that he balled like a baby for an hour in the alley after he heard the first reports of the family that died in a fireball.

"Did you hear?" Gutierrez broke Ramirez's line of thought. "The police had dogs out last night and they found the rifle and the gloves just like you said they would." Gutierrez flashed a broad smile. "They are going to run Griffin out, mi amigo."

"That's good…I guess."

"What is it, man? Why are you so down?"

"I'm not doing well, like I said."

"What is it?"

"It's the war I guess, I just can't get my head together?"

Gutierrez leaned back and furrowed his brow in a question. "If this is what you can do when you're head isn't together, I can't wait to see what you can do when your head is right." He pulled out a joint for Ramirez. "Here, this will take care of your head."

Ramirez looked around and took inventory. "No, I've got to get out of here."

"Huh? You'll be back right?"

"No, I don't think so."

"But I still owe you money if Griffin goes down."

Ramirez waved his hand. "Forget it. I gotta go."

"Where are you going?"

"I don't know, but I gotta go."

Gutierrez grabbed Ramirez's arm and studied his friend with concern. "What is it?"

Ramirez wrapped his palm around his forehead. "It's the war. I have these nightmares and headaches and...You know Teresa left me?"

"Yeah, we talked about that." Gutierrez let go of Ramirez. Suddenly Gutierrez sensed he was playing with fire. Ramirez' body started to tremble and his muscles flexed.

"Yeah, she left me because I beat the shit out of her." Ramirez's voice quakes and his body trembled. "If she would've stayed I would've killed her sooner or later."

Gutierrez considered the evil laced into the plot Ramirez spawned and knew his friend wasn't lying. His friend wasn't right. Maybe Ramirez wasn't good for the gang. "So, what do you think you're going to do?"

An idea had floated through Ramirez's mind and now he had the seed money to chase it. "I think I'm going to go up to Alaska and work on one of those fishing boats."

Gutierrez didn't want to argue although he thought Ramirez was delirious. Either way Ramirez did good work for him, but he couldn't trust him to do another job. He didn't have to mention to never speak about what went down. "That sounds like a good life," Gutierrez lied. Ramirez's fit subsided and Gutierrez relaxed some.

"Yeah, I need to...I need something different. I need...well, I need to get out of here."

16

"Sir?" Jennings said in the early morning light at the range as he walked up to Drake.

"What is it?" Drake smiled. He loved the shooting range. He loved any range. He loved being a Marine platoon leader.

"Birdwell."

"What is it this time?"

"He forgot to bring his camelback."

"Do you want me to talk to him?" Drake asked. Old salts took pride, and to some sick degree, pleasure in whipping boots into shape. Hazing wasn't beyond them. Tortuous calisthenics, public humiliation, and other resources all played into the training of young Marines.

"Nothing else seems to work. He's like a zombie. He just sits there and takes it. He says he cares, but he's…I dunno. I swear that if you asked him for his knife so you could stab him, he'd give you the damn knife."

"Maybe I'll try a different track."

Lizzy Birdwell looked back down to the bucket to count the eggs again, were there five or six? Her "stepfather," her mother never married the man so he could collect a welfare check, owned a "farm" with only a few chickens. Enough to lay about five or six eggs a day. They never married because her mother had a legitimate job as a waitress near the interstate that passed through the West Virginia hills in the next valley over. If they got married, he's loose his welfare.

Lizzy counted five and wondered if it she only collected five the day before. As she walked up the hill to the singlewide trailer, she stared into the bucket. Her heal caught a pile of dog scat. Her foot slipped out from under her and she shoved out her free arm to catch herself, careful not to drop the eggs. She slid down the hill but caught herself and save the eggs. Dog scat ran from her ankle to her hip, to her elbow and to her wrist.

The fourteen-year-old girl scrambled up the hill and into the trailer where her stepfather sat watching TV and drinking beer. She put the bucket in the sink and ran into the bathroom and shed her clothing. She bundled her clothes in a towel careful not to let the dog scat touch anything. She turned on the water and jumped into the shower and started scraping off the dirt. She made a mental checklist to get her clothes in the laundry and get the eggs in the fridge. When she got out of the shower she realized she didn't have a change of clothes. Her stepfather unnerved her, but she kept quiet. She didn't want her mother or herself to get hit by him any more than what he already dished out. She looked for another towel, but couldn't find one in the bathroom. She wasn't going to unravel the one around her clothes. She decided to hold the bundle in front of herself to cover her and make her way to her bedroom and hope that her stepfather didn't notice. She opened the door to see him standing there waiting to use the bathroom.

"What the hell are you doing running aroun' nakid fer!" He bellowed as he raised the back of his hand. With her arms full, Lizzy couldn't defend herself. His blow struck hard knocking her to the floor and exposing her. She didn't have a chance.

It outraged Lizzy's mother that her fourteen-year-old daughter got herself knocked up by one of the local boys. But to claim her stepfather raped her was too far. Lizzy's mother beat her—hard. She pummeled her with open and closed fists. Over the years the mother saw her daughter's looks ripen. The mother also saw how her husband looked at her. And finally, the mother knew the daughter told the truth, but that didn't stop the pain of her situation. Lizzy's mother made a choice and she chose her husband. She banished Lizzy.

Lizzy fled just over the hill from the valley where a cousin took her in. The cousin serviced truck drivers in their cabs at the local truck stop and made enough. She dabbled in dealing crack, but the authorities drew the line at drugs and she spent a spell in prison—prostitution OK, drugs, no. Lizzy wanted a girl but gave birth to a boy and never went back to school. Her cousin taught her the trade and they lived semi-comfortably.

Lizzy tried not to be an abusive mother, but just looking at her son, Shannon, brought on too much heartache. Shannon grew up awkwardly with no father figure. Some kids at school said her mother was gay. Others knew his mother served tricks. A rumor floated through the student body that he was the product of incest, which technically wasn't true. His senior year he tried to ask a girl out to senior ball. "But I thought you were gay?" she replied. "Oh, forget it," Shannon said and walked away. He skipped fifth and sixth period and went straight to his job stocking a local feed store and then home late. He avoided his homework as usual. Homework bored him and his lagging GPA revealed it. He would graduate—barely. It didn't matter. He was just going to work at the feed store after graduation anyways.

He looked at the dishes and decided to do them after another half hour of TV. He passed out on the couch before the show ended. At two in the morning Lizzy came in, saw the dirty dishes, and her son asleep on the couch. She stomped over to him and cracked her open hand across her son's head. "Get your lazy ass up!"

Shannon cowered and groaned.

Lizzy continued her assault. "Didn't you hear me! Get your lazy ass up and do them damn dishes."

"Okay, Okay, mama! I'm sorry. I'm sorry." Shannon held his arms up trying to block the onslaught.

Lizzy didn't have a good night. One of the Johns got rough. Another claimed not to have the money to pay her.

Shannon couldn't get to the dishes because of the attack. If he could just get by her, "Mama," he cried. Finally he forced himself up and overpowered the woman. He picked her up and threw her across the room. Her back cracked on the TV and knocked it off its stand. Her spine snapped when it fell on top of her.

"Shannon," she whimpered.

"Mama?"

"Shannon, baby."

"Yes, mama."

"I can't feel my legs."

Medicaid offered minimal assistance. Lizzy was still in the hospital when her son turned eighteen and joined the Marines. Once in the Marines he could claim his mother as a dependent and get her better healthcare.

Drake knew everything about everyone in his platoon. One of the hardest things though, was trusting his NCOs to lead. He wanted to be hands on with everything, but a good leader didn't micromanage. When Jennings came up to him, he felt the leeway to try his leadership on Private Shannon Birdwell. Drake prowled the firing line and watched. He knew Birdwell was one of the better marksmen. He watched Birdwell and considered his approach. "On the next one let a little more of your breath out," Drake advised Birdwell. Before squeezing the trigger a shooter should take in a breath, hold it and let half of it out.

Birdwell followed his commander's advice and his precision increased slightly. His rounds were already accurate, but slightly erratic. This last bit of advice tightened the grouping. "That's it," Drake said.

The platoon continued on the range for another hour. At the end Drake called out, "Birdwell, over here."

Birdwell double-timed over. "Yes, sir." Birdwell knew he was in trouble again.

Drake wrapped his arm around him and walked away from the rest of the platoon. "That worked for you, eh?"

"Ah, yes, sir."

"Right now, I would say that you are one of the best marksmen in the platoon."

"Yes, sir." Birdwell didn't know where his platoon commander was going with this.

"Look, I'm gonna need you when we go to Iraq."

"Yes, sir."

"I need a sniper, but we don't have one. You're the closest thing we got."

"Yes, sir."

"You know, a sniper, Gunny Cole, saved my ass in Iraq time and time again."

"Yes, sir."

Drake turned and squared his shoulders to Birdwell. "This is what I'm thinking. I'm going to see if I can get an M14 for you as a secondary weapon."

"Yes, sir."

Drake saw the smile growing on Birdwell's face and knew it was working. "And I'm going to see if I can get you some time with Gunny Cole, sound good?"

"Yes, sir."

"Good. But this is what I need from you."

"Yes, sir."

"I need you to be squared away every day. I'm going to depend on you. I need you to protect my ass when we go down range."

"Yes, sir."

"That means no more forgetting camelbacks or anything else, you copy?"

"Yes, sir."

"All right, just remember, squared away, every day."

17

"What was it like?"

"What?"

"When you got this?" Erika said running her fingertip along Doug's sweat soaked leg under the sheets. She couldn't ask, *when you got shot?* That brought the war a little too close. She controlled the Commandant's message to the public and military as the Marine Corps Director of Public Affairs. She kept the war sanitized and at a distance. Her office drafted statements about Marine Corps *loses*. They were loses, not young boys dying. She thought about the choices she made and how in a parallel universe one of those boys could've been hers. The thought seeped into her mind whenever she visited the wounded. To retain her sanity and professionalism, she buried some of the reflections prowling her soul.

"Oh, that?" Doug waved a hand to dismiss it and leaned in to kiss his cougar.

Erika leaned back. "No." She girded herself. "I need to hear how it happened." She paid no concern to the details of his injuries when she first met him along with all the other wounded. Even after sleeping with him she didn't concern herself about the details. At first she thought it might be a latent bucket list fantasy, *have cheap sleazy affair with a guy young enough to be my son—check.* But the enchanting young lieutenant seeped in beneath her hard shell.

She found herself looking at the clock on Friday afternoon, a first in her career. She never looked at the clock even when she was married. *Maybe that is why my marriage failed. Why am I looking at the clock? Stop it!* She would read an email and then find herself wondering how Doug's leg was coming along and what coital gymnastics they could perform with his leg.

"Why?"

"Because?"

"Because...why?"

"Look, I'm not going to play juvenile games. Just tell me how it happened."

Doug's eyes narrowed as he considered how to play her. "Fine," he said in an even voice. "But explain to me why I should answer your question if you won't answer mine?"

Erika huffed.

Doug continued, "I'm not one of your staff. You can't order me around. Well, not right now at least."

"I just can't. Why can't I just leave it at that."

"Because I won't let you."

"I'm not going to tell you because it is personal."

"Personal?" Doug laughed. "Oh, because what we just did was so impersonal."

"So you're not going to tell me?"

"Let me ask you this. What is more important to you, your secret, or knowing how this happened?"

Erika sneered in frustration. She was angrier with herself than him now. She underestimated his intellect. She knew she just violated some Sun Tzu axiom.

Erika huffed again and rolled over. "It's because I like you." She didn't want to see the look on his face.

"You *like* me?" Doug said mocking her. "Well, I guess that is a good thing considering..."

"Shut up. This is why I didn't want to tell you."

"Because you like me?"

"No, because I knew it would go right to your head."

"Huh?"

"I swear I hate men…and you."

"Do you like me, or hate me? I'm confused." Arrogance rolled through Doug's voice.

Erika rolled back over and faced him. "I hate that I like you."

Doug raised an eyebrow.

"I told only one man that I ever loved him and he decided to start a family with another woman while he was still married to me! Men suck and so do you!"

"I thought you liked that?" Doug said referring to some of the gymnastics he'd recently performed for her.

"You ass!" Erika rolled out of bed and grabbed a robe and stormed out of the bedroom.

Doug dragged himself to the side of the bed and reached for his boxers. He found Erika standing at the kitchen faucet filling a teakettle with water. She ignited a flame on the stove and set the kettle over it. When she saw Doug leaning on the counter she said, "What are you doing? C'mere, let me get you over to the couch." She set him down and then straddled him. She took his face in his hands and took in his gaze. "I'm scared." She let it sink in as she built up strength. "I'm very vulnerable here." She saw that he didn't comprehend. "I like you. I really do." She paused. "I don't love you. I don't believe in love…because…" She had already established why. Her thoughts confused herself and she considered what to say next. "I'm a coward. I joined the Marines to see if I could do it. I mean make it through." She stretched her neck and her gaze fell upon the ceiling. "I never thought about this part of it."

"What part of it?"

She looked back down at him. "Knowing the faces."

"Huh?"

"I care about you and I don't want to see you get hurt."

Doug scrunched his eyes as he tried to decipher her intent.

"Oh, this is stupid. I just don't want you to go back because I don't want anything to happen to you."

Doug tilted his head slightly. "And what if something did happen to me? It's not like this is love or anything."

Erika swallowed. "Oh, it is love though. I just tell you it isn't."

"What?"

Erika shook her head. "It's complicated."

"Yeah. I got that."

Erika couldn't tell if it was frustration or hurt she heard in his voice. "No, I do love you, but I won't let myself love you."

"Oh, that clears it up."

"Can't you see how different we are?"

"You mean besides ages and rank?"

Erika's eyes widened expressing her frustration with his stating the obvious. "That is plenty to be different between us."

"What if we were the same age and rank?"

Erika eyes slid shut and her mind slipped into a fantasy where she was young again and took a different path. Before she could censor herself she cooed, "I'd probably be pregnant by now."

"Really?"

"Oh, no. I'm sorry. I shouldn't have said that."

"So why can't we—"

"Because I won't let myself. I won't let myself love you. Besides…" Erika's sentence drifted off.

"Besides what?"

"I'm going ask to deploy to Iraq."

"You? Ask? Why?"

Erika lifted her brow indignantly. "What? Can't I deploy?"

Doug huffed. "Yeah, sure, but…"

"But what?"

"You just said you're a coward."

"Yeah, and I said I joined the Marines just to see if I could do it."

"What does that mean?"

"I want to deploy to Iraq to say I did it."

Doug tried to straighten up. "Hey, this isn't like the invasion. There are no safe areas right now. They have these IEDs and you never know who they'll take out."

"You sound worried about me?"

"Hell yeah!"

"Do you see why I don't want you to go over?"

"That's different."

"How's that different?"

Doug opened his mouth, but stopped himself.

"Because I'm a girl?"

"No," Doug protested. "Because I do love you and I don't want anything to happen to you."

"But I just told you that I love you too."

"No, you didn't."

"Yes, I did."

"Wait, it sounds like you love me if it is convenient in the conversation for you to love me and you don't when it isn't."

"That's it."

"Do you know how twisted that sounds?"

Erika adopted an airy tone. "Yes. I'm a mystery." She giggled to herself. "You really are naïve. You've haven't dealt with women in today's world have you?"

"No, I guess I haven't."

Erika saw his mind drift. "What are you thinking about?"

"Oh, a friend of mine. You know, Drake."

"Yes."

"He's had to deal with women like this."

"Us mysterious types?"

"Call it what you want. I think you all are psycho."

Erika flashed a pouty frown. Then turned serious. "Speaking of Lieutenant Scott," Erika stood up and fetched her Blackberry. "I need to call him," she said as she thumbed through her emails. She saw the confusion on Doug's face. "They have a date for the *Storming Baghdad* premier. Do you have his cell number?"

Doug rattled off the number by heart while she fingered it into her Blackberry. She hit SEND and held it to her ear.

"Hello?" Drake answered. He didn't recognize the phone number.

"Hello, Lieutenant Scott, this is Colonel Hess, Marine Corps Public Affairs."

"Yes, ma'am." He hesitated. The sultry voice conflicted with the Colonel image Drake painted in his mind. Then he quickly put the picture together. "Oh, are you calling about," he didn't know if he should say *Doug* or *Lieutenant English*, "Lieutenant English. Is he okay?"

Erika groaned. Her face fell limp with despair. *Damn Lieutenants gossip like teenage girls. You sleep with ONE lieutenant and the whole Corps knows.* "No, Lieutenant English is fine—"

Doug barked out a laugh and held his belly.

"I'm calling about your movie premier for *Storming Baghdad.*" Erika told him what her email said she had received about the premier. Then continued with slight trepidation. "I understand that you'd like to have an escort." Erika carefully skirted a name. The person in question could reel in a publicity mother lode for the Marine Corps. "Will she be available by that date? I understand she is filming overseas currently."

"Ah, the last I heard that will be about a week before she gets back."

"And you're deploying two weeks after the premier, so you will only have a week to spend with her before you leave?" Although Erika held the rank of Colonel, she still knew a woman's perspective. "Is there anyway," She stopped herself. She knew Drake couldn't do anything about getting her back sooner. He would have already tried everything he could to get her back sooner. "Is there anyone I can call?" Erika asked although she already knew she would call Grace's director John Sword to work that angle. She didn't know Sword, but could get a hold of him through Gary Buckhorn. She planned her tactful attack in her mind. Directors liked being told what to do about as much as Generals like to be told. Luckily for her, Erika was and expert at telling Generals what to do and making them think it was their idea.

"No, I think she is already trying to get home as soon as she can."

"Oh, I see," Erika said. *But I'm a Colonel in the Marine Corps and I'll MAKE it happen.* "Well, you have a good evening, Lieutenant Scott. I just wanted to give you the news."

"Thanks, Erika. You have a good evening too and say 'hi' to Doug for me," Drake said and hung up.

Erika's jaw dropped. Her gaze slid from her phone to Doug. "He is one cocky S.O.B." She got a broad smile in return and went on to explain. "He's all, 'Thanks Erika, say 'hi' to Doug for me.'" Erika's eyes grew. "Just who the hell does he think he is that he can just call a colonel by their first name?"

Doug held back a laugh. "Yes, ma'am, I mean Colonel ma'am."

Erika grimaced playfully and swatted Doug on the shoulder. "Lieutenants!" she grunted. "What am I going to do with you!" Mischief filtered from Doug's mind to his smile and Erika groaned once again. "I know the Corps is about as sexist as you can find in an organization, but I'm still a colonel dammit!"

"Do you want me at the position of attention again?"

Erika blinked ignoring the innuendo and tried to regain focus. "Anyway…changing subjects. Do you want to go to the premier?"

Doug's face transformed as concern creased his brow. "Yes, I would."

Erika saw the question behind his hesitation. "You'd be my escort."

"Yes."

"We'd have separate rooms."

"Yes."

"At the party and the premier, you will be my escort and n0thing more—oh, and please don't tell anyone else that…"

"What? That you are using your rank to defile my good name?" Doug said.

Erika half laughed and half groaned. "Ah, yes, whatever you want to call it. Could you just please keep this confidential to some extent?"

"Oh, so I probably shouldn't have told Stephanie Chandler?"

Erika's groans turned to whimpers. "Yes, telling a Hollywood tabloid probably didn't do me any favors."

"Hmm." Doug raised an eyebrow. "I guess you will have to keep, ah, what is it we have been doing? Dating? Seeing each other? Well," he waved his hand, "whatever we have I guess you'll just have to keep doing it, or I'll have to write a tell all book about my torrid affair with one of the Marine Corps top officers." His smile seethed arrogance.

"Fine, you go write a book," Erika conceded. She lacked any leverage to protest. "Seriously though. At the premier, you will act like my seeing eye lieutenant and just because we have separate rooms doesn't mean we need to use both." Frustration didn't dampen her libido. It heightened it if anything. "So do you want to go?"

Doug put his hand on her hips tenderly. "Of course, I would love to go."

"Fine. Now I have to make a phone call."

18

"Hello?" Drake answered his cell. He didn't recognize the number.

"Goose? It's Foxy."

"Hey, sir."

"Drop the 'sir' shit, gomer. What are you doing tonight?"

"Ah…"

"Gonna call your girlfriend and do the nasty over the phone again?"

"Would you—"

"Stop giving you shit? Oh, hell no, that is my job in life—"

"You're just jealous?"

"Of you? Ha! In your dreams! You're just lucky she met you first. Anyway, get your ass down here. I'm gonna take you out with some friends and teach you how to drink like a man."

Drake walked into the bar and at first felt underdressed. But then he heard the din erupting from the table of SEALs and knew his attire wouldn't steal any attention from the boisterous group.

"Goose!" Foxy said holding up a beer bottle.

Drake smiled and shook his head. He laughed to himself, *like I wouldn't have been able to find the loud group of SEALs?*

Foxy smiled a glassy smile. This wasn't his first beer. "Goose, these are the guys. Guys, this is Goose." He rattled off call signs as he pointed with his beer bottle.

"So, how did you get to be called *Goose*?" A SEAL called Dragon asked. Dragon got his call sign from a story about a girl he dated in college. The girl hunted him down like a dog and finally got him into bed and spent the night with him. In the morning his breath curled her nose hair and she never came back. Short for Dragon Breath, he was now known as Dragon. Drake explained his story.

"That's awesome!" a SEAL called Snowball, for his premature gray hair, said about Drake's story about the mongoose and the snake. "Yeah, all jarheads miss the mark," he said referring to Houston's incompetence.

Drake nodded and accepted the insult. He wasn't going to try to convince a group of drunk SEALs the value of the Marines.

"Except for Goose, here," Foxy said pointing his beer at Drake.

"How did you guys hook up anyway?" Dragon asked.

Foxy sucked down a swallow of beer and said, "I was doing an SR mission," Strategic Reconnaissance. "I was overwatching a Marine platoon take down this Imam in Iraq. He did pretty well." Foxy tipped his beer at Drake. "One of the most professional units I've ever seen operate...Marine units that is." He took another swallow and pointed back at Drake. "He would have made it in the teams. We got together to debrief and I overheard this guy Ramirez talking about the Farmhouse Shootout and it turns out that Goose here is the CMH guy."

"Not yet," Drake protested.

"Yeah, well, they're making a fucking movie about you, dude. That rates."

"You're the guy who went in and got that reporter?" Snowball asked with a hint of respect.

"Yeah," Foxy answered for him.

"Oh, hey." Drake brightened up. "Are you gonna be around for awhile?"

Foxy crossed his eyes. "Well, this isn't my last beer." He sucked it dry. "Waitress!" He yelled across the establishment.

Drake eyed the swanky establishment. He tried to evaluate how many people they were pissing off. "No, I mean are you going to be in town for awhile?"

Foxy tilted his head to the side. "You never know."

"I know, but if you happen to be around at the time, speaking about the movie, I was wondering if you'd be interested in coming to the premier?"

"Huh. Sounds interesting."

Something clicked in Drake's head. "There's someone I'd like you to meet."

"Really," Foxy said reaching for a beer from the waitress. "You better not introduce me to that Hollywood girl of yours." He twisted off the cap and sucked in a belly full. "She'd leave you in a heartbeat if she got sight of me. She looks like the kind of girl who dates only the first string." Foxy said identifying the professional and capability gap between the Marines and SEALs.

Drake conceded with a nod and took a sip of his beer. If he knew about the SEALs on 9/11 he would have hunted down a Navy recruiter and not a Marine one. For the first time since his freshman year in college he felt outclassed. His mind finally landed on a comeback. Military operators, as opposed to staff and other POGs, carry a certain swagger and there is a pace to their conversations. They lob insults at each other. The receiver can't answer too quickly because it shows insecurity. The receiver pauses a moment. That moment says, *that was a nice attack for someone as inferior as yourself.* Then a wittier rebuttal counterattack is launch that says, *this is how the big boys play.* "I don't know. From what she told me, she'd only date a CMH guy," Drake's said smoother than silk and took another sip of beer. Everyone else at the table burst into laughter. As sophisticated as operators could be intellectually, when push came to shove size mattered most. If they could have thrown out their members on the table for a measuring contest, they would have.

Even Foxy chuckled accepting defeat for the moment. "Like I said, you would have made it in the teams."

"Excuse me," a man from another table had walked over. His muscles bulged and stretched his short sleeves revealing a barbed wire tattoo around his bicep. "But would you all mind keeping it down. I'm trying to have dinner with my lady." From the looks of her, they could tell his lady was part human, silicon, peroxide, and collagen. It was clear her talents weren't in the workplace, but between the bed sheets. In fact her workplace might have actually been between the bed sheets. Evidently, her eye wandered to the table of well-built gregarious competition of the SEAL's table and her suitor wanted in on the Penile Olympics

Fresh off his defeat of wits with Drake, Foxy leapt at the chance to score a win. "Look buddy, I'll tell you what." Foxy reached his hand up to put it on the man's shoulder condescendingly. "You shut your pie hole, go back to your table and we won't rip you a new one and steal your *lady*." Foxy flashed a sappy smile displaying his utter lack of respect.

A woman driving to work can talk on the phone, put on makeup and switch lanes all at the same time. They have been driving so long that only the slightest thought is required to actually drive the vehicle. It is almost as if it is just a natural instinct. SEALs spend more time in Close Quarter Battle, CQB, than any other outfit. They react without the need to consciously think through their thoughts. They spend infinite hours training in a room with a man who may or may act as a hostile. They could be armed. They could attack but then concede. Or they could not attack at all. The SEALs are trained to match the threat level of the attacker. If they concede, the SEAL remains ready to escalate the violence, but restrains himself and may actually offer help if the person in question requires assistance. If the SEAL terminates the attacker, it is because the attacker earned the double tap. Someone has to do America's dirty work and go face to face with an ugly enemy. America chose the Navy SEALs to take that task. And America has done well to train Navy SEALs to be that pit bull on a leash. The problem is that when that pit bull is off his leash and another dog looks at it the wrong way, the pit bull reacts the way it was trained.

Foxy put his hand on the man's shoulder not only to establish dominance, but to also invite a reaction. One of the biggest mistakes ever made is to equate a SEAL's physical proportions inversely with their IQ. Foxy knew exactly what would happen next. The man's arm snapped to knock off Foxy's hand, but Foxy's other fist landed in the man's solar plexus before his arm got to Foxy's hand. The man doubled over and crashed into a table behind him.

Two bouncers that stood nearby in anticipation of such an occurrence jumped into the fray reaching for Foxy. Snowball sent a fist through the ribs of one bouncer and Dragon broke the other's jaw. Six more bouncers flew in from all corners of the bar. The three SEALS naturally fell into a defensive circle with an opening for Drake.

Holy shit! Drake thought. He was tossing away a fantastic career in the Corps. He might even lose his CMH. How could he ever discipline a guy for getting in a bar fight again? *But damn, this is fun.* It was camaraderie at its best. His sick combat smile returned. Drake felt the adrenaline rush of combat once again. He would trade everything for this moment.

Foxy sprung out and grabbed the first bouncer by the throat to neutralize him while flexing his forearm flashing the meaty part to block the next bouncer's billy club. He threw the first bouncer into the second and squared up his shoulders and hips. He lined up his toe and rammed it up the inside of the first bouncer's leg, landing on his testicles. Then he grabbed the second bouncer's shoulders and squared up to him. He lunged at him sending the crown of his forehead through the bouncer's nose. Blood sprayed onto both of their faces but the bouncer's body crumpled. He turned to jump in on another fight.

Two bouncers attacked Snowball since he was the smallest at the table. He threw a bottle at the lead one. The lead bouncer raised his arm to block the projectile. It was a critical error. His focus transferred to the bottle momentarily and in that moment Snowball landed a crippling blow to his ribs. Three distinctive snaps popped through the building indicating how many ribs Snowball busted. Snowball sidestepped the next attackers billy club swing and grabbed the fist holding the club. He twisted the attacker's wrist rotating his thumb in and downward so his elbow pointed upward. He tugged the fist with one hand and hammered his forearm into the back of the joint popping it out of socket and sending a sickening thunderbolt through the establishment. The bouncer's chest heaved and his stomach emptied its contents.

That left one bouncer each for Dragon and Drake. Dragon's arrived late enough to turn and run which pissed off Dragon. "Fuck!" He was going to be ridiculed for not getting any.

While the SEALs snapped and fell back on their CQB training, Drake didn't spend a tenth of the time on CQB that the SEALs did. He fell back to his roots, football. A bouncer launched a billy club attack at Drake, but Drake ran him down like the linebacker he was. The bouncer landed a blow to Drake's back, but Drake drove his shoulder into the bouncer's chest and ran him backward into a table. The table collapsed and Drake landed on top of the bouncer. In an instant Drake lost his ability to control his mind and he saw Anderson cut down. He held the bouncer down with one hand and landed blow after blow into the bouncer's face. He saw a mutilated Stephanie and his fists sped up. He was attacked by an A-10 and he stopped feeling the blows land. He saw Houston attacking Gabrielle and his furry peaked. The SEALs roared as Drake wound into a killing frenzy. Drake was in a fight to the death in his mind.

Foxy caught a glimpse of Drake's eyes and knew he was gone. "Hey!" Foxy reached for Drake's striking fist. The bouncer was unconscious and defenseless. "Stop!" Foxy looked at the other SEALs pleadingly. It took them a moment, but then they saw it too and reached to pull Drake off. While Foxy had his head turned Drake elbowed him in the cheek. "Son of a bitch!" Foxy slid into a full Nelson behind Drake and the other two sat on his legs.

Drake shrieked a death cry as he flexed every muscle he could to escape, but the SEALs knew their craft and locked him down. "Easy there, Goose." Foxy cooed in Drake's ear. "Slow down."

Drake shrieked again. His chest heaved air in and out.

"Hey, buddy, I need you to get it together. We need to bug out," Foxy said. He watched Drake's chest slow and bounce lower and lower with each breath. He looked at the other two SEALs then asked, "You good to go? Cause we need to go," he asked Drake.

"Ah…yeah," Drake shook his head to clear it. "I'm good."

Foxy didn't let up initially. He looked at the other two SEALs and received the nods he expected. They had trained so long together they communicated nonverbally as well as verbally. "Okay, killer we need to get out of her before—"

"Freeze! Don't anybody move." A female cop stood at the door with her weapon pointed in their direction. She keyed her mic and muttered something into it. She moved slowly to create a better shooting lane at the group.

"Shit," Foxy said under his breath. He wasn't just worried about going to jail, he worried that Drake wasn't under control or might lose it again. "He's—"

"Shut the fuck up and get your hands off of him and up in the air!" the cop ordered.

"Hey, look bitch, he's not well, and I don't know if I can let him go without him going crazy."

The cop's eyes narrowed. She studied the *crazy* man and saw there was reason for concern. She looked at the other two. "You two, back the fuck up and get on your knees, hands behind your head."

Two more cops came in with their pistols drawn. "You take these two," the female said indicating her partners to take Snowball and Dragon. "I've got these two."

The cops got Snowball and Dragon handcuffed and in their car. Then they got Foxy and Drake handcuffed and in her car. She watched the other car drive off and then she opened Foxy's door. "Hey, are you okay?" she said across Foxy to Drake. She didn't want to get to close to the crazy one. "Is he going to be okay?" she asked Foxy.

Foxy inspected Drake's eyes and said, "Yeah, he'll be alright," without any confidence.

The cop reached into the glove box, pulled out a baby wipe and tenderly wiped the blood off Foxy's face, "There, is that better for you?"

Foxy smiled back at the officer, "Yeah, thanks."

"You can thank me later."

Drake flashed a WTF look at Foxy as the officer closed the door and walked around to the driver's seat. Foxy shrugged his shoulders. They rode in silence to the station. The officer turned and looked at the two GIs. "Can I trust you to stay here for a moment?"

"Yes, ma'am," Foxy replied quickly. Drake still hadn't caught up with the circumstances. Foxy smelled out the events as they unraveled. The officer looked at her watch. "I'm just about off duty." She opened the car door and then looked back in before closing it. "I'll be back in a minute."

"Uh," Drake's jaw hung. He didn't even know what he wanted to ask. What was going on? How much trouble were they in? Was his Marine Corps career over? Why was Foxy so calm?

"Don't worry about it," Foxy said.

The officer returned in skintight jeans and a T. "Okay, guys. Let's go."

"Where are we going?" Drake asked.

"Shut up," Foxy replied.

The officer smiled over her shoulder as she led them to her car. "Don't worry guys, nothing is going to happen. Well, I wouldn't say nothing."

"I don't get it," Drake pressed.

"Would you shut the fuck up," Foxy insisted.

"I—" Drake started again before being shot down by Foxy's glare.

"You guys are vets, right?"

"Yes, ma'am," Foxy replied.

"Hi, I'm Jennifer Lee." She smiled and held her hand out to shake their hands. "You can call me Jenny, Officer Lee or Corporal Lee, as in Corporal Lee of the California National Guard."

"Oh, so you didn't—" Drake started

"Would you just leave it alone?" Foxy admonished once again.

"Relax," Jenny said as she slid her arm up Foxy's shoulder to calm him down. "Did I ever read you guys your Miranda rights?"

Drake searched the sky, "'Uh, no."

"Oops." Jenny raised her eyebrows and tilted her head. "I guess I screwed that arrest up."

Jenny drove back to the bar and pulled into the parking lot. "You're good to drive aren't you?" She asked Drake.

Drake calculated his alcohol intake and time elapsed from his last drink. "Yeah, I'm good to go. But I don't think you are," he said to Foxy.

"Don't worry about him. I'll take care of him," Jenny replied.

Drake sat trying to unravel the confusion clouding his mind.

"Would you leave already?" Foxy said.

"Uh…yeah…see ya." Drake stepped out of the car and reached for his keys. *Most bizarre night of my life.* He started up his Tahoe and slowly rolled towards Foxy's pickup. *Nothing will ever top this night. Oh, correction, it just got topped.* Through foggy windows Drake saw Foxy's face buried in Jenny's tits as his pickup gently rocked. Drake rolled to a stop. He pulled out his phone and texted, *Thanks for teaching me how to party like a rock star-hope to see you at premier.*

He checked his watch and then dialed another number.

"Hey, you," the iconic Britanic voice said.

"Hey, yourself. You would not believe the night I just had." Drake went on to explain his evening.

"So do you usually get into bar fights?" Grace asked with concern.

"No! I never do! That's the crazy part!"

"Oh, *that's* the crazy part, not your friend behaving badly in the parking lot with the officer?" Insecurity slipped from Grace's accent.

"Well, yeah, that is crazy too. But, I mean how it started."

"Would you ever?"

Drake waited for the rest of the question then asked, "Would I ever what?"

Grace sighed. "Would you ever…you know?"

"No, I don't."

"If a woman ever…" Grace tried her hardest to add dignity to the question. "Offered herself, would you?"

"No, of course not!" Drake answered.

"Yes, but weren't you engaged when Gabrielle came along?"

"Uh, yes…but…"

"But what?"

"That was different."

"How was that different! You were engaged to marry some other woman and you cheated on her!"

"But that's in the past."

"So it was in the past. Are you saying that you would never in the future? What has changed?"

"I could never do that to you."

"But you were in love with the woman you were engaged to right!"

"Yes."

"So how can you say you wouldn't," Grace paused to omit a word or two, "tomorrow?"

"I," Drake felt defeated. "I don't know."

"Darling," Grace sniffled through tears, "I want you to feel that you can do whatever you want. If you need to have a tawdry affair with some trollop, don't feel you can't because of me."

"Gracie!"

"What?"

"What's the matter?"

"I can't be there," she sobbed. "And you have needs. Every man has needs."

"Sweetheart. Relax."

"I don't want you to feel deprived."

"I don't."

"I don't want you to resent me because your friends can go off contracting diseases from less than wholesome women and you can't."

"Stop it, Grace!" Drake needed her to calm down. He listened to her sob on the other end. "There isn't any other woman. And there isn't going to be any other woman. Don't you realize you're my everything?"

"Yes," she sniffled, "and you're my everything too. But I can't be there for you now and I wish I was."

"I know."

"I just miss you so much, darling. I know it sounds odd since we've never met, but," she stopped herself abruptly. She treaded into dangerous territory. "I just want you to know that more than anything else, I want you to be happy even if it means for you to be with someone else."

"Grace, I don't want to be with anyone else."

"Neither do I."

"So what is the problem?"

"When you tell me stories about your friends going off...and doing God only knows what to disreputable women, I think that you are in some way jealous. That you'd like to have a cheap fling for yourself."

"Yeah, I'd like to have a cheap fling, but only if it involves you."

That bubbled a giggle out of Grace. "Promise."

"Yes, I promise. The next time I see you, I will have a cheap tawdry meaningless romp in the hay with you."

"Well," Grace said coyly, "you don't have to be so brash about it."

Drake laughed. "So, are you okay now?"

"Yes, I'm better. Thank you for tolerating my neurosis."

19

Grace threw open the tent flap and stormed in.

A half naked man sat up and threw a naked woman off of himself. The woman scrambled for the sheet to cover herself.

"So it's true!" Grace hissed. Fire shot from her eyes. Her tight jaw clenched onto the hatred burning her heart.

"Honey, it's not what you think!" the man pleaded.

"Don't 'honey' me!" Grace spotted a revolver near the tent entrance. Weapons littered the camp for defense against predators. She snatched it and lowered the barrel on the man's chest.

"No, please!" the woman protested.

Grace's eyes narrowed. She cocked the hammer. The woman squealed and ran out the back of the tent. "If I can't have you—"

"No!" the man begged.

BANG! Grace fired a slug into his belly. The man roared in agony. "Then she can't either," Grace continued. She stepped closer to the man. "You know what can have you?" Grace sneered as she cocked the hammer again.

"No, I don't. Please..." Blood burbled out of the man's mouth.

"Hell!" She pulled the trigger and the hammer fell driving the firing pin into another slug that tore into the man's belly. Hyena's howled in the distance. Grace studied the man and savored his agony. She smiled like the devil as she pulled back the hammer once again and placed the barrel above the man's heart. "But not before the jackals get theirs." The hammer fell once again and the man stopped breathing. Grace waited.

"All right," the director said looking up from a camera. "That was fantastic!" He smiled and looked at Grace. He enjoyed the moment seeing the anxiety and anticipation in Grace's face. He slouched in his chair. "That was…" he held his palms up, "absolute perfection, Grace."

"Oh, goodie!" Grace hopped up like a schoolgirl clapping and tucking her heels up to her backside as she leapt into the air. She was out of her mind with anticipation. "So…"

The director tortured Grace by not finishing her sentence right away. "Do we need another take? I don't know. What do you think?"

"No!" Grace squealed but then tempered her reply. "Unless you think we do."

"No, I don't think we need another take."

"So…"

"Go, get out of here. Go see that boyfriend of yours."

"Oh! Thank you! Thank you! Thank you!" Grace ran up to the director and kissed him on the cheek, then sprinted down to the road where a Range Rover waited for her.

The actor walked over to within whispering distance of the director with his eyes focused on Grace's inviting duff bounding down the hillside. The director shared the view. Lust swilled through them. The director didn't cast Grace by accident. "Such a waste," the actor said.

"How come?" the director said without shifting his gaze.

"She's going to waste that on a guy in the Army."

"She's an odd bird." The director then added, "But there is still hope."

"Huh?"

"Yeah. He could still get himself killed in Iraq."

"One could only hope."

Grace slid into the passenger seat and smiled at the driver. He started slow over the bumpy dirt path. "How long will it take to get to the airport?" Grace asked.

"About forty-five minutes."

"Thank, you." Grace ran times through her head. When it got to be too much she pulled out a notepad and wrote down times and calculated she would arrive in LA the next morning. She pulled out her cell phone and held it up to the top of the Range Rover. Nothing. It wasn't until about fifteen minutes away from the airport she caught a signal. She thumbed through her contacts and picked one and hit SEND then END immediately. She forgot to make that calculation. It was too late to call. She sent a text to her assistant and then texted Drake. *Finished early-pick me up for premier at 5 XOX.* When MESSAGE SENT rolled through her display she squealed and squirmed in anticipation.

20

"The blonde woman must be stopped," was the loose translation of the beginning of the message. The rest contained cryptic details, but it was good enough for Air Force Captain Barry Horton. He stood up and marched into his boss's office. Less than a minute later he walked out of his boss's office in search of his NCOIC, Non-Commissioned Officer in Charge. He found him on console at a bank of computer screens. "Hey, I'm going on a pass up to Baghdad tomorrow. You got things down here while I'm out, okay?"

"Okay, I got it, sir," the NCOIC said.

Horton sat at his desk and pulled out a notepad. He cross referenced a schedule and then dialed a number.

"Hello?"

"Fawn Hollings?"

"Yes, who is this?"

"It's Barry Horton, Captain Barry Horton, remember me?"

"Of course, Captain Horton."

"Barry, please."

"Excuse me?"

"Please call me Barry."

"Okay, Barry, call me Fawn."

"Okay Fawn."

"So why did you call, Barry?"

"The reason I called," Barry thought about how to approach what he had to say, "is because I'm going to be up on a three day pass in Baghdad starting tomorrow and I was wondering if we could meet up?" Horton knew she had a 0900 staff meeting that would last no later than 1100 and then she had nothing else on her schedule.

"Captain Horton, are you asking me on a date?"

Horton considered how to make his request from several angles. He didn't consider the romantic angle. "Uh, no, not really."

"Oh."

Horton heard disappointment in her voice. His mind churned. "But we can talk about that once I get there." He had seen pictures. She was attractive.

"No, that's fine."

"No, please don't misunderstand me. I would like to go out on a date with you…just not in Baghdad." *How big of an idiot am I?* The conversation's direction frustrated Horton. He needed to talk to her in person.

"Oh, I'm sorry."

Barry visited Hollings' blog daily to see her photos and read her daily entry. From afar he became attached to the feisty blonde. "That's not why I need to see you though." He took control of the conversation. "I'll meet you right after your staff meeting and we'll go to lunch, okay?"

"Yeah, sure."

"Okay, I'll see you tomorrow," Barry said and cut the connection.

"Barry?" Fawn looked at her phone trying to figure out what happened. Then she wondered, *how does he know I have a nine o'clock staff meeting?*

Fawn closed her notebook at the end of the meeting and then it struck her that someone might be standing outside the doors waiting for her. She hurried out of her seat and scampered to the door. People clustered around the door and then she found a bright smile focused on her. "Barry?"

"Yes."

Fawn drew close to him in the crowd and stuck her hand out in a cramped manner dictated by the situation. "Fawn Hollings," she said for an introduction.

"Nice to meet you, Barry Horton."

"So, where would you like to go?" Fawn's eyes dazzled. She brandished her long golden locks as if they were a weapon against male chauvinism. Barry noticed them in every picture of Fawn. She dotted her blog with pictures of her wielding her blonde hair in the midst of women in black burqas.

Barry hesitated stunned by her electric energy. "Uh, I wouldn't know where to go."

"C'mon, I know a place." Fawn took his hand and pulled him through the crowd. Uneasiness nagged at Barry he wasn't supposed to be holding hands with her. First of all, it was professional and second, it was culturally insensitive. But he feared that he'd never see her again if he let go. She moved quickly and with purpose.

Fawn abandoned her post as a Supreme Court clerk when the Iraq War started to go to Iraq and become the voice of all Iraqi women, Sunni, Shi'ite and Kurd. She wanted to break some cultural sensitivities in Iraq. A woman should be able to hold a man's hand in public.

"So, tell me, Captain Horton, what is with all the cloak and dagger?" she asked once she secured them a table at a local café. She continued to hold his hand.

Barry pulled his hand back finally to concentrate. A starting point eluded him.

"Barry, what is it?" she asked.

He needed to cover several items, but decided to work backwards and see where it took him. "Why did you hold my hand?" He had the advantage of studying her every electronic move and built a personality profile that seemed more accurate than not.

Fawn smiled disarmingly and ran her fingers through her long blonde hair and swept it over the front of her shoulder.

"Why can't a girl hold a boy's hand? I've always been a touchy feely person." She reached for his hand again.

"Ugh, Fawn." Barry pulled his hand back. His shoulders slumped and his gaze drifted to the ceiling. He dropped the inquisition. "You're in danger."

She smiled and leaned back. "We're all in danger. Iraq is a dangerous place."

"No! Fawn! *You* are in danger."

"So." She ran her fingers through her hair again.

Barry twitched. "And why do you do that?" He couldn't focus. His mind led him all over the place.

"What?"

"That—flashing your hair around as if you were proud of it."

"But I am proud of it."

A light bulb lit a corner of Barry's mind. His eyes widened. "You didn't go through any training before coming here, did you?"

"Training? What training would I need?"

"Cultural sensitivity, Antiterrorism…I don't know what else."

"Do you think that a government agency that walks around in helmets and flak vests knows anything about cultural sensitivity? How can you honestly bond with a person, or a people when you are physically isolated from them? When I go out and visit the women of Iraq I want them to feel my heartbeat, not an iron plate."

"But do you have to insult the men of Iraq, by flashing your God damn gorgeous hair at every opportunity?"

"Hey! First of all, we are here to change Iraq and that is one of the changes I'm here to make. The women of Iraq should be able to flash their God damn gorgeous hair. And second, you think my hair is gorgeous?"

"Yes, of course I do. Who doesn't? You know you have gorgeous hair. That is why you show it off."

"No, but I'm glad you think so…that it's gorgeous, not that other part," she said demurely.

"Look," Barry pointed a finger in her face. "You have a problem and the problem is that you are cute and—"

"So you think I'm cute?"

"Yes, and it is going to get you in trouble."

"How?"

"The problem with you is that you are cute and you know it and you are used to…uh…getting your way because of it."

"That's not true."

"Well, this time it isn't going to work I'm here to tell you. They don't see you as cute, they see you as Satan incarnate."

"Who?"

"The fucking jihadis! Who do you think?"

Fawn shook her head. She smiled weakly. "I'll be fine."

"What do you know about antiterrorism? Did you get any briefings?"

"No, did you?"

"I took a course in it before deploying. I couldn't take a shit without them being able to tell me what color it was they were so far up my ass."

Fawn giggled.

"It's not funny! People are watching all the time. And they're not just watching…" Barry stopped. He toed the line of what he could say.

"What do you mean?"

Barry's eyes scanned the café. He reached into his cargo pants pocked, pulled out some folded papers and handed them over.

Fawn cautiously reached for them. It wasn't funny anymore. Her eyes dove towards the print and immediately recognized it. "What! Have you been reading my email!"

"Yes."

Fawn's eyes darted at his. She waived the papers in the air. "You can't do this. You can't read my private emails."

"The hell I can't."

"These are private!"

"It's a fucking war zone!"

"That doesn't give you the right—"

"Oh, yes, it does."

Fawn stood up.

"Sit the fuck down!" Barry hissed. He grabbed her petite arm and bent it so she didn't have a choice. His eyes seared holes through her. "There's more."

"There's more?"

"Yes. It's my job to know this shit. So calm the fuck down. I'm here because no one else gives a shit about you because you're not military. As a matter of fact, most of the staff sees you as a pain in the ass."

"I know I'm a pain in their ass. That is part of my job."

"Fawn—stop—you're missing the point."

"Then what is the point?"

Barry took in a breath. His toe crossed the line. He grimaced as he reached in his other cargo pocket to pull out another wad of folded up papers. Slowly he slid them across the table. Fawn's finger's tentatively reached for them. She sucked down shallow breaths and then she swallowed hard. Barry watched her eyes crisscross the page. His eyes followed her free hand as it reached to cover her trembling lips. Dewiness glazed her eyes. "So," her voice cracked. "When is this going to happen?"

Sympathy filled Barry's eyes. "Fawn, you need to go home."

She raised a knuckle to her nose to stem an emotional display. "I won't. I won't be stopped by these cowards."

Barry reached across the table and took her hand. "You've done a wonderful job here, Fawn. But you need to go home."

"Just tell me where and when this is going to happen?" She shook the wad of papers defiantly.

Barry reached for the classified document and took it from her. "I don't know when, where or how?"

"I thought that was your job?" Tears cascaded over her eyelids.

"I'm sorry, but I don't know."

Fawn stood up and gritted her teeth. "Well if you can't tell me that, I'm going to keep going out to see the women of Iraq."

"Then let me go with you tomorrow?"

"How do you know I'm going out tomorrow? Oh, that's right. You're Big Brother, you know everything...except for what I need to know."

"I'm going with you tomorrow." Barry studied her face and watched the recognition cross her face.

"No, you can't."

"Why not?"

"Because..." Logic failed her.

"Because tomorrow might be the day?" he asked. He hoped the added responsibility would cause her to rethink her actions.

Fawn drew close to him and laid her hands on him. She looked up and said, "This is my fight. It's not yours."

"I'm going, and you can't stop me."

Fawn's Toyota Land Cruiser rolled up. From the back seat she flashed a bright smile with her golden locks prominently displayed cascading over her shoulders. If the Iraqi men understood her to be flaunting her femininity, they'd be correct. Her guide and translator occupied the front seats. Barry took a step and hesitated. Once he was in he had to press on with her. He knew the odds and explained them to her and she didn't bat an eye. It might not be this trip, but it would be some trip. Barry had read the electronic traffic and it was clear a host of characters meant her harm, fatal if possible.

This was the only one he could go with her on. What was the point? He couldn't save her. He'd just get killed along side her and after this trip he couldn't go with to even try to protect her. He studied her. There was no hesitation in her. She was going come what may and why dread the potential outcome when she could dream of a better future for Iraqi women. Barry lumbered forward and into the vehicle loaded with body armor, Kevlar helmet, M-16 and M9 pistol.

"Where do you think we're going?" Fawn asked with a laugh.

"Indian country."

"And who are you Wyatt Earp?"

Barry shook his head. "You know what you're up against. I laid it all out for you."

"So…"

He opened his mouth but couldn't argue with her. She was fearless. She occupied a separate plane in the universe than him. He couldn't talk to her.

"Don't worry," she continued. "There's no good that can come of worrying."

His head twitched up and down and then swung into a full nod when he submitted himself to the circumstances. He drew in a deep breath and slowly let the air slip out of his lungs.

"There, that's better," she said and reached for his hand. She held it and caressed the back of it to soothe his nerves. She asked him benign questions about his background. Easy conversation grew. They spent nearly an hour sharing stories about their past lives. They laughed often.

"What is it?" Fawn asked breaking the flow of the conversation.

Barry's head jerked forward. She didn't realize they were slowing down.

"A police checkpoint," the driver said.

"Oh," Fawn replied.

Barry saw the whiff of concern drift over Fawn's face. His fingers inched toward his M9. Fawn reached for his hand and wrapped hers around his, intertwining their fingers so he couldn't grab his weapon. She shook her head. She didn't want him to spook the Iraqi police. Barry froze. He starred across the cab to the officer on the opposite side of the SUV. He didn't want to look out his window and make eye contact with the officer approaching his side. Fawn smiled feebly at him. It was the last thing she did. If this was a set up, he thought, and there was a heaven, he would be going with Fawn. It was his last full coherent thought. The thunks against the side of the vehicle perplexed him. By the time he realized they were bullets he didn't understand the crashes. When he understood the crashes of bullets were shattering glass he was trying to process what caused Fawn's shoulder to explode, her chest to whipsaw and her jaw to come unhinged producing a fountain of blood. Bees stung him simultaneously throughout his limbs. His arms wailed around without command. His vision grayed. He was tired.

In less than twelve seconds two bright intelligent American's perished in the unforgiving Iraqi desert. Years of schooling and experience evaporated. Untapped potential squandered. Their stories ended in a wasteland. Instead of spending their lifetimes serving others in their own way and loving one another and creating life built on love, history will render them to insignificant footnotes of a war that is just another war, in a string of wars, man deemed necessary. This is where their story ends.

21

Drake studied the street sign. When he recognized it he slowed and turned the wheel. "Holy shit—What the fuck!" Cars and motorcycles clustered in the middle of the block. People hung from trees. Drake slowly rolled down the street looking at house addresses. Of course the mob centered around the house he targeted. The gate confused him. She didn't say anything about a gate. It made sense though. He imagined what the circus outside the gate would look like if there wasn't a gate. The sea of photographers swarmed his Tahoe when they noticed he was *the* Drake Scott. His nerves tingled. He sat upright and fought the temptation to gun the engine. *This isn't Iraq.* He reminded himself. He looked for a call box then spotted an outbound vehicle. He backed up to let the vehicle out and then rolled forward through the gate. To their credit the mob didn't pour through. Through his rearview mirror he watched the gate close behind him without a single squirter. The Tahoe idled up to the rear of a limo where he slowly applied pressure to the brake pedal to ease the vehicle to a stop. He put the car in PARK, removed the key and tossed it in the center console. His eye gazed into the distance. He raised his chest to open his lungs for a full breath and slowly exhaled. He could hear his heart beating in his ears. This was it. It was the first day of the rest of his life. It was his fourth first day. He stepped out of the car and clenched his hands hoping they would stop shaking. He took another deep breath. He felt less pressure breaching the farmhouse. He stood at the entry dumbfounded. Two ornate knockers adorned massive doors. Was he supposed to use the knockers? Then off to the side he saw what appeared to be a doorbell. He liked doorbells. They were his speed. Tentatively he raised a finger to it, pressed and released. A thunderous gong boomed twice. The racket nearly shook Drake off his feet.

"Drake?" A soft Britanic voice chirped through the speaker.

He recognized the accent. A chill shook his spine. It was her! He was finally going to see her! "Yes?"

"Come in, the door is open."

"Okay." His voice cracked and his face turned red. He stepped up to the to the door and worked the lever. He pushed on the heavy door until it gave. He gently closed the door behind him. Every sound echoed off the marble floor. He took two steps into the foyer and froze. The opulence overwhelmed him. His apartment would fit in the foyer alone. It wasn't the first time he'd been here, but this is the first time it felt real and not some obtuse alternate universe.

Grace heard the door close. She took one last look at the mirror. Starting at the top of her head she inspected her hair, eyebrows, eyeliner and shadow, blush, lipstick and earrings. She inspected their length for symmetry. Her eyes moved to her necklace, not overstated and not washed out. She held out her arms and watched how her strapless dress flowed over her breasts. Then she ran her hands down her sides over the gentle curves of her hips. She swung her hips side to side to gage the sway of the dress and the slit. She wanted the slit to be unassuming and yet occupy a corner of Drake's mind. She slid her weight to the balls of her feet while inspecting her heals. With the shift her back arched thrusting her chest forward and her backside high and tight. Perfect.

Softly she fingered the doorknob to her bedroom and twisted it open. She glided out of her room to the balcony where she peaked over the railing. HE WAS BEAUTIFUL!

She swallowed a whimper. He stood tall inspecting the art in the foyer. She toed her way to the top of the staircase and stopped. Her chest heaved. Trembles showered her body. She could never remember being so nervous. "Drake?" she said. He looked up with piercing blue eyes that bowled her over with their softness. Her fingers tightened on the railing as her knees buckled momentarily. Sensory overload paralyzed her.

"Grace?"

Ouch. His disarming smile physically hurt her. She needed to do something. She needed to move! *Oh God, please move my feet!* Her foot gingerly felt for the next step. *Now God, if you could please make my mouth work, I'd really appreciate it.* "Well, it is so very nice to see you finally." Her other foot continued to make progress down the staircase. Good.

"Yes, it is."

Grace couldn't say another thing. Her senses hammered her brain. She had to walk down the stars and breath. She spent the rest of her brainpower looking at his eyes. He crossed the room to the bottom of the staircase. She held out her hands to take his but she forgot he was 6' 4". When she reached eye level with him she stepped towards him. She missed the floor. There was another step. Her body lurched forward and into his arms.

"Oh, I'm so sorry," she said.

"So, I see where you get the name Grace."

Grace cracked into a nervous laugh. "I'm sorry, I'm just so nervous."

"I know!" Drake's eyes brightened. "I almost pissed in my pants when I saw you."

Grace giggled and blushed. "I felt the same way."

Drake rattled his head.

"What is it?" Grace worried she said so much.

"It's you."

"Yes, it is me."

"No, it's just," the corners of his lips curled into a smile that swept Grace away. "I guess I'm trying to put the picture with the voice. I mean, you think about all we've talked about. I mean *all* we've talked about—"

"I know!"

"And me talking about pissing myself doesn't sound so weird for a first conversation."

Grace giggled. "That's so true. But I just want to tell you right now that more than anything else, I just want to kiss you."

Drake's eyes lit up.

"I've been dying to kiss you for…I don't know how long, but the lady who does my makeup just left and she'll be very upset if I don't at least make it to the red carpet without mussing her work." Grace inhaled. "I'm sorry I'm so chatty, but I'm so nervous I can't stop myself." Grace stepped towards the door and then turned towards Drake and hovered her hands just over his chest. Her hands swayed while she considered what she wanted to do. She exhaled and laid them on his chest. "Are you nervous?" Then she realized how much he towered over her. "My goodness you're tall!"

"Yes, and yes."

"I'm sorry." Grace shook her head. Her eyes danced around his uniform, curiously inspecting the trinkets adorning it and the physique that filled it out.

"Yes, I'm nervous and yes, I'm tall."

Grace laughed nervously.

"I have to say this is the first time I ever opened a conversation with a girl I've never met with the condition of my bladder," Drake said.

Grace giggled again a little easier this time. Drake held an elbow out for her. Grace slid her arm through it. "No wait, stop." She pulled back. She held his hands at arms length. "I just want to look at you." Her eyes dazzled. "You're so pretty."

"Pretty? Don't *ever* call me pretty," Drake pleaded.

Grace snapped erect and saluted awkwardly. "Yes, sir, commander, sir."

Drake laughed regaining his composure. "At least not in front of the guys. They would never let me forget it."

"They wouldn't?"

"Oh, you bet."

"I can't wait to meet them."

"I can't wait to show you off. I mean for you to meet them."

Grace smiled. She swayed her arm towards the door. "Shall we?"

"If you say so. I'm all yours."

"All mine?" Grace cooed. "I like that. But if you were all mine, we wouldn't be going anywhere right now."

"No?"

"No, I really wanted to get in last night so we could spend some time together before going to this."

"Ah." Drake froze outside the door. The scene overwhelmed him tactically. Leading up to the premier and the unit's predeployment leave Drake had spent days and weeks nonstop in the field training for the deployment. He saw the mob and all he could imagine was a field exercise simulating an angry Iraqi mob. In fact he had a close call with an angry Iraqi mob before and it isn't a pretty scene. Flashbacks snapped at his mind.

"What is it?"

"Nothing."

"No, what is it Drake?"

"I was just thinking."

"About what?"

"How I would deal with this in a tactical environment."

"Deal with what?"

"That." Drake pointed at the swarm.

Grace laughed. "Oh, you get used to it."

"It doesn't bother you?"

"No, you have to realize they are just trying to make a living for themselves. Don't get me wrong, it's intrusive, but I can get away when I need to." Grace saw his eyes narrow. "Now what are you doing?"

His eyes softened. "Oh, nothing. It's just nerve wracking for someone like me."

"Really?"

"Yeah." Drake looked at her and then out at the crowd. "Imagine if somebody out there had a gun and was intent on killing you, or worse was a suicide bomber."

Grace scanned the crowd and caught her breath. She raised a hand to her chest. "Oh, my that would be terrifying."

"Welcome to my world."

"Really?"

"Pretty much."

"How do you deal with it?"

"What, being shot at?"

"Well, yes, but also this." She swept her hand towards the crowd.

"This? Oh, I've been trained on convoy training," Drake's mind replayed the drive up.

"So what do they teach you in convoy training."

Drake shifted uncomfortably. He didn't want to talk about work. "A lot of things, but most importantly is to never get pinned in the kill zone. You have to press through it."

"Kill zone? That sounds awful."

"It is. You're as good as dead if you get bogged down in the kill zone because the enemy will have fire superiority and will eat you alive."

Grace scrunched her face. "That doesn't sound good."

"No, it's not."

"But you've been trained in this?"

"Yes." Drake saw the wheels churning in her head now. "What are you thinking?"

"Do you want to drive?" Grace asked.

"Sure."

"I called for the limo, but we don't have to go in the limo. Do you want to show me some of your stuff?" Grace shook her hips.

Drake laughed and shook his head. "Sure if you think you can handle it."

"Oh, I can handle it."

"Wait here one moment." Grace ran over to the limo and cut the driver off as he stepped out to get her door. She whispered to him and then returned in a trot past Drake to the Tahoe's passenger door. She swung the door open and hopped in before Drake could open the door for her. Drake raced around to the driver's side, hopped in and started the car in one fluid motion.

"I have to warn you though." He looked up at her face. "Your stylist, or whoever does your hair, isn't going to like the way you look by the time you get to the carpet."

"I don't care." She pointed to the limo. "Jimmy is going to lead out and go to the right. If you wait and turn left you might be able to give some of them the slip."

"Cool." Drake pointed at the doorframe handle. "There's your *oh shit* handle. You better hang on. It's gonna be a ride."

The limo led out and the crowd gravitated toward it. When the majority left. Drake rolled up to the gate and waited for it to open. His fingers twitched on the steering wheel. When the Tahoe could fit through he rolled forward. He didn't want to gun the engine. That would alert the mob something was afoot. Slowly he continued to apply the accelerator until he reached 70 miles per hour by the end of the street. He jammed on the brakes engaging the antilock system. Some of the crowd reversed itself and charged the Tahoe. Drake snapped his head to the left to check for traffic. He released his fingers off the wheel and whipped the wheel around. He drove just on the edge of keeping the tires from squealing in the turn. He drove under a paranoid spell, cast upon him in Iraq. With no bogey's in sight he sped through the stop sign and accelerated for the highway. Some of the motorcycles caught up with him. He scanned the next intersection as he approached. He timed his approach to the red light so that he could scoot between two crossing cars. Three motorcycles squealed to a stop and then punched their accelerators when the traffic passed. Drake floored the accelerator and the Tahoe woofed forward towards another yellow light. "Hold on." Drake spun the wheel as the light turned red. The tires squealed straining to maintain the turn. The Tahoe shot down the on ramp. Drake gauged the traffic and slid through it to the far left lane. He eyed his speedometer and settled in at ninety miles per hour.

"You weren't exaggerating were you?" Grace asked.

"Huh?" Drake's eyes darted nervously at signs, vehicles and mirrors.

"That I needed to hang on."

"Oh…yes. No, I wasn't exaggerating." He stole a glance at her. "Aw, I'm sorry."

"What?"

"You're hair is," he check his mirrors for traffic, "out of place."

Grace used her free hand to run a finger across her brow. She didn't dare let go of the handle. "Oh, I guess so."

Drake glanced again and said, "Looks kinda sexy actually."

"Really. Maybe I should leave it then." Grace couldn't hide her delight. She sat back satisfied. "Drake!"

"What?"

"That was our exit."

"I know." Drake's eyes swung across the highway. He stomped on the brakes momentarily. Three motorcycles sped by. With one hand he spun the wheel and the other he tapped the four-wheel drive button and climbed up the off ramp embankment. "That should be the last of them."

"Does that mean you'll stop at red lights now?"

"Sure, why not." He weaved his car through neighborhoods to the premier. Another gaggle hovered over the premier's entrance. Drake pulled the car up.

"You ready to put on your face?" Grace asked.

"I guess I have to be." Drake hopped out of the car and gave his keys to the valet. A murmur ran through the crowd as it recognized Grace in the passenger seat and concluded the Marine must be *the* Drake Scott. He ran around the car and opened Grace's door. She held her hand out for him to take. She delicately stepped out of the vehicle and stood for a second to make sure her dress was in place and allow for pictures. Drake started to march off with her.

"Drake," She said softly. He stopped and she sauntered up to her him and whispered in his ear, "Let them take their pictures. We're in no rush, darling." Grace knew the ear whisper was a favorite shot for the tabloids. It meant *secret*, which tantalized their readers. Drake froze. "What is it, darling?"

"Ah, nothing." He melted. Just the word *darling* from that Britanic voice rushed a natural opiate through Drake's system.

Grace looked quizzically.

He had to come clean. She could cut him to the quick with just a look. "You called me 'darling.'"

"You don't like to be called 'darling?'"

"No, quite the contrary."

Grace straightened her back and squared her shoulders. Confidence washed over her. She hooked him. "We can go now, darling." She paced him down the red carpet.

Drake gathered his bearings once inside the lobby seeing Marine uniforms. He stopped and surveyed the area.

"Scott, you fucking piece of shit!"

"English, you fucking cocksucker! What the fuck are you doing here!"

Grace snapped her head. She had to look at Drake's mouth to confirm the string of profanity came from him. She looked at the man Drake called to and saw a Marine a little shorter than Drake hobbling up to him. Drake broke from Grace and stepped up to the crippled Marine. The two men engaged in a tight affectionate brace. She watched the two men tighten into a bear hug. Drake kissed the man on top of the head. Grace felt out of place until she realized there was a woman in a Marine uniform hanging back from English. Her eyes continued across the crowd. She noticed other Marines greeting each other similarly. She didn't realize how affectionate Marines could be. She swung her eyes back to the female Marine and didn't like the way she looked at Drake. Grace stepped in and grabbed Drake's arm. She'd be damned if the woman thought she was going to hug Drake like that.

"My girlfr—ah, Col Hess brought me with as her escort." Doug English said opening up and waving to the woman in uniform.

"Oh, and this is Grace," Drake said. "Grace, this is Doug English."

"It is very nice to meet you, Mr. English." Grace didn't know how to address him. She liked the way he lit up when he saw her though.

"Oh, my God!" Doug said.

"What?" Drake asked. "Did you think she was a blow up doll?"

"With you? No, it is just your luck to get set up with Grace Freemont." Doug drank in the sight of Grace Freemont. "And, please, call me Doug."

"Sure, Doug."

Doug realized he was gawking. "Oh, and this is Eri—ah, Col Hess."

"Ma'am," Drake said and shook her hand politely.

Grace resented the woman already. Somehow the woman was on the inside just because she wore a uniform. Grace turned up the charm. "It is such an honor to meet you, Col Hess."

"Please, call me, Erika," The woman said and held her hand out to Grace.

"Thanks, Erika, please call me, Grace."

The woman nodded. Grace turned her attention back to the two men as she considered the tall elegant blonde. Grace concluded she was cold. Maybe Doug liked cold women, but she was definitely too cold for someone like Drake she convinced herself. This was only the beginning to assaults on Grace's security. Her position with Drake would take a barrage before the night was over. Grace waited for a break then asked. "Doug," her soft voice cut through the men's foul dialogue. "May I ask what happened, or is that inappropriate." She despised that she didn't know more about Drake's world and the protocol. Why did Drake have to call the woman *ma'am*? Wasn't he going to be the most decorated Marine since Vietnam? Frustration percolated in Grace. A moment ago on the red carpet, she was the one at ease, in her element, and it vanished as soon as they stepped into the lobby.

"Oh, no, I don't mind—" Doug said.

"He was doing his John Wayne impersonation," Drake interrupted. "Stephanie went down in a street during a firefight and the Duke here," Drake nodded at Doug, "felt the need to go rescue her." Drake adopted a huffy sarcastic voice. "Personally, I would have left her out there."

"No, you wouldn't have," Stephanie scampered in from nowhere and threw herself into Drake's arms. "You love me too much."

"Okay, fine. I might have thought about it," Drake said.

"It is so nice to see you again. It's been too long." Stephanie said. She submitted her whole body to Drake who engulfed it intimately. Grace watched the couple enviously as the two savored their embrace with closed eyes. Stephanie clung to him. Grace looked away uneasily. She felt someone's eye surveying her. She was used to being gawked at but this was different. Her eyes drifted to a stunning brunette that challenged her stare momentarily before averting her eyes. She wore a different uniform. She wasn't a Marine. Grace wondered if that was the other woman. Grace turned back in time to see the two finally break their union and Stephanie kiss him on the cheek as they separated. Grace immediately stepped in and claimed her prize again by wrapping herself around Drake's arm. It bothered Grace that Stephanie seemed more interested in reuniting with Drake than her. Stephanie had seen Drake more recently than she had seen Grace.

Stephanie turned to Doug and Grace watched them embrace too. It comforted her to see this embrace almost as affectionate as the one with Drake. Grace eyed the Colonel to see if her hackles rose as much as her own. To Grace's dismay, the Colonel seemed to take it in stride, unaffected by the lavish display of affection.

When their embrace ended Stephanie finally turned to Grace and offered her a typical Hollywood half embrace and kiss on the cheek. "It's so nice to see you again," Grace offered hiding her growing angst. A stray thought trickled through her mind that Stephanie was intentionally trying to make her feel out of place. Grace buried the thought with the logic that Stephanie had set up her and Drake. "I can never say how grateful I am to you for finding this one for me." Grace tugged on Drake's arm.

"Oh, Stephanie," Doug interrupted. "This is Colonel Hess. Colonel Hess, Stephanie Chandler."

"How are you?" Erika asked earnestly. "I know you had a rough time in Iraq."

Grace cringed. She'd forgotten about Stephanie's ordeal and felt like a petty Hollywood starlet. Her feeling of isolation grew into inadequacy.

"I'm…I'm okay," Stephanie offered.

"Please let me know if there is anything I can do."

"So, why are you here?" Drake asked Doug.

"Oh, I'm just here as an escort."

"As Marine Corps Public Affairs, I'm here to cover the premier," Erika said. "And I thought that you might like to see Doug. He talks about you constantly." Doug considered Drake a big brother figure. "I won't share all the stories, but I knew he would've liked to come."

Grace wondered if she knew the secret stories about Drake.

"Also, I need to inform you," Erika focused in on Drake, "that after your Tuesday appearances in New York, you'll have a meeting with the Commandant on Thursday to discuss your awards ceremony on Friday and that the president wants to spend Friday night with you to watch *Storming Baghdad*."

"Can I bring Grace?" Drake asked then turned to Grace. "Do you want to go meet the president?"

"I would love to." Grace lit up. "All I have next week is an appearance on the *Tony Lopez Show* Monday?" Tony Lopez was a former comedian that hosted a late night TV talk show.

"You're going to be on *Tony Lopez*?" Drake asked.

"Yes, this is my movie too."

"Oh, I forgot that you're in it."

"Well..."

"She also financed it, at least part of it," Erika broke in to save Grace from having to sound conceited. "If it does well, she'll be even wealthier than she already is. So yes, she has a fair interest in building a buzz."

"Really?" Drake looked at her affectionately. Grace melted. She wished she had a camera to capture the moment. He smiled genuinely and with affection. Inside she whimpered.

"Hey, sir?" A voice interrupted them from behind. Grace turned as saw a tall black Marine even taller than Drake.

"Link!" Drake said to Jamal Lincoln. Drake hugged the Marine in the same way. Grace gained a familiarity with the scene. Drake pounded Lincoln's back. "How the hell are you?"

"Married. We eloped last night up in Vegas."

"Congratulations!" Drake opened up the circle to include Lincoln and a Middle Eastern woman. Drake turned to Grace and said. "This is Corporal Lincoln and Mrs. Nadia Lincoln."

Grace didn't know the protocol but she closed with the man, hugged him and kissed him on the cheek and did the same with his wife. A simple handshake seemed too cold to follow the two Marines' greeting. "It is very nice to meet you."

"Nadia, it's nice to see you. I haven't seen you since Iraq," Drake said.

"Iraq?" Grace asked.

"Yeah. I met her in Nasariyah." Drake turned to Jamal and Doug. "That was a scary place."

"Hell, yeah," Doug confirmed.

"What got me," Drake said turning back to Grace. "Is that when Lima Bravo was getting overrun and we went to go take them batteries and ammo," Drake chuckled. "We're bounding our way there and we stack up on this corner. Link, here, pies a corner and WHAM he get's his helmet blown off by a seven-six-two."

Grace wished she knew what a *seven-six-two* was, what *pieing a corner* meant or any of the other jargon Drake just listed off. She tightened her grip on his arm.

"So his helmet comes rolling across the ground in front of me and he's all, 'a little help,' like his basketball just rolled out of bounds. I laugh my ass off every time I think of it."

Grace laughed along with the rest of the group even though she wasn't too comfortable with the topic. *Didn't the man nearly die?*

"Then the next time he pies a corner..." Drake's chuckle died and he stopped midsentence.

Drake and Doug both dropped their eyes to the floor. "What happened?" Grace asked. Everyone but her seemed to know.

"Ah," Drake stammered.

"That is when he came face to face with Amir," Nadia Lincoln said in her Arabic accented British dialect.

"Amir?" Grace pressed. Drake squeezed her hand lightly and she knew she overstepped her bounds.

"Yes, my husband. My *former* husband."

Grace gasped knowing what was coming.

"He was foolish. He was going to regain his honor in the eyes of his family by taking on the Americans. He stepped out of the door with a rifle and into the barrel of Jamal's rifle. He passed quickly and painlessly. He won the respect of his family by being a fool."

"Oh, my." Grace reached for Nadia's hand.

"It is fine," Nadia continued taking Grace's hand. "He wasn't a good husband or father. He lacked character."

Grace withdrew her hand and possessively wrapped it around Drake's arm. She couldn't relate to this world but everyone else seemed to understand including Stephanie.

Nadia lifted up her purse and searched it.

"Oh, sir," Lincoln said. "Do you think we could," he pointed to a camera Nadia pulled out from her purse.

"Oh…ah, yeah…Grace, would you mind?"

Grace lit up. "I would love to!" This was more her territory, being the starlet. The one everyone wanted a picture with. She waved her hands for Jamal and Nadia to bookend her. She beamed as Drake snapped a series of photographs.

"Thank you so much," Nadia said. "It has been an honor to meet you, ma'am."

"Oooh, no! The honor is all mine to have my picture taken with you and your Marine." Grace snapped her head around to Drake. "Drake?"

"Hmm?"

Grace waved him over and then turned to Nadia. "Would you mind?"

"Of course not." Nadia snapped a string of photos. "You are such a beautiful couple. You will have lovely children."

Grace blushed and averted her eyes. Then she focused on Drake. The comment didn't seem to phase him. What was he thinking? Grace broke her train of thought and reached for her clutch. She pulled out a card and handed it to Nadia. "Would you mind emailing them to me?"

"Most definitely."

"And if there is anything I could ever do for you, please let me know."

"Yes, ma'am." The couple nodded respectfully and melted away into the crowd.

Grace turned back to the crowd. She looked around and only recognized Drake. "I have you all to myself again." Her voice turned low and sultry. She wrapped her arms around his waste and ran her hands up his back. She leaned into him to tantalize him with her ruby lips. She purred as she place her cheek on his. She whispered in his ear, "Why did they insist on calling me 'ma'am?'" Drake drew back to look in her eyes. The corners of Grace's lips curled up into a bow when she saw him drowning in her eyes. "Drake?"

"Oh, yeah. Well, technically they should."

"Why?"

"Because you're with me."

"Mmm," she purred again and pressed further into his body. She was getting the reaction she wanted. "I like hearing you say that I'm with you."

"You do, huh?"

"Yes, I do." Grace creased her lips and caressed them with her tongue. Drake's reaction grew stronger. "Did she have to call me 'ma'am' just because you outrank him?"

"Yep."

"I don't think I like it."

"Really?"

"No, not at all. It makes me sound so old. I'm much too young to be called 'ma'am.'"

"Sorry, but that is the way it is."

Grace narrowed her eyes. "So, technically could I call Erika 'ma'am?'"

Drake closed one eye and fixated the other on the ceiling as he worked through the protocol. "As my escort, yes. But you also have a business relationship with her that puts you on par with her, so maybe not. I don't think she'll get too wrapped up in whatever you decide to call her."

Grace smiled like a vixen. "I think I would like to call her 'ma'am.'" Grace swayed her hips back and forth against him to increase the stimulation. She liked having him all to herself. The rest of the world seemed to melt away. She felt wrapped in cocoon built just for the two of them. She savored the moment until she felt a pair of eyes on them. Without looking she asked, "Could I call Gabrielle 'ma'am' too?"

Instantly she lost all progress she made arousing Drake. "Ah, yeah, I guess so."

"She outranks you, right?"

"Ah, yeah."

"She's here, isn't she?"

"Ah, yeah. I think Stephanie brought her."

Grace swayed her hips. "I'm sorry. I guess I shouldn't have brought her up."

"Why's that?"

"I seemed to have dampened the mood."

"Huh?"

Grace pressed her breasts up against him and ground her hips into him. She tightened her calves to stand on her toes. She dropped her voice to a low whisper and breathed into his ear, "It's just that I'm so wet for you that I wanted to know you felt the same way about me." She leaned back to see the pained expression in his eyes and press her hips further into him. *And...he's back.*

"Hey, sir?"

Drake looked up to find Jennings standing behind Grace bringing his eye back up from Grace's backside.

"Sergeant Jennings!" Drake said red faced. He spun Grace around to face Jennings while hiding his pronounced problem by standing behind her. "Grace this is my platoon sergeant, Sergeant Jennings."

"Pleased to meet you Sergeant Jennings." Grace started to worry she was going to lose track of the ranks. "Does anyone use first names?"

"Yeah, sure, his first name is Sergeant and mine is Lieutenant." Drake teased. "I'm sorry, you can call him Dwight."

"Can you call him Dwight?"

"Yes, and I do on occasion."

"Can you call him Drake?"

"Only when I'm stupid drunk and he has to drive me home."

"So you two spend time together on occasion?" Grace didn't remember hearing about nights spent with Jennings.

"No, well on occasion, but not the time I'm thinking bout." Jennings thought about the time Drake had to bail

Ramirez out of jail. "You don't ever want to piss off the Goose by getting picked up for being stupid."

"Goose?" Grace asked.

"It's a nick name," Drake clarified.

"Speaking of Ramirez," Jennings said, "he's here."

"He is? I need to talk to him." Drake silenced the group with his tone.

Grace ended the awkward moment. "So what do you do as the platoon sergeant?"

"I'm his number two. I make sure the men do what he wants them to do." Jennings pulled out a camera. "Hey, sir, would you mind?"

"Oh, not at all." Drake took the camera, handed it to Grace and wrapped his arm around Jennings to pose for a photo. Grace took the camera and looked it over.

"Here, ma'am." Jennings stepped forward and pointed to a button on the top.

Grace snapped a series of photos and handed Jennings a card too. "Could you please email me copies?"

"Oh, sure, ma'am." Jennings eyes widened as he studied her card. He refocused. "Oh, ah, sir..." He handed Drake the camera again and inched towards Grace.

"What?" Drake continued the ruse.

"Could I..."

"Yeah, I know. I was just fuckin' with ya. I'm pretty sure the last thing you needed was a picture of you and me in our monkey suits." Drake took the camera and looked through the lens. He studied the subjects momentarily then captured a series of pictures.

"Thanks, sir," Jennings said and retrieved his camera.

"Sure," Drake said.

Jennings nodded to Grace and withdrew into the crowd.

Grace turned her attention back to Drake and found his eyes glazed over. "What is it, darling?"

Drake closed the distance with her. He hovered his hands over her hips to her waist and shoulders. He rested them on her face.

"Darling?"

"I'm sorry. It's just," Drake's eyes darted back and forth as he took in her eyes. "When I saw you through the camera I realized that you were real."

"Of course I'm real."

"I know. But I forgot how perfectly beautiful you are."

"Darling," Grace cooed and placed her hand on his chest.

"We've spent so much time talking and corresponding that…I guess I thought it was all a dream."

"I feel the same way. I want to pinch myself."

"Just let me look at you for a while."

22

"Are you all right?" Stephanie asked Gabrielle.

"Yech." Gabrielle fired disgust from her eyes.

"What are you drinking?" Stephanie asked trying to distract Gabrielle.

"Just water." She steamed. "They're nauseating."

Stephanie stole a glance. "They look happy."

"She'll never make him happy. He's too much for her."

"I wouldn't say that. They've spent a lot of time on the phone. They know each other well."

"Yes, but," Gabrielle held an advantage, "she doesn't *really* know him. She doesn't know who he is on the inside. She hasn't seen him they way you have."

"You haven't seen him like that either."

"Yes, but she has no idea what it is like to love a man who goes off to war. It's going to eat her alive."

"Love? Who's discussing love?"

Gabrielle ended her fixation and shook her head trying to dismiss the comment.

"Gabrielle, what are you thinking?"

"Nothing."

"Gabrielle," Stephanie pressed.

"Closure."

"Closure?"

"Yes."

"How? Don't forget Grace is my friend too. I love you both."

"I need to tell him."

"What?"

"If I don't tell him. I'll regret it for the rest of my life."

"Tell him what."

"That I love him."

Stephanie stole a look at Grace and Drake and then turned back to Gabrielle. "Don't do that."

"Why not? Are you afraid I might hurt the Hollywood bitch's feelings?"

"No, I'm afraid you will get hurt." Stephanie continued, "They look really happy." When Gabrielle didn't reply Stephanie asked. "Why do you want to hurt her? What did she ever do to you?"

"The bitch stole him away from me!"

"That's not true and you know it."

Gabrielle huffed.

"You let him go," Stephanie continued.

"Yes, I did, but he never knew how I felt about him and tonight I'm going to tell him."

Stephanie hugged her friend. "I don't want to see you get hurt. But if you need to do this…"

"Yes, I need to do this."

"Ramirez!" Drake bellowed. The tone unnerved Grace. She looked to see a Latino man in a suit walk up.

"Hey, sir." Ramirez turned to Grace, "ma'am." Grace watched the man lower his eyes. If he was a dog his tail would curl up between his legs. She felt this wasn't about getting a photo with Grace Freemont.

"What the fuck!" Drake belched out.

Grace's eyes found the floor too. She squeezed Drake's hand and took a step back.

"Why didn't you reenlist?" Drake asked.

"Sir, I just…"

"What?"

"I couldn't."

"So how's Teresa?"

"Gone."

Drake huffed and shook his head. He took a step forward and jabbed a finger in Ramirez's chest. "Look asshole, the Corps doesn't need you. You need the Corps," Drake growled.

"Sir, I can't."

"Why not? Are you clean?"

"No, I'm clean. I just can't do it."

"Why not?"

"It's the headaches and not sleeping."

Grace peeked up and saw tears welling up in the man's eyes. She dropped her gaze and tucked in behind Drake's shoulder. She frantically massaged the back of Drake's hand trying to soothe him.

"So life is better now?" Drake continued.

"No."

"I hear you're back in a gang?"

Ramirez turned his head in shame.

"And I read about some gang hit that looked like it was planned by a former military member, possibly an Iraqi War vet."

"Sir..." Ramirez whimpered.

"Fuck you, ya piece of shit!" Drake's body clenched and he squeezed down hard on Grace's hand.

Grace grimaced and bit her lip. She didn't want any part of this. She looked to escape. She searched for Stephanie but found her talking to the brunette. Grace didn't want to walk in on that either.

"You're not my brother," Drake fired at Ramirez. "You don't ever deserve to be called Marine. You know that hit killed children."

"Sir, don't say that."

Grace could hear the man openly weeping.

"So life is that much better on the outside?"

"Sir," the man pleaded. "I saw my best friend turned into a fucking Pez dispenser. And I see it over and over every night."

Grace tried to imagine what the man meant.

"And killing babies is better!" Drake tightened up again.

Grace whimpered.

"Sir…"

"What?"

"You're hurting her." The man pointed at Grace.

Drake turned and rubbed Grace's hands. "I'm sorry. Did I hurt you?" He said tenderly.

"No," Grace lied. "I'm fine."

Drake turned back and changed his demeanor back. "I'm going to pick you up at your mama's place—you staying with her?"

The man nodded. "For now."

"I'll pick you up at seven and we'll be at the recruiter's by eight—"

"Sir, tomorrow is Sunday. They'll be closed."

"I'll make sure one is open. Look, the reason you're here is because deep down inside you wanted to talk to me and you know how I would react. Deep down you know you need the Corps. That is why you are here."

"Yes, sir."

"You can hack it, Marine."

"Yes, sir."

"Bring it in here." Drake released Grace's hand and bear hugged the man.

Grace marveled at the effect Drake had on the man. The man couldn't exist without Drake's acceptance. The man nodded and withdrew without a photo.

"I'm sorry. Did I hurt you?" Drake said rubbing her hands.

"I'm fine, really," Grace replied relieved that the confrontation ended.

"Sir?"

Drake turned around, "Sergeant Connelly!"

Grace grew more accustomed to greeting. This Marine had a wife.

"Grace, this is Sergeant Connelly and his wife Lilly."

"Nice to meet you, ma'am," Sergeant Connelly said. Grace noted that Connelly was one of the few Marines who weren't big and burly. She knew Lilly was probably below the century mark on the scale.

"Nice to meet you, ma'am," Lilly parroted. She timidly offered a hand from behind her husband who she seemed to be hiding behind.

"Oh, the pleasure is all mine." Grace said brightly. She noticed Lilly withering further behind her husband.

"Lilly, have you been married long?"

"Nearly five years, ma'am."

"Five years!" They looked too young to be married five years. "And please call me Grace."

"Yes, ma'am," Lilly replied unable to break her southern upbringing.

"Do you have any children?"

"Yes, ma'am, we have a three year old girl."

"She must keep you busy?"

"Yes, ma'am."

"My this feels so overwhelming doesn't it?" Grace lied. She was perfectly at home in Hollywood, but knew Lilly was in over her head.

"Yes, ma'am. This is nothing like Valdosta."

"That's in Georgia right?"

"Yes, ma'am."

"Lilly, did you bring a camera?" Grace knew the reticent girl would never muster the courage to ask.

"Yes, ma'am," she replied as she hurriedly searched her purse.

"Maybe we could get a picture together…all of us."

"That would be wonderful, ma'am, ah, Grace."

"That sounds better," Grace said.

A puzzled look crossed Lilly's face.

"Grace. I much rather you call me Grace. Ma'am makes me feel so old."

"Awwl right, Grace," Lilly said with her southern accent breaking through her nervousness.

"Jawhn, Grace, here would like us all here to take a picture. Do you think y'all could find someone one to take it?"

"Link!" Drake bellowed. Lincoln was the closest Marine. "A little help," he said mimicking the infamous words from Nasariyah.

"I got this," Lincoln replied and stepped in to take the camera.

Grace and Lilly straightened their dresses and stood next to each other with their Marines bracketing them. Grace put her arm around Lilly. Lilly replied in kind. When Lincoln finished Grace pulled out another card and handed it to Lilly. "Here, Lilly, would you do me a tremendous favor and email me a copy when you download them?"

"Of, course," Lilly took the card and then looked at the picture in the camera to make sure the pictures came out. "My Gawd!" Lilly said training her eyes from the camera to Grace. "You are one lovely lady." Lilly had spent so much time averting her eyes, she never really looked at Grace.

"Aww, you're too sweet." Grace said touching Lilly's shoulder. "But I have a lot of help. Trust me, in the morning, the thing I fear the most is the mirror. Some girls spend up to a quarter million a year to look like this with facials, personal trainers, dieticians and what have you."

"My, Lord," Lilly couldn't conceptualize a quarter million dollars. "I'm sure you don't have to spend a penny on any of that."

"Sorry to disappoint you, but I'm one of those girls," Grace giggled.

"Lilly," Connelly said. "We'd better go and get our seats."

"Awl right." She turned to Grace. "I'll email these to you in the morning."

"Thank you so much," Grace replied. She continued to smile until they were out of earshot. She tried to figure out what was different about the couple. "They're not like the others?" she asked Drake.

"No," Drake sounded melancholy.

"What is it about them."

Drake wondered which part to tell. He lowered his voice. "He froze up in Iraq and," Drake stopped himself from saying Connelly got some of his men killed. "Some people questioned his courage."

"But she seems out of place too."

Drake lowered his voice more and leaned to whisper in her ear. "They're from Georgia and he got her pregnant in High School. It was an ugly scene. I guess her father beat her until she lost the child."

"Oh, how awful. He should be put in jail!"

Drake shrugged then said, "Hey, lets go get Chandler and get our seats."

"Chandler?" Grace laughed. "You mean Stephanie?"

"Whatever."

"Oh, you're adorable." Grace wrapped herself around his arm tightly.

Drake took a step towards Stephanie and stopped.

"What is it?" Grace asked. She turned and saw Stephanie with the brunette. "Oh."

"Oh, shit, I gotta go," Gabrielle said.

"Why?" Stephanie asked.

"Here they come."

"Who?"

"Drake and the bitch."

Stephanie glanced quickly and saw the couple looming towards them. "Oh…what are you going to do?"

"I don't know." Gabrielle's eyes desperately darted around the room. She lunged forward a few steps. "Hey, Doug."

"Gabrielle!" Doug said turning to open himself to Gabrielle and Erika.

"Hey, are you sitting with Drake?"

"I didn't think about it." Doug was more interested in sitting next to Erika.

"Would you mind sitting a little away from him so could I sit with you?"

"Oh, yeah, sure thing," Doug said placing the whole picture together. He turned to Erika. "You don't mind do you?"

"No, not at all," Erika replied.

"Thank you, ma'am." Then she stepped forward and offered Erika a hand to complete the military protocol. "I'm Gabrielle Noccionni from the JAG's office. Nice to meet you."

"Erika Hess, Public Affairs. Nice to meet you Gabrielle." She could've added *I've heard a lot about you,* but that would've made her vulnerable to Gabrielle replying *likewise.*

"Hey, chicky," Drake said to Stephanie once Gabrielle had cleared out. "Do you want to sit with us?"

"Of course," Stephanie said latching onto Drake's other arm. They filed in and Grace noted that Stephanie sat on the other side of Drake, not her. She tried to disregard it, but it gnawed at her. Stephanie's relationship with Drake was obviously closer than Grace imagined.

"Isn't this exciting," Grace whispered in Drake's ear. "Having a movie made about you?"

"It is. I guess I still don't believe it. But what about you, this must be routine for you?"

"No, this is the first time I played myself in a movie…and it is the first movie I produced."

"How big of a deal is it to be a producer?"

"Oh, it is a very big deal. There are girls younger and prettier than me moving to Hollywood every day. Hollywood is cruel. It is all about your face and looks. I don't want to be one of those people who try to hold onto their looks with surgery and makeup. I'm sure it works for some people, but I would find it exhausting."

"So are you going to continue to make movies?"

"Yes, but only on my own terms and in all likelihood only ones I produce."

"Won't you miss the spotlight?"

"No, I never wanted it in the first place. All I wanted was to make some money so I didn't have to rely on my father for financial support. I told you about how he just about disowned me when I told him I was in a movie and wasn't going into premed."

"Do you talk to him at all?" Drake whispered as the action started.

"Him? No, I talk to my mother on birthdays and other special occasions."

Drake wanted to ask her if she felt lonely, but the movie was rolling and he needed to quiet down. He half watched the movie and half watched her to see how she reacted to the opening scene that had some blood in it. Drake looked at the screen. The actor didn't look like him, but he had the mannerisms and played Drake convincingly. He shifted his eyes back to Grace. She cringed a little as the bodies fell.

"Oh, my God!" She whispered in his ear. "You did this?"

"Pretty stupid huh?"

Grace brought her eyes back to Drake. "I can't watch. I forgot that that is actually you up there and it really happened and that this isn't just a move. What were you thinking?"

Drake ran a sweaty palm down his pant leg. "Ah, you'll see later on. It'll explain itself."

Drake continued to watch Grace as the movie played along and the joke Jennings pulled on him with the *Grace Freemont died joke*. He wondered how she would take it. She covered her mouth and stifled a hearty laugh when she saw the on screen Drake pout and sink into depression because his dream girl died.

"Oh, how sweet," Grace said looking at him and weaving her fingers into his.

"I'm here to tell you that everything Stephanie told you about me being obsessed with you is true." Then Drake turned to Stephanie. "Remind me to kick Jennings' ass."

Stephanie chuckled.

"I never knew he started the rumor. Did you know?"

Stephanie flashed a *well, duh* look at Drake and waved to the screen.

"Oh, yeah, you wrote this didn't you. Do you know everything?"

Stephanie leaned towards Drake and said, "That's my job...to know everything," without breaking her fixation on her story playing out on the big screen. "As a matter of fact..." she stopped herself from revealing Gabrielle's secret. Her loyalties crossed and she didn't know who to protect.

"What?"

"Oh, nothing."

"No, tell me."

Stephanie knew she would have to offer him something. "Gabrielle is here." Stephanie didn't offer any information about why Gabrielle was there.

"I know. I saw you two talking."

"Oh. I didn't know you knew," she lied.

The movie progressed and the music turned ominous leading up to the Marines crossing the border. The music faded without the shock the audience expected. Marines laughed and joked that all the Iraqis already surrendered in the next scene where they set up a roadblock. The ominous music returned and the audience couldn't tell if it was another tease or if something was really going to happen this time.

"Here, they're all coming to surrender!" a Marine said as a white bongo truck, a pickup truck with no hood to speak of commonly used in Iraq, approached. White flags stuck out of the windows.

"That's Ramirez, the man we talked to in civilian clothes?"

"Yes." Drake leaned over. "You may not want to watch this." He raised his free hand to just under her eyes. If she lowered her head she wouldn't be able to see the screen. If she raised it she would have a full view.

Grace took his hand with her free one. Shots fired and blood spattered the camera. Grace choked down a squeal and drove her face behind Drake's shoulder. She heard Marines shouting but no more shots so she glanced at the screen and then buried her head behind his shoulder again after seeing Pfc Anderson cut down. "Is that what Mr. Ramirez meant by Pez dispenser?"

"Yes." Then Drake added. "I told you not to look."

"I know."

"You can look now."

Grace turned her eyes back to the screen.

"Will you believe me now?"

"Uh huh." Grace nodded.

When the movie finished the Basra chapter Drake turned to Stephanie. "Wow, you did some great work getting all that. That's impressive how you captured everything that went down. I didn't even know that the guy in the street was the guy's brother. I knew he knew the guy, but I didn't know it was his brother."

Stephanie smiled contently.

"Okay, you and I got to go," Drake said to Stephanie when Cameron showed up on screen."

"The bloody hell I'll leave now."

"Stephanie, let's not do this now." Drake released himself from Grace and grabbed Stephanie's arm—hard.

"You're hurting me."

"Yeah, I know."

"Drake."

"What is it?" Grace asked.

"You might now want to watch this," Drake told Grace.

"I want to see this, Drake," Stephanie protested.

"Fine, I've got a DVD. We'll watch it somewhere else. You don't have to watch it now."

Drake sat at the back of the theatre next to the aisle and next to Stephanie for a reason. "C'mon, let's go." Drake tightened his grip until Stephanie relented.

Stephanie walked out on her tiptoes trying to ease the pain in the arm that Drake was holding her up by. Outside the door Stephanie ripped her arm free and hissed, "Who the hell do you think you are?"

"I'm your friend I thought."

"I'm a big girl Drake—"

"What's going on out here?" Grace asked as she passed through the door.

"She shouldn't be in there right now," Drake said.

"Drake's trying to be my big brother," Stephanie said.

"You might want to stay out here too for a little bit," Drake said.

A crash from the theatre startled Grace. *How will I ever know what his world is like if I can't even watch what he lived.* Grace thought to herself. *I'm going to try to watch it.* She nodded hesitantly towards the theatre.

"Okay."

Grace slipped into the theatre and stood near the door. The screen flashed a beastly vial image of human jackals attacking the character playing her friend. A blood-curdling shriek shook the theatre. Grace jumped and covered her eyes. She lowered her quivering hand only to see a woman exposed and strapped down inhumanely. The sights and sounds pummeled her senses causing her body to revolt. She slipped out of the theatre before she lost control of herself. She looked up and saw Stephanie buried in Drake's arms. Stephanie's arms hung on to him for dear life. Drake had one arm around her and another over her exposed ear pressing her head and other ear into Drake's chest so Stephanie couldn't hear anything. Grace shuffled to a stop. Breaking in seemed inappropriate. Out of options she closed her eyes and covered her own ears. She looked pathetic and knew it. She changed her mind once again and walked back in. When she reached for the door handle the door came swinging open at her. "Oh, pardon me." Grace said and looked up and stood face to face with the brunette. The brunette sneered at her and pushed past Grace. Grace turned to say something but didn't know what to say. She didn't want to look petty in front of Drake. Besides that wasn't who she was. Backstabbers littered Hollywood, but at least they did it discreetly and through proxies—tabloids. Grace didn't know how to handle open confrontation. She sat in her seat and considered Drake. Was it for real or was she misguided? He seemed completely taken with her, but his loyalties seemed all over the place—the Marine Corps, his men and Stephanie. Then there was the brunette, what loyalties did he have towards her?

23

"Hey, are you all right?" Gabrielle said rubbing Stephanie's back.

Stephanie broke from Drake's chest and saw Gabrielle looking at her with soft reddened eyes. "Yes, I'm fine." Stephanie rolled into Gabrielle's embrace.

"I'm so sorry," Gabrielle said. "I never imagined...I mean I could imagine, but when I saw it..."

"I know."

With Stephanie in caring hands, Drake disappeared back into the theatre. Discreetly he avoided speaking or making eye contact with Gabrielle.

"Is everything all right?" Grace asked when he sat down.

"Yeah, everything's fine."

Grace opened her mouth but then thought the better of it. If she asked where Stephanie was, Drake would say that she was with the brunette and that was a subject Grace didn't want to discuss. Reeling from the tension Grace lifted the armrest and rested her head against Drake. She possessively wrapped her fingers through Drake's and massaged the back of his hand with her other hand. Her mind raced and ebbed from the movie. She glanced up and saw Drake shooting again, but he always seemed to be shooting. Her mind wandered again. Then a roar of bullets caught her attention. She refocused on the screen just in time to see a hail of bullets shred a Marine with blood splatting the camera again.

Grace jumped at the sight but hadn't followed the story close enough to understand who the Marine was. Then she heard soft sobs floating from an individual in the theatre. "Who was that?" Grace asked.

"Rodney."

Grace noticed Drake didn't use rank or last name. She saw a glaze in his eyes where his eyes tried to hold back tears. "Who's that?" Grace asked. Then clarified she meant the person crying in the theatre, "His wife?"

"No."

"His girlfriend." She didn't understand why he didn't elaborate.

"Gabrielle," Drake said inspecting Grace's reaction.

Shit! Grace cursed to herself. She'd been so careful, then blundered into the one topic she wanted to avoid. "Was she close to Rodney?" Grace knew Gabrielle's reputation and hoped Rodney was another notch on Gabrielle's bedpost.

Drake returned his gaze back to the screen and leaned towards Grace. "Doug, Jon Kim, Rodney, Grace—I mean Gabrielle, and I spent Christmas together just before we deployed."

"Oh." Grace's voice tailed off. She mindlessly watched the screen as thoughts bombarded her.

"…A little help," a tall black man on the screen said.

The familiar dialogue caught Grace's attention and she watched Drake running through streets getting shot at again. Then the tall black Marine turned a corner and rammed his rifle into the chest of an Iraqi. The Marine pulled the trigger twice and the Iraqi slumped to the ground. "That's Nadia isn't it," Grace said. It excited her to see something or someone she could relate to.

"Yep."

Grace wished Drake had introduced her to more Marines so she had personal connection to more of the players. She realized she would probably meet everyone else at the after party so she took mental notes for the rest of the movie trying to keep track of all the players. Besides, it took her mind off of the brunette. Before she knew it the movie ended.

"So what do you think?" Drake asked. "Was it worth eight-fifty?"

"I hope so."

"Yeah, you better," Drake chuckled. "You own it."

"Do you want to ride with us?" Drake asked Stephanie. He knew what the answer was, but it seemed appropriate to ask since she sat with them through the movie.

"Oh, we would love it if you would," Grace added. She wanted to pick Stephanie's brain and possibly isolate Gabrielle enough that she wouldn't go to the after party.

"No," Stephanie said tentatively. "I have a ride." She pointed a thumb over her shoulder.

"So it's just you and me again," Drake said with an oversized smile.

"Fine, but this time let's try not to break any laws."

"Why, what happened?" Stephanie asked.

"Drake showed me what it was like to…what?" Grace asked Drake.

"How to avoid being caught in a kill zone."

Stephanie smiled and rolled her eyes. "Okay, I'll see you there."

Grace wrapped herself around his arm. "So, I have you all to myself again." The corners of her mouth curled up into a delighted smile. "This time could we perhaps abide by some of the traffic laws?"

"Sure." Drake handed a ticket to the valet before walking out into the crowd.

"Don't forget to smile," Grace whispered in his ear.

"Okay," Drake chuckled.

A man waved to street and they exited out to the red carpet as Drake's Tahoe pulled up. Drake put on his best smile and walked Grace down the carpet and opened the door for her in a choreographed manner.

When Drake hopped in, Grace said, "Now, remember, you promised."

"Okay."

Grace spent a minute smiling for cameras taking pictures of them through the window. On the open road Grace said, "You seem to be very close with your Marines."

"Yeah, we're pretty tight."

"I can't say I've ever seen so much hugging, by men that is."

"We've been through a lot." Drake eyed the road and glanced at his side view mirror as he change lanes. "And we're going to go through a lot more," he added without thinking.

The statement landed like a bomb on Grace. "You all seem so affectionate."

"Combat brings you together," Drake continued without considering his audience. "I love those guys—don't ever say that though."

"That you love them?"

"Well, yeah." Drake shrugged.

"Not macho enough, eh?"

"Oh, I dunno," Drake blushed.

"I wish I could have come home sooner—"

"Yeah, me too."

"No, I mean, I would have liked to have seen what you do." Grace watched Drake's eyes narrow. "What are you thinking?"

"Oh, nothing," Drake replied.

"No, what were you thinking? Do you usually keep your thoughts to yourself?"

"Huh?"

Grace carefully selected her next words. "I know something crossed your mind and I would like it if you shared it with me." She reached for his hand. "I only have a short time with you and I want to learn everything I can about you and your world." Grace giggled "I've introduced you to my world tonight, I would think it appropriate if you introduced me to yours."

"It wouldn't be appropriate."

"What?"

"What I was thinking."

"I think you owe it to me," Grace pressed lightly.

"How bad do you—I mean, do you really want to see my world."

"Absolutely."

"How much of it."

Grace thought about the bond Stephanie talked about and how she envied Stephanie for it. "All of it."

Drake's mind worked. "I'm not sure you're going to like it."

"I don't care."

"I don't think you can handle it."

Grace felt insulted. "It can't be any worse than what Stephanie went through."

"Funny you should say."

"Huh?"

"Nothing, this secret I keep to myself."

"I told you I don't like secrets."

"I'll let you in on it Monday. Are you free Monday?"

"I just have that taping. I have to be at the studio by four."

Drake made some calculations. "That'll be fine. I'll just have to pick you up at four."

"I told you I have to be at the studio by four."

Drake turned to her and offered an evil smile. "Four in the morning."

"Oh." Grace massaged the back of Drake's hand and tried to imagine what he would do with her at four in the morning. "Maybe you should just spend Sunday night at my place—"

"Oh, make sure you wear comfortable clothes and no makeup." Drake's speeding mind drowned out Grace's offer.

"No makeup!"

"No, no makeup. It can catch fire."

Grace stifled a gasp. She asked for it all. Drake pulled up to a valet and handed over his keys again as he ran around to open Grace's door. Grace delicately offered her hand and smiled despite the disappointment growing from her overlooked offer.

"Captain Kim!" Drake said as they walked into the party.

"Mongoose!" Jon replied looking past him and onto Grace.

"Mongoose?" Grace asked.

"Yeah, Mongoose or Goose, it is a nickname he got for this routine he did with a snake and a mongoose," Jon said.

"Oh, I remember Drake telling me about that." Grace offered her hand. "Nice to meet you Captain Kim, I'm Grace."

"Uh," Jon's Asian face turned red. "Yeah, I know. Please call me Jon."

"Jon, really, not 'sir' or 'Captain Kim?'"

"Jon will be fine."

"All right, Jon." This new turn confused Grace more. Everyone was rank or last name, but Drake's immediate boss went by his first name. She didn't understand that behind closed doors Jon and Drake were still friends and on a first name basis. "I saw you in the movie right?"

"There were a couple scenes with my character in it."

"And you're friends with Stephanie too, right?"

"She's taken some of my poker money."

Grace laughed dutifully. "Speaking of Stephanie, I should go find her."

"Okay, sweetheart, I'm going to stay here and talk with Captain Kim. I need to see what I can set up for Monday."

Sweetheart! Grace melted. She wondered if Drake saw the goose bumps blanketing her arms. She understood what Drake tried to say about being called *Darling*. Grace's voice slipped into a low sultry tone. "All right, Darling." She savored paralyzing her Marine with her spell. When it was over she shuddered. She dreaded what she might find next. Her fears came true when she saw the brunette with Stephanie. Grace still slipped away and decided to find Nadia or Lilly and tried to get a wife's perspective. Maybe they could quell the wave of insecurity washing over her.

"Just a water," Gabrielle said to the waitress.

"Just water?" Stephanie asked.

"Yes, I would like to have my wits about me when I do this."

"I still think no good can come from this endeavor. But if you insist on going through with this I would have imagined you would have chosen liquid courage instead of just water."

"No," Gabrielle said sipping her water. "I need to have a clear mind. Now I need that bitch to leave him alone for just a minute."

"You shouldn't say that about her. She really is a wonderful person."

"She stole him from me."

"If you're going to make that claim, you should blame me. I'm the one who put them together. Besides, didn't you steal him from someone."

"Yes," Gabrielle said defiantly, "and I'm going to steal him back."

"Gabrielle, don't do that!"

"Why not?" Gabrielle's stare bore down on the woman. "Fucking bitch! Is she ever going to let go of him?" Gabrielle turned to Stephanie. "Is she always this clingy."

"Yeah, when there is a vulture circling over." Stephanie challenged Gabrielle's eyes.

"Just whose side are you on?"

"Nobody's. Remember, I'm her friend too."

Gabrielle huffed. "She's a bitch."

"I love you both, dear." Stephanie's voice softened. "This is not going to help you."

"What?"

"This anger. It will be your undoing. And really, she is a nice person."

"But—"

"I know you're hurting. But if he's happy, what can you do."

"I owe it to him to tell him how I feel though right?" Gabrielle pleaded.

Stephanie worked the idea through her mind. "I think you owe it to yourself."

"Fine."

"But…"

"No 'buts.'" Gabrielle stewed. "Oh, fine, but what?"

"But it's not fair to her—"

"Like I care about that fucking bitch."

"Or him."

Gabrielle's anger retreated.

"If you care about him," Stephanie continued. "You'll suffer in silence."

Gabrielle's past ran through her mind, her husband and the long trail of lovers she's left on the roadside. "I suffered enough. I'm sorry." Gabrielle reached for Stephanie's hand to stop her from interrupting. "I have to do this for myself." Gabrielle glanced back at Drake and noticed the blonde left him unprotected. "She's gone. I'm going after him."

"She's lovely," Grace said looking at a picture of Lilly's daughter. Grace got Lilly and Nadia to show pictures of their girls. It there was one way to get a woman to open up was to ask about their children. Grace had made strides opening lines of communication. "Oh, please excuse me." Grace saw that the brunette had finally left Stephanie's side.

Grace swept across the room dragging the attention of most of the men in the room with her. Stephanie chuckled to herself. Grace validated, once again, her thoughts about mankind.

"I'm so sorry. About everything you had to go through." Grace said referring back to the movie. She didn't know what she really wanted to say. She wrapped her arms around Stephanie and held her tight. She typically wasn't this affectionate with Stephanie, but she wanted to hug someone the way everyone else had been hugging. "I never…It was…" Grace didn't want to actually say it.

"It was."

"I'm sorry, you probably don't want to talk about it."

"No, I don't."

"I must say though, I love how you extracted your revenge."

A laugh burped out of Stephanie, "I forgot about that."

"Well, that's enough of that," Grace said closing the subject. "I missed you."

"I missed you too," Stephanie replied.

"We need to get together and catch up."

"Yes, we do." The conversation stagnated. Gabrielle preoccupied Stephanie's mind. "You seem to be getting along well with the wives," Stephanie offered to make small talk.

"Yes, they are wonderful." The conversation stuttered again. "But they insist on calling me 'ma'am.'"

"That's because you're the alpha female."

"Alpha female?"

"You're their pack leader."

"You make it sound so primal."

"Because we are." Stephanie studied Grace's reaction. "We're all just animals."

"I would like to think there is more to us as human beings." Grace's mind reached back to Drake's conversation with Ramirez. It was like two dogs snarling at each other and the alpha putting the other in his place.

"You can think what you want. From what I've seen, from what I've experienced, we are all just animals. Just now when you walked across the room at least a half dozen men imagined you naked or worse."

"I guess men can be that way."

"Men? Really? Women are worse. You've seen Drake. He's the alpha." Stephanie looked for Drake and saw that his head stood above the crowd but Gabrielle's was lost in the sea of people. Grace couldn't see Gabrielle. "Look around, half the women here would jump out of their panties at the chance to breed with him."

"Stephanie! Really!" Grace didn't know if she wanted to address the language or the content. "Most of the women here are married or involved with someone else."

"Doesn't matter, he's the alpha. He offers the best offspring."

"Now, Stephanie!" Grace protested.

"Be honest with yourself, Grace. You dropped an egg the moment you laid eyes on him."

Grace gasped.

Stephanie's eyes narrowed. "And you'd be lying to me if you told me that on the way here you didn't think about skipping out to take him home and put your stink on him."

"Stephanie, please!" Grace's mouth hung open. Iraq changed her friend more than she imagined. A couple images from the movie passed through her mind. "What about you?"

"What about me?"

"You shared some intimate moments with Drake. Are you part of the half that would like to breed with him?"

"It's not like that. We've been in combat together and when you've been in combat with someone you grow a bond that can't compare to anything else. There is no love greater than that shared between people who've taken fire together."

"So you are you trying to tell me you are one of the ones that would like to breed with him?"

Stephanie realized she had gone too far. "No, after what I've been through, I could never look at a man like that again," she lied. "It's just, we've had the common bond of surviving combat together."

"Oh, I'm so sorry. I didn't mean…"

"No, that's fine. But it's good to see you stand up for yourself."

Grace flashed a quizzical look.

"Because you're going to need it."

"I'm going to need it?"

"Well, not if you think that there is more to mankind than just our animal instincts."

"I do think there is more to mankind."

"Good, because if you didn't I would tell you that you're position of alpha female is in jeopardy." The crowd thinned momentarily. Stephanie nodded towards Drake and Gabrielle. "But since you do, you have nothing to worry about, right?"

"Excuse me," Grace said and rushed off.

No Grace, we're not just animals, but your claws are showing and you're about to mark your territory.

24

"Hello, Drake," Gabrielle offered.

"Gabrielle." Ice clung to Drake's response.

"I haven't heard from you in a while."

"That is because you and Stephanie stopped returning my calls."

"I know. I'm sorry. It was childish." Gabrielle took a half step closer to Drake and focused on her water. When Drake didn't respond she said. "It was sad to see Rodney."

"Yeah, it was."

Gabrielle welcomed the tears filling her eyes. She knew Drake. She knew him better than that Hollywood bitch. Gabrielle knew she could treat him better than the Hollywood bitch ever could. She understood the military. She knew what it took to be a military wife. "I just couldn't stop crying." Gabrielle thought about the Christmas they all spent together and wallowed in sadness. When the tears overflowed she knew it was time to strike. She lifted her head and locked onto his eyes.

"I know." Drake closed the gap. "I heard you," he said and wrapped his arms around her protectively. He lowered his head and kissed her on top of her head.

Got'em! Gabrielle exulted inside. She knew his protective instincts and turned them on. The Hollywood bitch didn't have a chance against her. "Oh," she moaned with her head resting on his shoulder. "I've missed you so much." She waited for a response. When it didn't come she said, "I have to tell you something." She drew in a deep breath. "I love you."

"What?"

"I love you."

"You love me?"

"I'm in love with you," she clarified.

"Well, I certainly hope I'm not interrupting anything," Grace said with dignity.

"Oh, nothing," Drake said pushing Gabrielle away. "Grace, this is Gabrielle. Gabrielle, Grace."

"I'm so pleased to meet you," Grace said pleasantly while wrapping herself around Drake's arm and offering Gabrielle a stiff hand.

Gabrielle took the hand and smiled as best she could.

"I'm sorry. Did I interrupt a tearful reunion?" Grace said.

Gabrielle did underestimate her enemy. The Hollywood bitch fought ruthlessly. "No." Gabrielle wiped away a tear. "I was just leaving."

Drake and Grace both watched her walk off. Drake waited for Gabrielle to build some distance before turning to Grace. "That's was nothing."

"I know, darling," Grace said with her eyes narrowed on the brunette. It wasn't soft or tender. She said it with purpose. "Excuse me a moment." Grace raced off after Gabrielle. She had protected her prize from the predator. Now she was going to hunt down the predator and kill it— with kindness. "Gabrielle," she said within earshot of Gabrielle. "Gabrielle!" she said a little closer so Gabrielle couldn't ignore her without it being obvious.

Gabrielle turned and wiped another tear away. "What is it?"

The tear caught Grace off guard. It wasn't just for show. "I'm sorry. I truly am."

"Why? You got him. What do you need to be sorry for?"

"I didn't know how close you were."

"We were very intimate."

"Intimate?"

"Is that so hard to believe?"

"Drake and I have an intimate relationship. You had a loveless infatuation, as I understand it. He was just another in a string of lovers for you"

"Oh," Gabrielle huffed. "You *are* a bitch. I just thought you were a bitch. But you truly are a bitch. Are you going to use the railroad analogy too?"

"Railroad analogy?"

"Yeah, been laid all over the country."

"No, I didn't know anything about that. But you had your chance with him and now I have him and I don't intend on letting go of him."

"You don't, eh?" Gabrielle scoffed. "That doesn't scare me because I know that I can take him away from you anytime I want."

Grace gasped. Gabrielle wasn't bluffing and Grace knew Gabrielle could take him if she put her mind too it. She was that type of a woman. Grace ran her eyes over Gabrielle's body. Grace envied the assets. Gabrielle wasn't a Hollywood pixy. She stacked lean muscle into shapely curves.

"I scare the shit out of you don't I," Gabrielle hissed at Grace closing the distance to flash a sneer.

Panic overwhelmed Grace. She was in over her head. She couldn't compete with her. "Then why don't you?" It wasn't a challenge, but a concession.

Gabrielle withdrew but kept the sneer. "Because he's always been hung up on you." Gabrielle turned on the charm. "I hated fucking him at his place because of all the pictures of you he had around. I swear you were in bed with us whenever he was fucking me." Gabrielle let Grace build the picture in her mind. "I just need him to get over you. You are just a little virus he needs get over. You don't know him like I do. You have no idea what it is like to be involved with a military man. You won't be able to take it. You don't have what it takes. You're too soft." Gabrielle jabbed a finger in Grace's chest.

"Well," Grace said slow and deliberately. "I guess I should hope he's not thinking of you later tonight when I take him home and break—his—bones, eh."

Gabrielle gasped this time. She didn't expect Grace to lower herself to her level. "You are a bitch." A smile almost cracked Gabrielle's mask. A fond memory seeped into the cracks of Gabrielle's armor. "I have to say you were good for one thing."

"Really? What was that?" Grace saw Gabrielle's ice melting and smiled delightfully.

"If I ever had an itch I needed Drake to scratch," Gabrielle lowered the lethality of the language, "all I had to do was put in a Grace Freemont DVD and he was good to go." A smile broke through Gabrielle.

"So do you have any…" Grace stopped midsentence. She didn't want to hear the answer.

"We do as a matter of fact."

"Do you or does he…" Again she didn't want to know the answer.

"We both do."

"After tonight it'll be just you that does."

Gabrielle laughed at Grace's false bravado.

"Gabrielle," Grace's voice turned tender. "I would like to be friends though. No matter what happens with Drake, Stephanie is my best friend."

"Yeah, well, she's my best friend and roommate."

"I know. So we are going to spend time together and if we are both going to be friends with Stephanie, you and I are going to have to be friends."

"I hate you," Gabrielle said unconvincingly. "She said that you were the nicest person on earth and it's hard for me to not like you."

"So could we be friends?"

"Sure." Then Gabrielle's turned stern for the last time. "But as your friend I need to warn you. If you ever question your relationship with him for even the briefest of moments, if you falter, if you disappoint him he will be mine and I will never let go. I swear to you, Grace, as your friend, I love him with all my heart and I still think I'm what is best for him. So, don't ever say I didn't warn you."

"Yes, ma'am."

Drake followed Grace for a step then reconsidered. Grace seemed to know what she was doing. More importantly she didn't seem upset that she caught another woman in Drake's arms.

"Did the fireworks start yet?" Stephanie said startling Drake.

"Huh? Oh, I don't know what is going on." Drake said. Gabrielle built enough distance from Drake that he couldn't hear the confrontation. "Do you know what this is all about?"

"I imagine a bloody cat fight."

"Why?"

"Did Gabrielle have anything to say to you?"

Drake looked at Stephanie to calculate what she knew. "Yeah."

"She did, eh?"

"You knew about that."

"I tried to persuade her not to."

"You couldn't stop her! Chandler, you're worthless."

"I swear you enjoy being upset with me, Drake."

"I don't get you. You set me up with Grace and then let Gabrielle try to break it up. What kind of sick bitch are you?"

"Look here, you pompous ass, Grace and Gabrielle are both big girls. They can take care of themselves."

"Yeah, and you'll have the opportunity to write all about it."

"I would never!"

"I thought that was your job."

Stephanie gritted her teeth clenched her fists and growled with frustration. "I hate you. You not good enough for either of them."

"Goose! What is up, my man?"

Stephanie turned to see a familiar face that she couldn't place immediately.

"Foxy!" Drake shook the sailor's hand and patted him hard on the shoulder. "You remember Stephanie, right?"

"How could I forget?" Foxy said rolling his eyes over the journalist and former lingerie model. "Hottest little embed I ever saw."

Stephanie rolled her eyes.

"So what is going on?"

"A cat fight," Stephanie replied.

"Drake, you shouldn't pick on her like that."

"No, stupid." Stephanie didn't realize it looked like she and Drake were in as heated a battle as Gabrielle and Grace. She nodded toward the female power struggle.

"Hey, that's!" Foxy said looking at Grace. "And...that's..." He stopped his sentence. His brain sped through files in his brain. The brunette matched one he stored away years ago.

"Yes, it is," Stephanie said. She looked at Foxy to see what happened with the other part of the sentence. What she found surprised her. The cockiness evaporated. His eyes narrowed. Something was there.

"Hey, there is someone I want you to meet," Drake said to Foxy. "Grace, Gabrielle, c'mere I want you to meet someone," Drake bellowed across the room. He wondered if he needed to do damage control.

"Grace Freemont? I thought she was here with you?" Foxy asked.

"Well, yes, but I actually thought the other one you might get along with. She was married to a SEAL."

The picture in Foxy's mind grew clearer, but he couldn't make it out completely.

Gabrielle turned and saw Drake with Stephanie. She nodded towards the two and Grace led the way. Gabrielle's tried to wrap her brain aournd what just happened. She regained focus when she and Grace arrived at the group. That was when Gabrielle saw the third party. Visions from her past assaulted her. She caught herself just before her knees buckled. The uniform was familiar, sure. But it was the menacing eagle with the lowered head clutching a trident that ripped into her psyche. She was such a different person then. A person she admired and loved being. Her mind waded into dangerous waters. It took years to bury that person. She took a step back. He was handsome. He was cocky. He was familiar. Already overwhelmed with emotion from the night, she couldn't take anymore. She took another step back and then turned before her tears flowed over again. "Excuse me…excuse me…excuse me," She repeated as she bumped her way towards to front door.

"Dude, one look at your ugly mug and girls run away?" Drake nudged Foxy.

"Fuck you," Foxy replied.

"I'm going to go see how she is," Stephanie said.

Grace grabbed Stephanie's arm. "No, let me."

Stephanie turned to protest then saw the sweet caring smile she saw when she first met Grace as a terrified nineteen year old actress making her first movie. "Sure."

Grace slipped through the crowd in Gabrielle's wake. "Gabrielle." She followed her outside where Gabrielle broke into a faltering sprint. Grace accelerated and called again, "Gabrielle!"

Gabrielle couldn't fight her mind and run at the same time. She stopped. She spun around and hissed, "What do you want? Do you want to see what a mess I really am?"

"No, darling." Grace slowly approached the wounded woman. "Not at all." Grace ran a hand up her back. She could feel her back bob rhythmically to stifled sobs. Grace walked around her until she could wrap her arms around her. She pressed Gabrielle into her embrace and patted her on the back. "What is it, darling?"

Gabrielle didn't trust her airway with words fearing sobs would get the better of her.

"It's all right. Let it go," Grace said.

Gabrielle leaned back in Grace's embrace so Grace could see her face. "This is what happens to you, you know."

Grace looked on sympathetically though she didn't understand.

"Someday, Grace, he's going to break your heart."

Grace still didn't understand. This time Gabrielle saw the confusion.

"I was married once you know." Gabrielle brought up a finger to wipe away a tear.

Grace couldn't remember if she knew that or not. "Oh."

"Yes," Gabrielle said wrapping her arm back around Grace. Gabrielle's eyes rolled upwards and her eyelids fluttered. "Oh, I was so in love—We were so in love—It was perfect. And then one day he didn't come home." Gabrielle looked for understanding in Grace's eyes but came up empty. "He was a SEAL." Grace still didn't understand. "Drake's friend is a SEAL and it just reminded me how much I miss him and how lonely I am." Now Grace understood so Gabrielle rested her head back on Grace's shoulder. "And he's gone now and there's nothing left of him."

Nothing left of him. The words echoed in Grace's mind.

"And my memory of him is fading and…and…" Gabrielle sniffled, "I miss him so much." Gabrielle took a breath. "He's going to do it to you too, Grace."

"Who? Who's going to do what to me?"

"Drake."

"What's he going to do to me?"

"Grace, I want to be your friend. I wasn't lying when I said I don't think you have what it takes to love a Marine. I wouldn't wish this on my worst enemy. I know it sounds perverse, but I would be doing you a favor if I stole him from you."

"You would, eh?"

Gabrielle coughed up a laugh. "I know you love him—"

"I never said anything about loving him."

Gabrielle's head snapped up. "Then you're lucky. Don't."

"Don't what?"

"Don't fall in love with him."

"I'll try not to." Grace scrunched her forehead in confusion.

"Damn."

"What?"

"It's too late."

"Too late for what?"

"You're already in love with him."

"Says who?"

"Grace, you can try to deny it all you want, but you love him."

"Be serious, this is our first date."

Gabrielle rolled her eyes. "Believe what you want." Her voice turned serious. "But know that I am here to be your friend too."

"Yes, ma'am." Grace smiled. "Are you ready to go back in?"

"No, I think I've had enough for one night."

"Really?" Grace lifted her brows sympathetically.

"Yes."

"I'm sorry. I really wish you would stay."

"Really?"

"Yes, I would like the opportunity to talk to you more."

"Keep your friends close and your enemies closer?"

Grace smiled. "Something like that."

"I still hate you."

"Now, why?"

"Because you really are nice and I can't think of any reason to hate you so I'm going to hate you for cause."

"All right," Grace giggled.

Gabrielle leaned forward and pulled in Grace. She wrapped her arms around Grace and held her. She may have lost Drake, but gaining a friend might be consolation enough. Besides she really only had herself to blame. Her cowardice and inability to open up to Drake when he was still hers sent him into the arms of his fantasy. "Please tell Stephanie I took a cab home."

"I will."

"Goodnight, Grace." Gabrielle cracked a pain filled smile. "Enjoy your evening with Drake."

"Goodnight, darling," Grace said. Anything more would've been gloating. She waived a diffident hand and retreated to the party. She walked in and watched Drake. Stephanie was right. He was the alpha. Grace watched him talking with a crowd around him. She watched until curiosity caught up with her and she wanted to hear his story.

"...At that point..." Drake looked up and saw Grace. "Well, I think you've heard enough of it. Do you want to plan on it?"

Foxy rubbed his jaw. "Sure, I'll work my end if you work yours. Call me tomorrow afternoon and we'll confirm it all."

"Great. Hey, Grace," Drake said. "This is Jake, Jake Netaceretachuvski. But call him Foxy. Foxy, Grace."

"Pleased to meet you, Foxy."

"Grace," Foxy said shaking her hand. "How is she?" Foxy nodded towards the door.

"Oh, she's fine. She just decided to go home."

"I should probably go too," Foxy said.

"Yeah, I forget how you squids lack the stamina to stay up past your bedtime," Drake said.

"Fucking Gomer," Foxy said and moved towards to door.

"Did I interrupt something?" Grace asked.

"Oh, nothing."

"You're lying, darling." Grace said.

"It's classified."

"Oh," Grace said looking guilty of some infraction she didn't fully understand.

"Colt!" Drake shouted across the room.

"Goose!"

"C'mere." Drake waved him over. "I want you to meet another a friend of mine," Drake said to Grace.

Drake made introductions and then asked. "So how's your evening? And why don't you have a drink?"

"I dunno, just trying to keep it together I guess," Colt replied.

"Hey, what's bothering you, bro?"

"Did you see who is with Bill?" Colt threw a thumb over his shoulder.

Drake cranked his head around. "Yeah, that's that waitress from the bar."

"I know, Nika."

"Nika? You remember her name?"

"Yeah, so."

Drake chuckled and raised an eyebrow. "I guess that was a hundred dollars well spent."

"Hundred dollars?" Grace asked.

"Yeah," Drake said. "We paid her a hundred dollars to go out with him. He really needed to get laid. And I have to say he's calmed down a bit."

"I had no idea they were still seeing each other," Colt said.

"You sound jealous," Drake said.

"I just don't see…"

"Yeah, he doesn't rate that," Drake said admiring the slight but attractive figure. "Hold on, here he comes."

"Hey, guys," Houston said. His eyes darted around. Colt watched him spy Nika and then a blonde.

"Bill, this is Grace, Grace, Bill," Drake said dutifully and not particularly friendly.

"Pleased to meet you," Grace said.

"Yeah, you too," Houston said dismissively. His eyes darted from Grace to Drake and then to Colt. When he realized Colt wasn't with a girl he asked, "Colt, I need you to do me a favor."

"Yeah, what is it?"

"I need you to go over there and ask that girl to dance."

"Nika?"

Houston scrunched his face, "Yeah, how did you know her name?"

"Dude, I was there when you met her," *and when Drake paid her a one spot to go out with you.*

"Oh, that's right." Houston's face lit up like he'd just been caught with his hand in the cookie jar. "So, will you go ask her to dance for me?"

"Sure, whatever."

25

Colt slowly approached the girl and analyzed her. She stood staring at her drink just outside a cluster of girls talking. She felt Colt's stare and looked around to see who was watching her. When she met Colt's eyes she lit up into a smile. She recognized him from the night she met Houston. She opened up to him, relieved to find a familiar face. "Would you like to dance?" she asked with a soft Russian accent.

"Uh, yeah, sure." Colt didn't know what to make of the situation, but she grabbed his hand and tugged him towards the beach where a DJ pumped music out over the pool, small dance floor, beach and ocean. Their bodies swayed back and forth in the crowd. Colt kept his distance and his hands off of her. Nika kept closing the distance though. His gyrations were half-hearted. He didn't understand what the game was and didn't want any part of it. Then he saw Houston with the blonde and then understood. Still, Colt didn't want any part of it. At the end of the songs he said, "Thank you," and turned to leave.

"Is that all I get?" Nika touched his arm softly.

Colt turned and said, "Oh, I just thought that…" he had no idea how to end his sentence. Nika's eyes pleaded with him. "You want to keep dancing with me?"

Nika nodded. Their bodies bounced to the beat again. This time Colt unscrewed the vice in his mind allowing himself to enjoy the dance. That was until he noticed her left ring finger.

"Are you married!" Colt's mind searched for an explanation he could imagine.

"No."

"So what is this?" Colt asked grabbing her hand.

"Oh," Nika said disheartened. "I have to get married next week."

"Oh."

"No, it's not like that," she placed her hand over her womb. "I mean, I'm not—he's deploying."

"Where is he?" Colt asked. He regretted asking. He wanted some certainty, that it was Houston. Houston hadn't told him anything even though they had spent plenty of time together over the past several months. Colt also knew Houston was sizing up his chances with a blonde in the corner.

"Over there," Nika said pointing out Houston as he worked on the blonde.

"Oh." Colt got his confirmation that Houston was in fact engaged. He also knew that he wanted bail on this drama. Colt treaded on thin ice with his next question. "So why aren't you dancing with him?"

Nika leaned in close to Colt and whispered in his ear. Her breath sent shudders down his spine. "He got injured out in the field this week and he has a bad leg. He said he can't dance on it."

BULLSHIT! I was with him all week and there isn't a thing wrong with his legs. Nevertheless, he played along. "Oh, okay, that makes sense."

Nika continued to pursue Colt around the dance floor song after song until a slow song drifted through the night air.

"Well, thank you for the dances," Colt said.

Nika closed the distance once again and took his hand. "Don't leave me now?" she pleaded.

Colt fought his desire and failed. "Oh, I just thought…" Again, he didn't know how to finish his sentence. He held her at arms length with his hands gingerly placed on her waist. Nika swayed her hips and slowly glided towards him as the song continued. While his brain raced his body weakened and enveloped the girl. She glued herself to his body. "I take it you're from Russia?" Colt asked trying to stem the heat growing between them. He had already asked the question and knew the answer but hoped anything would divert them off the track they were headed on.

"Yes." The question caught Nika off guard. Houston never asked about her heritage.

"So how did you end up in the US?"

Nika raised her head off his shoulder and looked at Colt's warm eyes. Nobody had ever seemed to take an interest in her or her story. "My father was a newspaper writer and he made lots of enemies in the government. So we came her on a political asylum visa."

"Oh, so does he still write for a newspaper?"

"No, he is a custodian at an elementary school."

"Hmm. Does your mother work?"

"Yes, she is a chamber maid at a motel."

"Do you have any brothers or sisters?"

I have two brothers and a sister—all younger than me. What about you? Why did you join the military?" Their conversation continued. Nika kept herself wrapped in his cocoon regardless of the music.

Colt finally thought of his exit. Sweat poured out of his body from all the dancing. He must have smelled horrible and couldn't imagine why she was still attached to him. "I'm dying of thirst. I need to go get a drink."

"That sounds wonderful."

Colt's manners, or desires, got the best of him. "What would you like?" The idea was to ditch her. Instead he invited her along.

"Just water."

"Hey, Colt," Houston said tapping Colt on the shoulder.

"Hey, Bill. We just finished dancing."

"You two should go back out there. You looked good together," Houston said.

Colt rolled his eyes.

"Then would you mind taking Nika home?" Houston asked. "I have to go finish that equipment list for Captain Kim that was due yesterday."

Colt cocked his head off to the side. *What fucking equipment list, you lying sack of shit.*

Houston widened his eyes as if to say, *C'mon help me out here.*

"Oh, sure." Colt felt Nika's hand grab his while she stood on her tiptoes to kiss Houston on his cheek.

"Good night, dear," Nika said to Houston.

"Good night," Houston said and disappeared.

Nika watched him disappear and then drug Colt back out to the dance floor and wrapped herself back into Colt.

Colt stood dumbfounded. "I can't believe you are getting married in a week," Colt said.

"Why not?"

"Oh, I dunno. Are you happy?"

"I'm as happy as I deserve to be."

"That's not what I asked. Are you happy?"

"I get lonely."

"Really?"

"Yes, he spends a lot of time at work and with the boys."

"I know, we play a lot of poker and..." the sentence headed into dangerous territory.

"And what?"

"Oh, nothing."

"No, tell me."

"Well, he's never mentioned that he was seeing someone."

"Oh," Nika said with a shrug, "Bill is a private person."

"I know, but..." Colt didn't know how much he wanted to know. It was twisted whatever it was.

Grace spent the next hour mingling, juggling several interests without Drake by her side. First, she watched Drake. She observed his actions and conversations, how he treated people and how people treated him. She watched from a distance. She watched the other Marines and talked with them and the women they brought. She made herself available to everyone she could. She knew her role as an icon and that most of them would want a picture with her. She charmed her way into hearts and tried to build bonds with the women who would be left behind just like her. Lastly she attended her Hollywood duties by ingratiating herself to the right people who would continue to promote her career and speak well of the movie she so heavily invested in.

Time after time she scanned the area for Drake and each time people huddled around him deferring to him as the alpha. Grace had been patient. She's played naughty and nice. She was tired of waiting. She fought to temper her appetite. Two enticing thumps pounded over the sound system followed by three more. Grace's lower lip quivered as she stifled a whimper. She shook off a chill that rattled her spine and swelled her longing. She stormed for her objective as a sultry woman's voice with a Mississippi tone washed over the crowd. "Ladies, gentlemen, this dance is mine." She sped through the group, snatched Drake's hand and led him out the back to the terrazzo that butted up against the beach. She found a clear area near the beach, led him to the spot and pressed herself up against him. She swayed her hips into him in time with the melodic song about the power of moonlight. A fire burned inside Grace and she wanted to know Drake felt the same. She dug her hips further into him. The steamy voice continued hypnotically about the heart's inability to fight against its true feelings after sunset. Grace applied a full court press. She leaned her head to the side to offer her neck and its sweet scent to Drake's lips. Her chest heaved with anticipation. She could feel her nipples grow tender and sensitive. The song spoke how a heart would eventually surrender in the magic of the night. Grace pulled out every last stop and moaned softly when Drake squeezed her. She rose to her tiptoes and ran her fingers over his ear and through his hair. She leaned back fully exposing her throat. She felt him fight the power of her spell when his fingers dug into her back. The song admonished any attempt to resist. Grace's patience ran out. Her finger crossed back over his ear to his chin when she led his chin towards her. "You can't fight it," she concluded and locked onto his lips with hers. A low moan growled from her throat. His lips locked onto hers. Her blood pressure spiked and she couldn't control her legs. She tightened her arms around his neck and held on. And then it was over. "What is it?" Grace asked. Her heart shattered. Her fingers trembled. Then she saw a smile cross Drake's face. She was able to breath again.

"Oh, nothing, I'm just not supposed to do that?"

"Dance with a girl?"

"No, PDA."

"PDA?"

"Yeah, Public Display of Affection, it is against regulations."

"Oh, how ridiculous," Grace chided, disappointed that the regulation existed and relieved that it was the regulation that ended the kiss and not the thought of Drake's former lover that he had just learned was in love with him.

2002

The helicopter hovered over the stern of the oil vessel as SEALs fastroped onto the deck. With each SEAL that dropped from the rope the pilot had to let up to compensate for the loss of 250-300 pounds. The maneuver required a sensitive touch on the controls considering the pilot had to also keep the helicopter over the same spot as the oil tanker wallowed to the side as the ship turned hard to race for friendly waters out and out of international waters. Saddam played cat and mouse with the US military trying to sell oil illegally. This was the game. Saddam tried to sneak oil out. Navy SEALs tried to intercept the illegal shipments. But they could only board the vessels in international waters. The crews had orders from Saddam himself to avoid capture at all costs. The crews skimmed just inside of international waters and when necessary darted into territorial waters of whatever country was closest, even enemy waters such as Iran. In the beginning, SEALs were able to board a tanker and take it over before it hit territorial waters. To combat this, Iraq welded up every passage that accessed the pilothouse, so the SEALs couldn't stop the tankers from reaching territorial waters. The cat and mouse game continued until this particular time when a third party showed up.

It started by SEALs dropping down security teams and teams that used hooligans, a crowbar like device, or Quicksaws to gain access to the pilothouse and stop the oil tanker before it escaped international waters. Two SEALs raced for the top of the pilothouse where they ran to the front. A burly SEAL, called Snowball, belayed a squadron third-O, the junior officer of the platoon, Mr. Phillips, over the front where there was a window pane the crew used to look down on the forward deck. To look down, the glass leaned in a reverse slope. When Mr. Phillips swung in and grabbed the rebar he used carabineers to latch onto the rebar that was welded on the glass. "Son of a bitch!"

"What is it?" Snowball asked.

"The fuckers used half-inch rebar this time instead of three-eighths."

Saddam succeeded in eluding the US military until the SEALs started coming in from the front window. Usually the tankers only needed ten minutes before they could escape international waters. When the SEALs came in through the front window they could stop the tankers in time. Saddam countered by welding three-eighths in rebar over the window. The SEALs fought back with a Quicksaw and again were able to seize the tankers in time. This time Saddam used half-inch rebar.

"Your call," Snowball replied.

"Time me. Let's see how far I can get before we extract."

"Sounds good."

The saw whined as Phillips worked diligently to gain access. A SEAL with a hooligan banged on a bulkhead hoping it would give. "Do you have something, Dragon?" Snowball asked.

"No, I'm just fucking with them."

Inside, Saddam's merchant marines cowered in the corners of the pilothouse. If the SEALs breached the pilothouse they would have to provide evidence to Saddam that they fought valiantly against the SEALS. But if they fought the SEALs at all they could end up dead. It was a lose—lose proposition for the merchant marines.

"That's it, we're out," Snowball called out looking at his watch.

"Let me know when everyone else is up. Let me keep cutting. I'll be the last one up."

"We're it. They're all up already."

"Fuck!" Phillips pointed his finger at each cut as he counted how many bars he cut.

"Move," Phillips commanded as he reached the top and unbuckled himself.

The VBSS, Visit, Board Search and Seizure operation ended in a draw. The tanker got away and no SEALs got hurt. Snowball sent the VBSS harness back down for Mr. Phillips. The third party boat appeared when the harness rose and the helicopter pulled away from the tanker.

"RPGs!" someone yelled. Al Qaeda knew the US military tried to board Saddam's ships and decided to use it to their advantage. Al Qaeda dispatched a small speedboat to shadow this tanker with three potential martyrs. One drove the boat, the other two shot RPGs." When the helicopter was at its most vulnerable, with someone on the rope, it would attack.

"Copy," the pilot said with a calmness that belied the urgency. His hands twitched and helicopter dropped and corkscrewed violently to evade the incoming rockets. A door gunner tracked his minigun at the boat. Hot lead evaporated the small boat and churned up a cloud of pink mist.

A crack ripped through the helicopter hull. SEALs excelled at controlling situations. The problem was they couldn't control this situation.

"Two's on fire—One's losing oil," the copilot said.

"Copy. Run the Fire/Failure checklist on two. Then read to me the Loss of Oil checklist," the aircraft commander replied. He keyed the mic. "Raptor, Swallow 21, pan...pan...pan. We are an emergency aircraft, we have..." He turned to the SEAL sitting closest to the door, "Do we have everyone?" The aircraft commander had to provide an accurate number of souls on board to any rescue operation.

The Chief who sat closest to the pilots nodded to Snowball, "Do we got'em?"

Snowball looked down and only saw a frayed cable. The second RPG tore it and Mr. Phillips from the helicopter. "No!"

"Negative," The chief said to the pilot. "Missing one." The pilot continued with his emergency.

"Chief! We gotta go back! We can't leave him there!" Snowball demanded.

"Sit down, Snowball!"

"Chief, we don't leave a man behind," Snowball said trying to stand up and approach the cockpit. For morale purposes, all units in the US military vow to never leave a man behind. But for SEALs and other special operators there is another reason. Sometimes leaving a team member behind can be devastating for national security purposes and plausible deniability. A dead US special operator showing up in Iran, Russia, China, North Korea, or on the soil of some other enemy of the US could create a political hell storm.

The military dedicates a portion of their special operators to the extraction of the wounded. For Snowball, if Mr. Phillips was going down, he felt they should all go down trying to save him. The helo pitched again and Snowball floated for a second. He grabbed the seat harness just before being tossed out the door.

"Sit your ass down Snowball! It's not our call." The chief knew enough to know they wouldn't make it back to the ship as it was.

"Chief," the pilot called back over his shoulder.

"Sir."

"Can you coordinate rescue while we run checklists and try to get this back."

"Yes, sir."

One rescue helicopter located the downed helicopter five minutes from the carrier. The second rescue copter performed a concentric circle search of the last known location of Mr. Phillips. Fuel ran low. Saddam's tanker, long gone, was nowhere to be seen. "That's it, we're bingo," the aircraft commander called over the intercom.

"Standby, I think I see him," the rescue swimmer said over the intercom. He directed the pilot over the location.

"Are you good to go? You've got to make this fast," the pilot said as he hovered over the location.

"No, we have to abort." The rescue swimmer watched helplessly as the SEALs body bobbed in the water. The swimmer was just about to go in when he noticed the blood. When he saw the blood he looked for fins. When he saw the fins his face grew white with fear. He'd almost jumped to his own death.

26

Gabrielle worked the key into her and Stephanie's apartment door. When it gave way she pushed through the door, turned on the light and took off her shoes. She picked up her shoes and headed to her bedroom where she opened the closet and tucked her shoes in the back of the closet. Then she emptied her purse and tucked the purse on a shelf for the next formal occasion. She spent a couple minutes removing the accouterments off her mess dress and stored them in a box. The simple tasks occupied her mind enough to thwart the loneliness bearing down on her. She slipped off her pantyhose and tossed them into the hamper. She hung her mess dress over a hook so she could take it to the dry cleaners on Monday. Then she foraged for some sweat pants and a T-shirt. She wiggled into the sweatpants and swam into the T-shirt. She pulled back her sheets and looked at the bed. She wasn't tired. She walked into the kitchen and opened a wine fridge she and Stephanie had bought. She pulled out a bottle of 14 Hands Hot To Trot. She opened a cabinet and pulled down a wine glass. She gripped the bottle and a corkscrew when a knock broke the silence. She put the corkscrew and bottle down and sighed. She couldn't even wallow in self-pity by herself. She looked at her watch. "What the hell?" She wondered who would bother her 12:38 in the morning. Then concluded Stephanie must've forgotten her key. "Steph?" she asked as she walked to the door.

No answer.

"Steph?" She wasn't going to open the door if it wasn't Stephanie. She looked through the peephole and didn't see anyone. Gabrielle backed up looking at the door suspiciously.

"It's Foxy," a man's voice said.

"Foxy?" Stephanie walked up and looked at the peephole again. It was the SEAL from the party.

"What do you want?" Gabrielle asked awkwardly. She knew what he wanted. She just wanted to hear what line he would you.

"I just want to talk to you."

"Talk?" Gabrielle rolled her eyes. *Fuck it*. Drake was gone anyway. She opened the door and waved him in. "How did you find me? Don't tell me let me guess. Drake told you."

"Ah, yeah."

Gabrielle walked over and put the wine away. "Do you want a margarita?"

"A margarita?" Foxy asked following her into the kitchen. His mind was elsewhere but keyed in on the margarita. SEALs have a vast array of talents, one of which was memory. Foxy stood for a moment recalling what Drake had said about the girl he dated before the invasion and how margaritas turned her into a sexual beast. "Ah..."

Gabrielle already had the tequila, ice and mix out. "The blender is over there." She pointed to a corner of the countertop. While Foxy tentatively reached for the blender, Gabrielle crossed her arms in front of herself, grabbed the bottom of her shirt and lifted it. The she reached behind her back and unclasped her bra. She rolled her shoulders forward and slipped off her bra.

Foxy didn't want a margarita, and didn't want Gabrielle to have a margarita either but he didn't want to sound confrontational either. He reached for the tequila and caught a glimpse of the amply endowed topless woman next to him. "What the hell are you doing!" Foxy said. He averted his eyes while he reached for her top. He held it out for her.

"What the hell am I doing? What the hell are you doing!" Gabrielle matched his indignant tone. "You're here to get laid, right?" Gabrielle took the shirt, but didn't put it on. She had a power over men and she used it to her benefit. Her naked body occupied a part of his brain muddling anything else he might say. Lying would be extremely difficult for him. For Gabrielle, her tits were a truth serum. "Your friend, Drake, told you," Gabrielle took on a husky voice to emulate a guy fixing up one of his friends. "Dude, you could totally get this chick into bed! Man, I'm tellin' you. She'd fuck anybody, even you." She dropped the voice. "Isn't that why you're here?"

"No, no, NO!" Foxy fought to avert his eyes and took a step back.

"Look, I made it easy for you. I even started on the margaritas." Gabrielle took a step toward him. "Isn't that what your friend, Drake, told you? She adopted the voice again. "Dude, get a margarita or two in her and you'll get her to drop her panties so quick your head will spin."

"No!"

"He didn't tell you that?"

"No—yeah, he told me that but—" Foxy backed up to the counter.

"So what is your problem?" Gabrielle closed in on him. "The last I heard about you, you were nose deep in the tits of some cop."

Foxy's jaw dropped. He was on his heels and reeling. *How the hell does she know that!* In his mind he drew the story's journey from Drake to Grace, to her reporter friend, who was Gabrielle's roommate.

"Yeah, I have my sources," Gabrielle said.

Foxy turned around. "Just put on your shirt. I told you I just wanted to talk to you."

Gabrielle shook her head. This was out of character, a SEAL turning down sex? "You're single aren't you?"

"Yeah."

Gabrielle wormed into her top. "So what's your story, sailor?"

"Do you have your shirt on?" Foxy snuck a peek at her.

"Yes."

Foxy studied her face and overlaid it on an image of his past. They didn't match up perfectly. This one was older—angrier. "No, I'm not married. I don't think I'll ever get married."

"Oh, now there is a line that will work on a girl."

Foxy huffed. "Look I'm not trying to get laid here. I explained to you, I'm not here for that."

"Oh, that's right—"

"You were married once before weren't you?"

"Yes," Gabrielle recoiled. When she saw the SEAL trident on Foxy's uniform at the party, the image of her husband haunted her. For a moment she was a new bride with the love of her life and dreams of children and lifelong joy. Then reality came crashing back, dozens of lovers, many of them married, devastated wives. She played the bitch for so long she started to believe it until Drake came along and rekindled the tender girl she was. Drake possessed a boyish quality, good and bad, playful and bratty, that turned back time for Gabrielle and allowed her to love again.

"When I got with the teams." Foxy rushed ahead with his story like he wanted to get it all out before he lost his nerve. "When I finished all my training and reported to my first operational unit, one of the first formations I attended was a funeral for the guy I replaced."

"Yes." Gabrielle backed up and turned for the living room. "Sit down." She waved at a couch. She curled up a leg under her and perched on the end of the couch while Foxy sat down at the other end. Foxy continued studying her face while she tried to understand what he was looking for.

"I was still drinking from a fire hose since I was just there. I didn't know the guy at all. But it was important to the rest of the team. I went, but my mind wasn't really there. I was still trying to orient myself in the team," Foxy paused and his eyes wandered as he organized his thoughts.

"Yes."

"Then I saw her."

"Who?"

"The guy's wife." Foxy focused back on Gabrielle.

"The widow?"

"Yes. She was the most beautiful woman I had ever seen. I don't know why I thought it at the time. It might have been just because I felt so sorry for her. You could see she was absolutely devastated. I'll never forget her vacant stare. It was my first funeral. I never imagined...I couldn't imagine the pain she was going through."

"I could imagine," Gabrielle said. Her vacant stare returned from so long ago.

"I mean I could see she was watching her whole life blow up in front of her."

"It happens." Gabrielle looked up and saw his soft eyes brimming with tears. She opened her mouth but decided against mentioning it. Instead she reached across and laid and hand on his knee. "So why did you want to tell me this?"

"I was so caught up in trying to get through training. I mean even before I went off to BUD/S I was obsessed with making it through."

Gabrielle struggled to follow. "And."

"Well, I mean I dated before, but nothing serious. But when I saw her I swore I would never do that to any woman. I decided right then and there that I would never get serious about any girl."

"Look, Foxy, this isn't working for me." Gabrielle shook her head. First of all, I hate Foxy, what is your first name?"

"Jake."

"Jake? Seriously?" It was just Gabrielle's luck that his name would only be a couple letters off from Drake.

"Yep."

Gabrielle took his hand in hers and patted it. "Look, Foxy—Jake, your name is Jacob. I'm going to call you Jacob, okay?"

"Okay."

"Cause…well, that is what I want to call you." Gabrielle flipped her hair. "And again, this only wanting cheap sex for one night is not a good line even if that is what you're after."

"No, you're not getting it."

"I'm not?"

"No."

"What am I not getting?"

"Noccionni is you maiden name isn't it?"

"Yeah."

"What was your married name?"

"Phillips."

"I'm sorry. It's not considered professional."

"Not professional!" Grace huffed. The speakers continued to pump out the sensual beat of the song.

"I don't know what to say."

"Well, I don't like it," Grace pouted.

Drake chuckled, "You're precious."

Grace huffed, "I still don't like it." An impish smile curled the corners of Graces lips. "What if I kiss you here?" Grace pressed her lips against his neck. "Is that against regulations?"

"Honestly, I don't know."

Grace worked her way up to his earlobe, which she took between her teeth. She felt his skin heat up among other indications revealing his positive reaction. She let her breath fall on his ear as she whispered. "I'm not bad for doing this am I?"

"Aaoohh…" Drake's voice shook. "No."

Grace's lips worked their way down to his cheek. She laid her eyes on him and watched him suffer. She worked her way down to his lower lip and bit it. She continued to watch his expression to see if it protested. He was powerless. She heaved her chest into him and locked her lips on his again and purred.

The song ended and Drake awoke from the spell. Grace found herself at arm's length. The impish smile remained though.

"You're…you're wicked," he stammered.

"Me?" Grace closed the gap again. She ran her finger over his ear again and then found herself at arm's length again.

"Oh, no."

Confidence grew behind Grace's grin. "Drake, I'm a grown woman." She closed the gap again and whispered in his ear and pressed her body up against him. She dropped her voice into a low sultry tone. "I have needs." She rotated her hips forward. "And so do you."

"Are you ready to leave?"

"Only if you are," Grace said coyly.

"You're going to be trouble for me aren't you?"

"How could I *ever* be trouble for you?"

Drake groaned. "Evil, pure evil, that is what you are."

Grace laid her head on his shoulder and held him. "I'm glad you think so."

"And strange."

Grace looked up at him. "I'm not like this." She saw the confusion on his face. "I'm having fun. I feel so comfortable with you. I guess it is because I know you so well."

"I'm having fun too," he said.

"You really make me happy."

"You make me pretty happy too." Drake leaned down and kissed her softly on the lips.

"Lieutenant Scott! Isn't that against regulations!" she protested.

"Yeah, but it isn't the first time I broke the regs."

She rose up on her tiptoes and returned the kiss. "You ready?"

"Yep, you?"

"Yes." Grace clung to his arm.

Drake took a step and stopped. He grabbed a pant leg and shook it.

"Having a problem there, soldier?" Grace said.

"Marine."

"Marine?"

"Yes, I'm a Marine, not a soldier and, yes, I have a problem."

"What seems to be the problem?"

"My girlfriend is evil. That is my problem."

"Aren't you the lucky boy?"

"What am I going to do with you?"

"I don't know, but I hope it involves being naked," she said.

"Would you stop already?"

"I'll stop when I'm satisfied."

"Okay, we're leaving," Drake pleaded. "Now go say your goodbyes."

He handed his ticket to the valet after they said their obligatory goodbyes. It was well into the morning and there weren't many people left to say goodbye to so it was quick. Grace watched Drake as he maneuvered out the gate and into the throng of paparazzi. She watched him grimace and twitch. "What was it like?" Grace didn't know if it was the paparazzi or the training that caused the reaction, or both.

"What was what like?"

"The war?" She saw his face actually relax.

Drake tried to find the words to sum it up. "For the most part it was boring. There is a lot of sitting around and waiting."

"What about when there was shooting?"

Drake thought again. "How do you mean?"

"Were you scared?"

"Scared?" Drake tilted his head to the side trying to think back. "No, not really."

"You were never scared?"

"No, it wasn't that I was never scared." Drake rolled his finger around in the air as he tried to get traction on his thoughts. "It was more like it was overwhelming. I never thought that I was going to die, but I was more worried about screwing up. I guess there was so much I had to do and control that I had no time to worry about getting killed myself."

"Did you like combat?"

Drake fought between saying the politically correct thing and what he felt.

"Stephanie said you always had a smile when you were shooting," Grace continued.

"I have to say it was...it was...I can't describe it. When you're not in a firefirght you're all tense and wondering when you're going to get hit. When it finally comes it is like you don't have to wonder anymore. They actually did a study about this in Vietnam and it turns out that guys actually relaxed more the closer they got to combat. Then there is the other aspect of it."

"What's that?"

"It was like you were never more alive knowing that you could be dead the next moment. Some guys actually said it was better than sex."

"Really? What about you?"

"Yeah, I might have said that."

Grace huffed indignantly. "Well, we'll just see about that."

"We will?"

"I think I'll need to test that when we get to my place."

"That combat is more stimulating than sex?"

"Yes."

"Well, I guess I haven't had sex with you so..."

"We're going to take care of that first thing." A sudden fear shook Grace. Stephanie had shared some of Drake's history with Gabrielle with her. It was the sexual history that ate at Grace. Grace was a complete novice compared to Gabrielle. If that is how Drake felt after his sexual escapades with Gabrielle, Grace knew she couldn't shake his feelings about the stimulation of combat. If she was to affect his feelings it had to be through his emotions. "Is it true about what they say about combat and how close you get to other soldiers—I mean Marines?"

"What?"

"Stephanie said that the bond between people who have been in combat together is stronger than any other relationship."

"I'd have to say that's true." Drake realized he forgot his audience. "Well, to an extent that is true. I wouldn't say that is always true. I mean—"

"No, that's fine."

"I mean…" Drake pulled to a stop in Grace's driveway.

"You don't have to explain."

Drake looked at her and saw the worry. "No, I should."

"You can't explain it Drake. There is no way I can understand unless I've been in combat myself, right?"

Drake leaned back surprised with her intuition. "Yeah, I'm afraid so."

"That is what Stephanie told me."

Drake waved the thought off. "Oh, don't believe her. She sensationalizes everything. She's just trying to sell a story."

Grace thought back to the movie and the scene where the enemy captured Stephanie. "I don't think she sensationalized everything."

"Okay, well, maybe not."

Grace took his hands and looked into his eyes. "Drake, I want to hear everything. I want to know what you were feeling. I want to know what you were thinking through everything." Grace started at the beginning of the movie and asked questions about every scene she could remember. When she got to the Farmhouse Shootout she asked, "What was it like to kill all those men?"

"I dunno. I just kinda went on autopilot. I knew I had to get Stephanie. I knew they were going to do bad things to her." Drake turned to look at Grace. "I had no idea that it would get that bad though." Drake eyes drifted into the past. "I think I told you before that I only thought that there were two guys alive in there when I went in, so I didn't think it was that bad. It was my fault that Stephanie was in there—"

"How was it your fault?"

"Oh, I let her go off looking for a story and I shouldn't have."

"Did you have the option to stop her?"

"In a way, yes. It's complicated. Embeds aren't part of the military so you can't order them around, but you try to steer them in the right direction."

"So you went in thinking you'd only kill two people, but there were a lot more?"

"Yep." Drake looked at Grace and saw her furrowed brow. He smiled at her to lighten her mood.

"When did you know there were more?"

"When they kept coming at us."

"So you just ran around the house and killed everyone you saw."

"Well, it's a little more complicated than that."

"How so?"

"First of all you have to make sure they don't kill you."

"So what is going on in your mind when you're doing all this?"

"Nothing, really. You kinda go on autopilot. That is why we train this stuff up over and over so that your body just reacts."

"What happened to Sergeant Connelly then?"

"He was put in a bad position. He had to lead his squad into a meat grinder. Whenever he sent guys forward they got killed. So he locked up and stopped sending guys forward. So the enemy just chewed him his squad up until the other two squads flanked the enemy."

"What would you have done in his case?"

"Me?" Drake stole another look at Grace. Her concern drifted into outright worry. Drake tilted his head and tried to sugarcoat the truth enough so he was still telling the truth and also stemming Grace's fears. "I would've consolidated and pushed en masse to gain fire superiority."

"A suicide charge, like a bonsai charge?"

"No," Drake chuckled.

"That's what it sounds like."

"No," Drake shifted himself to orient his shoulders towards Grace. "Well, I guess in their own way the Japanese were trying to establish fire superiority."

"So you would make a suicide charge."

"No," Drake fumbled for words. "We do it in such a way that it isn't suicide."

"I don't understand. All I know is that you would go out there and get yourself killed."

"Well, I'm gonna get killed if I let the enemy keep hammering me too." Drake fought to contain his frustration. "Let's say that you and I are in a boxing match—"

"That's hardly fair."

"I know, but just for argument sake. Let's say we're in a boxing match and I'm punching you. What would you do? Just curl up in a ball and let me keep hitting you?"

"What other choice do I have?"

"You can fight back. You start punching me harder and faster so that I curl up in a ball."

"And it is just that easy?" Grace asked incredulously.

"No, but it is that or die."

"I don't think I like those options."

"Well, in combat there are no timeouts or second takes."

"That doesn't make me feel any better."

"I'm sorry, but that is my business."

Grace twitched in frustration. "So what happens once you get this fire superiority, do you just kill all the enemy?"

"No, with fire superiority some of the enemy usually gets away?"

"What it called when you kill all the enemy?"

"That's fire supremacy."

"What's fire supremacy?"

"That is when they are down and out and you're just kicking the living shit out of them."

Grace swallowed hard. "My Goodness, you're business is a beastly one."

"I never said it wasn't."

"I'm having a hard time," Grace said.

Drake stole another quick glance. "With what?"

"Putting the soft tender Drake Scott that I know so well, with the man who smiles while killing people."

"I'm a mystery," Drake teased trying to lighten the mood.

"So when you went into the farmhouse, you had fire supremacy because you killed them all."

"No," Drake shook his head in frustration. His poor examples weren't connecting the dots for Grace. "When the enemy takes cover, they have to hide, but they can still shoot back. That is fire superiority. But if you have them pinned down and they can barely move to the point that they can barely return fire if at all, that is fire supremacy."

Grace nervously ran her hand through her hair and tugged at it. "So this war stuff isn't as easy as just walking through a house and killing everyone?"

Drake chuckled. "No, not at all. And I haven't even talked about a combined arms attack."

"Combined arms attack? Is that where you stand shoulder to shoulder and march forward? I didn't think you did anything like that anymore?"

Drake chuckled again. "No, that is when you have to call in airstrikes and artillery." He squared up to Grace again. "Remember in the movie with the bridge scene?"

"The one where Doug got shot?"

"Yes,"

"Remember how my character was on the radio all the time?"

"Yes."

"He was calling in artillery and that is a whole other level of complexity."

Grace pursed her lips. "You're good at it aren't you?"

Drake continued to smile. "At what exactly?"

"Being a Marine? I mean it isn't anything like I thought. I just thought you ran around and shot people, but in reality that is a very small part of it."

"Yeah, that is a small part of it."

"But you are good at it?" Grace didn't let him avoid the question.

"I can always get better. There is someone who is out there that is always training harder than you are. I would say I'm competent. But that is only for today. Tomorrow if I don't train as hard as I possibly can, I'm not the best I can be."

"Be all that you can be," Grace said referring back to the 1970s Army slogan.

"That's Army, but essentially, yes."

"So this takes total dedication all the time."

"If I don't want to get my ass shot off it is."

Grace sighed.

Drake reached across and held her hand. He ran his thumb over the back of her hand trying to soothe her worry. "I'm sorry, it is a lot to take in isn't it?"

"It is," Grace said. "What about that kiss Stephanie's character gave you in the movie?"

Drake grew nervous, "What about it?"

It was a sensual kiss usually reserved for lovers, not friends. "Did she really kiss you like that?" Grace asked.

"Stephanie?"

"Yes."

Drake tilted his head tipping his lie. "No, it was nothing like that."

"Really, I told her to give you a real kiss, one from me, like in the movie." Grace watched him squirm.

"Yeah, it was like that."

"Good, I'm glad she gave you the kiss I wanted you to get." She saw him sigh with relief. "But," she laid into him. She sat up in her passenger seat. "Drake Scott, promise me you will never lie to me ever again! I don't mind if you cheat on me. No, I will mind. But if you do, please don't lie to me about it. I could never forgive you for lying to me. I don't think I could ever forgive you." Her tone softened. "I would be very hurt, Drake. And I can't take being hurt again."

"Yes, ma'am."

"That's right, 'yes, ma'am,'" she crowed. "So, on Monday will you show me what it is like?"

"I will put on the best show I know how."

"Will it be realistic?"

"Grace, trust me it will be very realistic." Drake stepped out of the car and walked around to get her door. Grace had already popped out and she reached for his arm. She wasn't nervous at all. She would have a glass of wine and take him upstairs and he would finally be hers. She opened the door, "You're coming in, right?"

"Of course." Drake stepped in and looked at his watch. "Oh, shit!"

"What is it?" Grace asked as she watched Drake scan the room for a clock.

"Is it really five AM?"

Grace looked over at a clock. "Yes, is that a problem?"

"Son of a bitch!"

"What is it?"

"I didn't realize how late it was. I got a whole lot of stuff I got to get done." Lists of things he needed to accomplish to set up for Monday passed through his head along with items he needed to pack to go to New York and DC. Then he started adding how many hours of sleep he could get between then and Tuesday when he would appear on over a dozen TV shows. He bent over and kissed Grace before rushing off. "I'm sorry, but I have to go. I have so much to do it is unbelievable."

Grace nearly broke down in tears. "But I'll see you tomorrow right?"

"Yeah, four AM."

"I mean today, will I see you today?"

"No, I have to get ready for my trip and everything. Oh, and that's right. I have to go get Ramirez—shit!"

"All right I'll see you Monday."

"See you then." Drake ran out to the Tahoe, fired it up and took off on a tear."

Grace closed the door and headed for the wine fridge but not for the reason she originally planned.

27

"I don't think I've ever had so much fun before."

"Really?" Colt said in disbelief. He took his eyes off the road momentarily to examine her expression.

Nika continued to give him directions then added. "I don't get out much."

"I guess you don't. What do you do most of the time?"

"I work. I wait tables and I take care of my brothers and sister."

"Do you live at home?"

"Sometimes."

"Is that where I'm taking you?"

"To an apartment Bill is renting for me."

Sirens went off in Colt's head. "Where's Bill?" he asked before thinking about the answer.

"He's probably out with the boys playing poker."

It was a lie and Colt knew it. "I know he likes to play poker a lot." Colt wanted to ask something that would make sense of it all but couldn't think of what to ask. Eventually he asked. "Are you happy?"

"Yes," she said in her Russian accent. "I'm as happy as I deserve to be."

"What does that mean?"

"It means that Bill takes care of me and I don't have to worry about how I will live."

"And that's it?"

"Why? What else is there?"

Colt wanted to come out and say, *Because Bill is knee deep in some blonde right now!* But he knew she must have known that. "What about love, companionship and—"

"I don't get too emotional. Marriage is a contract. Love is an emotion."

"Wow, that sounds cold."

"It's cold in Russia."

"I don't believe you."

"What don't you believe?"

"Nika, I've spent all night with you and I know that there is more to you than just a contract. Don't sell yourself short."

"Don't talk about what you don't know. Yes, I like to have fun but fun sometimes comes at a price."

"Do you have fun with Bill."

Nika searched her memory bank and tried to think of a time. "He takes care of me."

"That's not what I asked."

"I don't want to talk about this anymore."

Colt realized he overstepped his bounds long ago. "I'm sorry, you're right. It is none of my business."

"Here it is," Nika said pointing to a shabby apartment complex.

Colt pulled in. "Do you want me to walk you in?"

"That would be nice."

Colt put his F150 into PARK and turned off the engine. He followed Nika upstairs while lusting for her figure. It was late and he was tired. His mind wandered. And yet, his heart pounded.

Nika fetched her keys out, worked the lock and swung the door open. "Would you like to come in?"

Might as well at this point. "Sure," Colt said. He stepped into her apartment. Nika turned on the lights and set her purse and keys down on the table. The diminutive apartment had one bedroom and offered little room. Nika said something, but it didn't register with Colt. He stared at her figure under her sweat soaked dress. They dance long and hard into the night. The dress clung to her body. He could see every curve.

His strength waned. He leaned in. Nika didn't need more than the slightest suggestion. She sprang into him and kissed him passionately. Colt ran his hand up from her waist into her hair. *She lied. She can at least feel lust.* Their lips melded together lighting off a dangerous cocktail of hormones. Colt heard her moan and press her body up against him. He brought his hand back down from her hair and ran it across the back of her bra. He ran his finger across the back to see if the clasp was in the front or the back. "I've got to go!" Colt said pushing Nika away. He had to stop now. The next step was to get her bra off, then her dress, then his shirt and eventually they would commit the inevitable. He tried to find the emotion behind her eyes. Was she hurt, disappointed, angry?

"Can I get you a cup of coffee?" Nika offered.

Sadness filled her eyes. That's what he saw. "No, I've got to go." His morals twisted and poured acid in his system. He wanted her. He wanted to make her happy. He shouldn't have done this to a comrade. Bile boiled up in his throat. There was no good answer. Someone was going to get burned if he stayed a moment longer. He had to leave. Staying might provide the two of them some hedonistic pleasurable moments, which in the long run could destroy them.

"All right," Nika said dejectedly. She opened the door to let Colt walk out of her life for good. She watched him walk down the hallway. When he started down the stairs she ran over to her window to watch him get in his car.

Colt shook his head trying to clear it. He walked up to his F150 and stood a moment before getting his keys out. His head swirled in a cloud trying to put all the pieces together about what really happened. Finally he got his keys out and opened the door when he heard footsteps running across the parking lot.

"It was you."

"Who?" Gabrielle asked.

"The wife."

"Of the SEAL?" Gabrielle's hand's started trembling.

Jacob nodded and slid closer to Gabrielle. He took her hands in his.

Gabrielle's mind rolled back to the day. She saw the green lawn of the military cemetery, the box that didn't hold her husband's body, the flag in her hands, the shots assaulting her ears causing her to jump. She was back sitting in a folding chair on a dreary day watching her life evaporate before her eyes.

Tears boiled over her eyelids like they did on that day. She pulled her hands free from Jacob's hands and wiped her eyes. Jacob wrapped his arms around her. She laid her head on his shoulder then snapped up. "Oh my, God!" She stood up and paced around the coffee table and TV. "You know, don't you?"

"Know what?" Jacob asked.

Gabrielle wrapped one arm around her waist clinging to herself. With the other she rubbed her temple. Tears returned followed by shaking hands and then trembling shoulders.

Jacob stood up and walked towards her. Gabrielle stopped him with a stare. He backed down and returned to the couch. She was working through something and didn't want the distraction. "What is it?" he asked.

"You know. I know you know."

"What? What do I know?"

Gabrielle stopped pacing. "Ah," she stopped herself. She couldn't take it back once she asked so she wanted to ask it in a way that would provide her the most protection. "If…"

Jacob couldn't imagine what rattled her. He sat on the edge of the couch with his elbows on his knees.

"Would I," Gabrielle stammered on. "Don't tell me anything."

"Okay, I won't tell you anything," Jacob chuckled and shook his head.

Gabrielle shot a look at him that frightened his testicles. "I want you to lie to me if you think I don't want to know the truth."

"What? What are you talking about? You're not making any sense."

"Dammit! Don't you think I know that!"

"Sorry," Jacob said just short of sarcastically.

"I'm glad you think this is so fucking funny."

"No, I'm sorry," Jacob said contritely.

Gabrielle kneeled next to the coffee table and placed her head in her hands with her eyes firmly focused on the table's edge. She rocked her body back and forth over her knees as if she was trying to muster up enough courage to ask, "How did he die?"

"How did he die?"

"Yes, I know you know how he died. I want you to tell me how he died."

Jacob leaned back and placed his hand over his mouth. His eyes searched the room as he considered his reply. "You don't know how he died?"

Gabrielle's head shot up and she shot a look that made Jacob's testicles retreat further. "Why the hell would I be asking you if I knew!"

"Okay, okay, he went down in the Gulf, the Persian Gulf." He saw some relief crack through her anxiety. "His helicopter went down in the Persian Gulf." He saw her shoulders recede from trying to attach themselves to her earlobes.

"How did it go down?"

"How much do you want to know?"

"Everything." She saw Jacob wring his hands and his eyes dart around the room. "What is it?"

"Some of it isn't pretty."

Knowledge brought relief. Gabrielle wanted it all. The unknown haunted her, not the truth. "I don't care."

"He was part of a classified VBSS operation when a terrorist vessel showed up and took the helicopter out with RPGs."

"So everyone on the helicopter died?"

"No."

When it was clear Jacob wasn't going to continue she asked, "What happened?"

Like a Band-Aid, Jacob decided to power through the rest of the story and get it over. "One RPG took out the helo which was able to get close enough to the ship for the survivors to be picked up. Phillips was on the harness when the second one severed the cable and he fell into the gulf. When the rescue bird found him, or what was left of him, the sharks had already gotten him."

"He was eaten by sharks!" Gabrielle wailed.

"Yes." This time he wasn't going to stop. He crossed the room and wrapped his arms around her and allowed her to cry. He cradled her head onto his shoulder. He laid his cheek on the top of her head. She tightened her grip on him. He rose up and kissed her on top of her head.

"What the hell is going on here!" Stephanie demanded. Gabrielle and Jacob didn't hear her come in. Stephanie's protective maternal instincts kicked in once she heard the wailing.

"It's not what you think," Jacob pleaded.

Gabrielle shook her head.

"Gabrielle?" Stephanie said.

Gabrielle looked up and shook her head. She concentrated and squeaked out, "It's not," and then stood up.

Stephanie dropped her purse on the spot and walked up to Gabrielle and held her. "What is it, love?" Stephanie said in her South African accent. "Tell me."

When Gabrielle gained some composure she explained, "He told me how he died."

"Who?"

"Pete."

"Your husband, Pete?"

Gabrielle nodded.

"Oh, poor dear."

"I should be going," Jacob said.

"No, don't go," Gabrielle protested.

"Okay."

"Oh, then I'll leave you two alone," Stephanie said.

"No, I don't want to be alone," Gabrielle objected again. "I know it's late, but I don't want to think about it right now." She pointed to the kitchen. "Jacob, would you open that bottle of Hot To Trot."

"Yeah, sure."

"Jacob?" Stephanie asked.

"Yeah, Gabbi here doesn't want to call my by my call sign and Jake is too close to..." Jacob shrugged stating the obvious.

"Oh, that's precious," Stephanie giggled.

"Gabbi!" Gabrielle asked with playful irritation. "Where the hell do you get off calling me Gabbi?"

"Oh, ever since you started calling me Jacob." Jacob scanned the area. "Where did you put the corkscrew?"

"Here, I'll get it," Stephanie offered.

"Don't you call me Gabbi," Gabrielle hissed and punched Jacob as hard as she could in the shoulder.

Jacob didn't flinch, but took the corkscrew from Stephanie and started twisting it in. "Fine, then you don't call me Jacob."

"But I can't call you Foxy or Jake."

"Whatever you want, Gabbi."

Gabrielle seethed.

Stephanie giggled and pulled out three glasses. Then she ran over to her purse and pulled out a DVD. "Hey, look what I got."

"This isn't over, Jacob," Gabrielle warned.

"Okay, Gabbi."

Gabrielle huffed and flipped a hand waving him off. "What is it?"

"It is one of Grace's movies that hasn't been released yet. Do you want to put it in?"

"Is it the one where he husband is trying to kill her?" Gabrielle asked.

"I believe so."

"Good, that's one I'd like to see," Gabrielle said.

"That's real nice," Jacob said.

"Shut up, Jacob."

"Whatever, Gabbi."

"Am I going to have to separate you two?" Stephanie said as she pushed PLAY on the remote and sat on the couch next to the other two. "So, why are you here?" Stephanie asked Jacob delicately.

"Oh," Gabrielle broke in. "He saw me at Pete's funeral years ago and it became a significant emotional event for him. He said he could never marry because of me. He would never want to put a woman through what I had to go through." After hearing the statement and processing it she turned to Jacob. "You're not like the others are you?"

"Huh?"

"You're sensitive," Gabrielle said.

"What?"

"You go around having sex with any woman who will offer it up," Gabrielle lifted her hand, turned to Stephanie and lowered her voice as if she was sharing a secret, but really not, "like every other special operator or Marine." Then she returned to Jacob, "But you do it for a reason."

"What are you talking about?" he asked.

"Let me ask you this," Gabrielle continued. "If you loved a woman, really loved her, would you leave the teams for her if she asked you to?"

Jacob considered the question. "If I really loved her?"

"Yes, you really loved her."

"I would."

"You would?"

"Yes. Why? Is that so hard to believe?"

"Oh, I don't know. I guess I'm just disappointed that you'd let a woman dictate your life to you."

"What?"

"I'm just saying that a real operator would tell her," Gabrielle adopted her low voice again, "'hey bitch, I am what I am and you have to deal with it,'" she returned to her normal voice, "that is what a real man would say. I could never be involved with a man who was so spineless."

"Fine, I wouldn't leave the teams then."

"So you'd put the one woman you truly love through a living hell wondering if you were ever going to come home every time you walked out the door. I can't believe you'd do that to her. Then you don't really love her if you didn't leave the teams."

"What the hell?"

Stephanie giggled and took a sip of wine.

"Stephanie?" Jacob asked across Gabrielle. "What the hell am I supposed to say?"

Stephanie shrugged.

"You can't say anything," Gabrielle continued. "You're damned if you do and you're damned if you don't. You're a man. Just accept it. No matter what you do you're wrong. Now, can we just watch Grace get killed?"

Jacob looked across to Stephanie for sympathy. "You're going to try arguing with a lawyer?" Stephanie said shrugging her shoulders.

"Nika?" Colt asked trying to understand what was going on.

Nika picked up speed and launched into Colt from five feet away. She zeroed her lips on his and hit her mark. She wrapped her arms around his neck and dangled with her feet off the ground. Colt's strong hand clasped onto her waist to support her. He returned her kiss. His mind short-circuited. He broke free momentarily. She locked her lips onto his neck and sucked the sweat from his hot skin. "Why are you here?"

Nika pulled herself up and guided his head lower. She leaned her head back to offer nher eck to him as she replied, "I needed," she whimpered as his lips locked down on her neck, "I needed to kiss you one last time." She released her arms and dropped to her feet and met his lips with hers. Securely wrapped in his arms she drove one hand down his pants and used the other to unbuckle his pants. She dropped to her knees.

Opiates flooded Colt's tired mind. His conscious struggled to gain control. Finally he said, "Stop," and lifted her. He lost himself in her eyes. "I don't understand?"

"What don't you understand?"

Colt rolled his head side to side, "What are you—what are you doing?"

"I'm trying to make you happy?"

"Huh?" Adrenaline fought off the exhaustion weighing on Colt.

"What do you want me to do for you, Colt? What would make you happy?" Her gray eyes darted between his eyes searching for an answer.

"Nothing."

"Nothing?" she said dejectedly.

"I want…"

"Tell me what you want, Colt." Hope filled her alert eyes. When he couldn't find the words she offered, "Do you want me, Colt?"

Colt's eyes rolled. His head nodded just enough to encourage Nika.

Nika saw her opening and struck. She rose to her tiptoes and leaned into him. She caressed his earlobes with her lips and breathed, "Then take me."

A truck passing by outside broke through Jacob's unconsciousness. He oriented himself. He was lying on a couch. Gabrielle slept on his chest. The TV was off. Gabrielle or Stephanie must have turned it off. One leg was stretched out on the couch. The other was on the floor. There wasn't a light on. He reached his arm around Gabrielle and looked at his watch, 05:34.

"What is it?" Gabrielle asked in her sleep. Her eyes were closed. She snuggled her face into the crook of his neck and kissed his neck.

"I need to get going."

"No," Gabrielle mumbled in her sleep. "Don't go." She squeezed him.

Jacob rolled Gabrielle off of his chest. "No, I should go. I wouldn't want to ruin your good name."

"Hah, my good name," she babbled still half a sleep. "How about you dirty my good name?" She slid her hand up his inner thigh.

Jacob grabbed her hands and placed them under Gabrielle's cheek for a pillow. He pulled the blanket off the back of the couch and covered her up. "How about we get dressed up Friday night and I take you out and treat you like a real lady?"

"Really?" Gabrielle's mind wandered to thoughts of fine dining and a classy place to dance.

"Yeah, sure. Or, you could just take me out surfing." An impish smirk grew over Jacob's face.

"Hey! That's not funny!" Gabrielle was wide awake now. Fire shot from her eyes.

"I'm kidding."

"That's not funny."

"Maybe not for you, but I found it funny."

Gabrielle relaxed and closed her eyes. "I still don't see why you can't stay for just a little while." When Jacob didn't reply right away, she added. "Stephanie is sound asleep." She waited. Then added, "I can be quiet."

"It's not that."

Curiosity poked one of Gabrielle's eyes open. "Then what is it?"

"Nothing."

"Huh?"

"Nothing we need to discuss right now."

"What is it?" she demanded as she propped herself up on her elbow. Lucidity flowed from both her eyes. She watched his soft expression search the floor for words.

"It's just," Jacob debated what to reveal. "I'm just looking for something real I guess."

"I thought that you would never get serious. Are you thinking of leaving the teams?"

"No."

"I don't understand."

"You know, as an officer, your time out on ops is limited. I'm probably on my last legs as an operator in the field."

"Yeah."

"The likely hood of whoever I marry turning into a widow in the short term is diminishing."

"Oh."

"And I fell in love with you at first sight when I first saw you."

"Oh, Jacob." Gabrielle caressed his face. "I feel bad. I don't know how to say this, but I'm in love with Drake."

"Oh really? How's that working out for ya?"

Gabrielle rolled her eyes. "Yeah, right."

"But you would still be willing to close the deal with me hear tonight?"

"Yeah, so. I figure Drake is trying out everything I taught him out on the fucking Hollywood bitch right now." Images of Drake and Grace's bodies wrapped up in a lustful explosion sickened her. "I might as well get mine."

"That is all I am to you?"

"Did you expect more?"

"I guess not. But I was hoping it could grow into something."

"Just get naked and we'll see if something grows." Gabrielle smiled, please with her witty remark. Her eyes were closed again and her head was resting on one hand and the other had a hold of his hand so he couldn't leave without having to pull it away.

"I'm sorry, forget it." Jacob pulled away his hand and headed for the door.

"Hey!" Gabrielle was up again. This time propped up on both elbows. "Wait." Her mind raced to zero in on her feelings before it was too late and he was gone. She had to make a decision now. Was she really going to wait Grace out or not? "Give me your phone number," she asked. "I'll do Friday." She had nothing better to do. "Please understand though, right now, I'm not looking for anything."

"That's fine. I can work with that."

Nika kissed Colt's sleeping body and worked her way down below his waist and then began working on him. She enjoyed controlling his sleeping body. He woke up with a bang.

"Hey, hey, hey. What are you doing?"

"I thought you would like that?" Nika said, running a finger across her lips.

"I did, but you don't have to do that for me."

"I know, but I like pleasing you." Nika said straddling him and wondering how long it would take for him to regenerate. "Especially after what you did for me last night."

"Why, doesn't Bill do that for you?"

"No. I just do it for him."

Colt felt intimidated. "He's that good in bed?"

"I don't know."

Colt propped himself up on his elbows. "What do you mean, you don't know?"

"I mean I don't know."

"How do you not know?" Worry crept into Drake's voice.

"We have never had the sex," she said in her Russian accent.

"Nika," panic rushed into Drake's voice. "You've had sex before, you're not a virgin are you?"

"Not anymore. Not after last night."

"HOLY SHIT, NIKA!"

"What, Colt? Don't worry. Bill trusts me."

"Bill trusts you? What the hell does that mean."

"It means that he will never know."

"You mean to tell me that you aren't going to tell him about this?"

"No."

"Nika!" Colt shook his head trying to reign in his thoughts. "You can't marry him now."

"Why not?"

"Well, for one thing, he's off fucking some girl and you're here fucking me." Colt shook his head. "And you're a virgin."

"I'm not a virgin anymore."

"Nika!" Colt growled with frustration. "You can't do this and then marry someone else next week."

"Why not?"

"It'll never work."

"Are you willing to marry me? Are you willing to take care of me?"

Colt was stumped. He wanted Nika, but did he *love* her? "Maybe."

"Maybe isn't good enough. If I marry Bill, he will take care of me."

"You could just wait."

"What if he doesn't come back?"

"What?"

"If I marry him now, I at least get his insurance."

"But if you wait maybe I will marry you."

"Maybe isn't good enough and besides..." Nika's face lacked emotion. It was all business, but it didn't want to venture further with her last sentence.

"Besides what?"

"What if you don't come back? What if neither of you come back."

"You shouldn't have to—" Colt's phone buzzed. He looked at it. He chortled at the irony. "Hey, Bill what is it?"

"Hey, buddy, I need you to do me a favor."

Colt looked at Nika and rolled his eyes. "Yeah, sure, what is it?"

"I got a little wasted—"

"A little!"

"Yeah, anyways, I ended up at this girl's house and I need you to come pick me up and take me back to get my car."

Colt studied Nika. She could easily overhear Houston's confession, but she showed no regard for the story. "Uh…okay."

"I'll text you the address, okay. Just call me when you pull up."

"Sure thing," Colt replied.

"Oh, hey, you don't think Nika suspects anything do you?"

"No, I don't think so." Colt rolled his eyes. His personal Twilight Zone twisted once again.

When they hung up Colt turned to Nika. "You're still going to get married?"

"I don't have another choice."

"Yes, you do," Colt pleaded. Nika drew close to him and laid her head on his chest. Colt instinctively wrapped her in his arms. His phone broke the spell when it buzzed with Houston's text. "I guess I'll be leaving."

Nika rose to her tiptoes, wrapped her arms around his neck and tenderly laid a full kiss on his lips. She didn't want it to end, but she had to let him go. She pulled back, "Thank you, for a wonderful night."

"Sure," Colt said.

Nika raised a finger to his cheek and wiped away a tear. "What's the matter?"

"You hurt me—really bad, Nika."

"Please don't feel that way. We shared a magical night together and I will never forget it."

"I'm glad you're happy."

"You're not? You didn't enjoy last night?"

"No, Nika, this ruins it all."

"Don't let it."

"How?"

"Remember the beauty that it was."

"I can't."

Nika's gazed fell to the floor defeated. "I will write to you, okay?"

"I don't—uh—whatever." Colt turned and stormed out.

Nika hesitated and then ran to the door. She realized in the daylight people might see them. She couldn't follow him to his truck this time. She ran back to the window and watched his truck disappear around the corner. It was then a lightning bolt of doubt shuddered her soul. She missed him already—desperately. Maybe Colt was right.

28

Grace opened the passenger door before Drake even had the Tahoe in PARK. "You ready to go?" he asked.

"I think so." She tossed a bag in the back seat and then reaching across to kiss Drake on the cheek.

"Is that a change of clothes?"

"For the taping this afternoon in case I need it."

"Wow, I'm impressed. You're all over this. I was going to say that you should bring a change of clothes for just that reason." Grace closed the door and the light went out. "Let me see what you have on?" Drake said opening his door to turn the light back on. Grace wore a loose fitting T-shirt and sweatshirt, jeans and sneakers. Drake's gaze ran over her from top to bottom. Grace followed his gaze over her outfit until it reached her feet and she saw the clipboard. "Looks good," Drake said. He closed the door and the light went out. Drake wore a red USMC T-shirt, jeans and boots.

"What's this?" Grace said reaching for the clipboard. The header and footer scrawl caught her attention. She tapped the overhead light and saw SECRET NOFORN in red letters at the top and bottom of the page. "Oh, am I not supposed to see this!"

Drake leaned over and glanced at the document. "No that's declassified now. It's nothing."

Grace read the document to see what a classified document read like. She gasped, "Were there really Al Qaeda operatives here in Southern California trying to kidnap or kill military members?"

"I dunno," Drake said weaving his way through the paparazzi. "After 9/11 there were all sorts of things going on and I'm not sure anyone knows what was really happening." Then he said, "Oh, hey, I can't wait to show you this thing," to redirect the conversation.

"What?"

"It's a surprise."

"Oh," Grace said. "So what are we going to do first?"

"Well, the first thing we are going to do is look at a MOUT site, M-O-U-T, Military Operations in Urban Terrain. Then we're going to do some shooting and then finally I'll show you what an assault is like."

"Sounds exciting."

"It'll be fun." Drake reached for her hand.

She took his hand held it up to her lips. "Thank you for showing me all this."

"Don't thank me yet. Not until you've had the full tour."

When Drake rolled up to the gate the guard checked Drake's ID, saluted him and passed him through.

"Wow, impressive."

"What?"

"Seeing him salute you. Do they all have to do that?"

"The guards?"

"Yes."

"Yeah. But that isn't the impressive part. Look behind you."

Grace looked back and didn't see any paparazzi. "Oh, my God. That's right. They can't follow you onto the base can they?"

"Nope," Drake said smugly. "That's the surprise."

Grace took in the sights. She saw humvees following Marines in full gear marching. She saw other Marines running in formation. It was a little after 0500 and Marines were already crawling all over the base. Drake drove to the end of a paved road and pulled out a piece of cardboard and put it in the widow. "What is that?" Grace asked pointing at the cardboard.

"Oh, that there? That's a range pass. We have about an hour drive or so until we get to the range and this allows me to drive back here without a Range Control Officer pulling me over." Drake pointed out to the side. "You see, these are all different ranges."

"I saw a sign that showed where Range One was."

"Yeah, Range One is like a personal firing range that we can use on the weekends to shoot our own weapons. Range Five there," Drake said pointing, "is for hand grenades. There are other ranges that are built for special weapons and then there are just open areas for basic maneuvers. We're going to start off at Camp Red Devil."

"That's a MOUT site, right?"

"Yeah, that's right. It looks like a typical town. It has a hospital, a school, city hall, a chapel, you'll see. It looks just like a town."

"This is nice. It is like a ride out in the country and no paparazzi."

"Yep."

When Drake turned into Camp Red Devil he pulled up next to the city hall. "Here we are," he said jumping out of the Tahoe. "This is the newest most modern MOUT site in the country. It's pretty cool."

"I can see that," Grace said not knowing any different since she'd never seen a MOUT site before.

"C'mon, let's go up to the roof and I'll show you what's here." Drake led her up to the top. "Over there you can see a crashed UH-60."

"UH-60?"

"Helicopter." A crimson tinge crested the horizon, but it was still just a little too dark to see everything. "Wait here a second. I'm going to go turn on some lights." Drake scooted down the stairs and left Grace to look around. She looked around and saw a city bus and several shot up cars. It was getting lighter. She was seeing more.

BOOM! An explosion knocked Grace off of her feet. "Drake!" Grace popped up and looked for Drake. Then she heard the POP-POP-POP of small arms fire. "Drake!" Dread filled Grace's voice. When she heard men chattering in Arabic the dread turned to panic. "DRAKE!" she shrieked out of her mind with terror when she spotted two men in black with headscarves carrying away Drake's lifeless body in its red T-shirt and jeans.